MAGIC AND MACAROONS

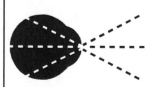

This Large Print Book carries the
Seal of Approval of N.A.V.H.

A MAGICAL BAKERY MYSTERY

MAGIC AND MACAROONS

BAILEY CATES

KENNEBEC LARGE PRINT
A part of Gale, Cengage Learning

GALE
CENGAGE Learning®

Farmington Hills, Mich • San Francisco • New York • Waterville, Maine
Meriden, Conn • Mason, Ohio • Chicago

GALE
CENGAGE Learning·

LIBRARY OF CONGRESS CATALOGING-IN-PUBLICATION DATA

Cates, Bailey.
    Magic and macaroons : a magical bakery mystery / Bailey Cates. — Large print edition.
        pages cm. — (A magical bakery mystery) (Kennebec Large Print superior collection)
    ISBN 978-1-4104-8407-9 (paperback) — ISBN 1-4104-8407-6 (softcover)
    I. Title.
    PS3603.A8955M34 2015
    813'.6—dc23   2015029135

Published in 2015 by arrangement with New American Library, an imprint of Penguin Publishing Group, a division of Penguin Random House LLC

Printed in the United States of America
1 2 3 4 5 6 7 19 18 17 16 15

ACKNOWLEDGMENTS

I'm incredibly lucky to have such an able and creative group of people who participated in various stages of this book. My team at Penguin/New American Library includes editor extraordinaire (and paragon of patience) Jessica Wade, Isabel Farhi, Ashley Polikoff, and Danielle Dill. Kim Lionetti continues to offer stellar advice and expertise. Other writers in my life who have helped shape this story and the words that tell it include Mark Figlozzi, Laura Pritchett, Laura Resau, and Bob Trott. My sincere gratitude for their feedback and counsel. Dana Masden first served me Brazilian cheese bread and inspired me to try my hand at it. Thanks also to any and all voodoo practitioners and experts who answered my questions, and one in particular who wishes to remain anonymous. I learned so much about this ancient and multifaceted religion and am richer for it.

And, as ever, thank you to Kevin, who buoys me, makes me laugh, and keeps me grounded.

CHAPTER 1

"Abracadabra?" Mimsey snorted. "Lord love a duck. No one who can so much as cast a circle would use that word in an actual spell." She tossed her head, causing her white pageboy haircut to whip against her round cheeks. The sky blue bow affixed to the left side of her hair didn't budge.

Aunt Lucy nodded. "It does create a certain, er, doubt about the author's experience."

Jaida banged her mocha latte down on the coffee table. "You think? Not to mention her abilities in general. Who picked this one for us to talk about?"

Bianca's eyes cut to Cookie, who sat to my left on the poufy brocade sofa in the Honeybee Bakery's reading area. It had been best for everyone's schedules to hold our monthly spellbook-club meeting in the bakery after hours. My Cairn terrier, Mungo, snoozed in his bed at the bottom of one of the many bookshelves that reached from floor to ceiling. Lucy's orange-striped tabby cat, the very Honeybee that the bakery was named after, sat in the window, watching the sporadic traffic out on Broughton Street. The tip of her tail twitched every few seconds as she studiously ignored us. Heckle, Mimsey's colorful parrot, perched on the back of her chair.

Cookie's eyes flashed jade green. "I'd never select this ridiculous spellbook!" The vestiges of a Haitian accent lilted beneath her words.

I raised my hand and twiddled my fingers. "I did. Remember when I missed the meeting last month and asked Cookie to pass on my suggestion?" I wrinkled my nose. "Sorry. It's pretty awful, isn't it?"

Jaida raised one sardonic eyebrow. For a moment I felt like a witness on the stand. It didn't help that she still wore a conservative linen suit from her day in court.

Aunt Lucy shifted on her oversized chair, slipping off the Birkenstocks she typically wore to work at the Honeybee and tucking her legs up under her tie-dyed maxi skirt. She had already freed her mop of gray-blond hair from its twisted bun. "Why did you choose this book, Katie, honey? I'm sure you had a good reason."

I felt heat in my cheeks, and it wasn't from the ovens in the kitchen. At six p.m. we were long done with the day's baking, and, mercifully, the sweltering August evening outside was held at bay by the building's efficient air-conditioning. "I did have a reason, but I don't know how good it was," I said. "I was browsing online, and the description said Rowanna Bronhilde was a young witch who had recently come to the Craft and wanted to share with others what she'd learned from her mentor."

Lucy beamed affection at me, which made me feel a bit less foolish. She was one of the sweetest people on earth, and I could always count her on my side.

Jaida made a noise of derision. "*Rowanna Bronhilde?* There couldn't be a more made-up name."

"Made-up!" the parrot screeched, loud enough to make me jump.

Ignoring him, Mimsey let her expression soften. "Many witches take on new names for whatever reason. Perfectly reputable ones, too. That's certainly not the most unusual name I've heard. What about Rainbow Daxel and Amethyst Angeline? Or Juniper Sunbeam?"

"I kind of like Juniper," Bianca's red-limned lips pursed in amusement. "Not so

9

much Sunbeam, though." She crossed her long legs, and as she turned, a huge Tahitian black pearl strung on a silver chain glinted from the V of her white silk blouse. I marveled at the understated elegance money like hers could buy. Of course, Bianca possessed so much natural grace that it would have shone through a burlap sack.

Jaida looked somewhat chastened, something only the oldest member of our spellbook club — and informal coven — could affect. Not that Mimsey was trying to put anyone in their place, but she would have been our high priestess if our group had been so formal as to have one. Jaida respected her as much as any of us did.

"I should have read it first," I said, "before bringing it to everyone. It's just that I was curious how Bronhilde's experience as a new witch compared with mine."

Bianca tossed her long black braid over her shoulder and grinned. "So what do you think?"

I half smiled. "She seems like more of a newbie than I was last year. I feel like I could tell *her* a few things. I wonder why she decided to write a book when she's still such a neophyte." I paused, then: "There's something else that bothers me."

"What's that?" Cookie asked, tipping her

head. The gesture reminded me of a playful colt, as did her slim physique, which was shown to advantage in a green miniskirt and striped crop top. In the two days since I'd last seen her, she'd changed the blue streaks in her dark hair to deep magenta.

"Well, her attitude," I said. "As if spell work is supposed to be a bunch of pat formulas, simple recipes a witch follows without any . . ." I trailed off. After all, who was I to criticize? I called my own grimoire, where I kept track of spells and techniques, my recipe book.

"Without any intention," Lucy finished for me. "It's disturbingly lacking in everything she says. She forgets that spells are tools by which we send intentions into the universe. Not to say that physical things like water and salt and herbs and stones —"

"Flowers," Mimsey broke in with an enthusiastic nod. "And colors." Two areas of magic in which she happened to have special skills.

"Yes," Lucy continued. "All those things have power of their own to be tapped and shaped. But without intention, that power is chaotic and ineffective."

Cookie leaned forward and put one hand on the book that sat between us and her other on the arm of the sofa. It was a simple

11

gesture, but it garnered all our attention. "Perhaps this Rowanna didn't forget. Perhaps she never knew."

"But," I began. "She has a mentor —"

"Not a very good one," Jaida said.

Mimsey turned over her copy of *Spells for Everyone* and perused the back. Shaking her head, she opened the front flap and scanned the copy. She looked up at the group. "Her mentor goes by the name Astroy."

We exchanged glances. Jaida asked, "Astroy what?"

"Just Astroy." Mimsey leafed through the pages. "There's a picture of them together at the end of the text. He looks much older."

"Oh?" Bianca flipped her book open, too. "Oh! You're not kidding. She barely looks twenty — if that. Do you think they're . . . ?"

"It's not impossible." Mimsey sounded resigned.

"If not, they soon will be," Cookie said with conviction. "He is a sham, a fake guru, and she's an innocent."

I stared at her, surprised at her fervor.

She met my eyes and said, a bit defensively, "I know that look. The mentor is too self-satisfied. Unfortunately, that expression on the author's face, this Rowanna girl, is devotion. Blind devotion. It's easy to fool the young, and I suspect this one has either been fooled for a very long time or is a very young soul to begin with." She frowned. "Their union will not end well."

Silence settled over the six of us, broken only by Mungo's soft grunt as he rolled over on his back. At twenty-five, Cookie was four years younger than my twenty-nine, and I found it intriguing to hear her make such a proclamation about someone she'd never met. Still, I couldn't disagree with her.

"Well!" Lucy said with forced cheer. "Did anyone find a spell or two in here they would like to discuss?"

I sprang to my feet. "Who needs a refill? More coffee? Or I can brew tea."

Jaida directed a pleading look up at me. "I don't suppose there's any wine?"

I laughed. "What kind of joint do you think we run here? Of course there is — and mint julep blondies were the special today. I'll grab what's left." Faces brightened at that.

"Winos!" Heckle squawked.

"Oh, hush," Mimsey absently said to her familiar. "This is why you aren't invited to our meetings very often."

"Lushy witches," he announced, ignoring her admonition. She turned and gave him a firm look. He quieted immediately.

Grinning, I hurried to the kitchen to retrieve the bottle of Malbec breathing on the counter and a chilled Moscato from the industrial fridge. As I piled a variety of biscotti on one plate and sweet, bourbon-laced treats on another, I listened to the murmurs of my friends. A deep gratitude settled into my chest. How lucky I was! More than a year before, Aunt Lucy and Uncle Ben had invited me to quit my loathsome job in Akron and use my pastry-school training to open the Honeybee Bakery in Savannah with them. I'd bought the cutest carriage house in Midtown and gone from practically being dumped at the altar in Ohio to dating a sweet, good-looking fireman who liked to cook for me. Yeah, maybe Declan McCarthy and I had encountered a few bumps as our relationship got off the ground, but things were going smoothly now. On top of all that good fortune, I'd discovered my true nature as a hereditary hedgewitch, and now had the amazing opportunity to learn the different aspects of magic from the ladies gathered in the other room.

Okay, so I had to admit the whole witchcraft thing had started off a little rocky, too, with a woman murdered in front of the bakery and my reluctance to believe in my

14

own power. However, the spellbook club, and Lucy especially, had guided me to both belief and understanding. Not to mention that we'd brought a killer to justice and saved my uncle Ben from being arrested for something he hadn't done.

Unfortunately, that murder case wasn't the last one I'd been involved with since moving south. Guess you can't be lucky in everything.

Lucy was my mother's little sister, and, much to Mama's chagrin, had spilled the beans about our family history of hedge-witchery soon after we started working out recipes and baking up bespelled goodies for our clientele. Mama was pretty much over that by now, but things had been a little tense there for a while.

Mimsey Carmichael was the youngest-looking seventy-nine I could imagine, but Lucy and the others insisted she didn't use magic to hide her age. Comfortably padded and shorter than Lucy's five-two, she was from a longstanding Savannah family. Jaida French also looked younger than her forty-something years, her chocolate-toned skin smooth and utterly unwrinkled even around her expressive, almost hyperintelligent eyes. A defense attorney, she had been schooling me in tarot magic. Bianca Devereaux fo-

15

cused on traditional Wiccan methods and moon magic. The divorced mom of seven-year-old Colette, she supported them partially with Moon Grapes, her wine shop on Factors Walk, but her real money came from playing the stock market for big bucks. And then there was Cookie Rios. She'd immigrated to Savannah from Haiti when she was only nine, and her magical heritage included some slightly darker elements than the rest of ours.

I carried the tray to the Honeybee's library and set it on the coffee table. The ladies filled their glasses and chatted away about their lives. Jaida and her boyfriend were thinking about a trip to France the next spring. Mimsey and her husband were going to visit their daughter in California, along with their granddaughter, Wren. Bianca, still single after her husband had dumped her for practicing magic, had dropped her memberships to online-dating sites, deciding to let the man chips fall where they might. Then the conversation turned to Cookie's new husband, Oscar Sanchez, his position at a local lab that tested buildings for mold and other toxins, and her new job managing commercial real-estate properties.

No one was talking spells. At least they'd

16

stopped tearing apart the lame spellbook I'd chosen for discussion. For a moment I felt embarrassed that I'd ruined our meeting, but then I glanced at my aunt, who was happily listening to our friends, and I realized there was no ruining our gatherings. The last time we'd all been together had been at Lucy and Ben's town house on the first of August to celebrate the sabbat Lughnasadh with a fire and a harvest feast. With our busy lives, it had been another two weeks before we'd managed to dovetail our schedules, and it was obvious that a little social time with each other was better than discussing spells a kinderwitch could do.

"How's Iris working out?" Bianca asked. She was referring to our new employee, the eighteen-year-old stepdaughter of the cheesemonger down the block. Beneath her Goth makeup, Iris Grant sparkled with creativity and latent magical talent. She would be starting her studies at the Savannah College of Art and Design in a few more weeks.

Lucy's smile deepened, crinkling the fine lines around her eyes. "She's wonderful! We really do need someone here part-time, and she's taken to the work remarkably well." Her eyes twinkled. "And Katie was right about her potential power. We haven't so much as hinted at the idea yet, but I think she may be open to learning more about the 'special amendments' we add to the Honeybee pastries to help out our customers."

Mimsey had opened her mouth to say something when a loud rapping on the front door made us all jump. I let out a little laugh and glanced over my shoulder. The angle of the sofa prevented me from seeing who it was. The door handle rattled as someone shook it, then knocked again.

"We're closed," I called out.

Lucy waved her hand. "They'll see the sign in a second."

Sure enough, the knocking stopped.

"How could anyone miss it?" Bianca asked. "It's as big as your head and right at eye level. Not to mention the hours you're open are listed right below."

Bam! This time a fist pounded on the thick glass door.

Mungo rolled to his feet and barked, loud and high-pitched. His whole body quivered with alarm.

"Heavens to Betsy!" Mimsey craned her neck to try to see the door. Behind her, Heckle launched into the air and flew up to the speaker mounted high in the corner.

I bolted to my feet. "Now, that's just

downright rude." I leaned down and scooped up Mungo, who was still barking. "It's okay, little guy. Hush now."

He fell silent. Honeybee had shifted on the windowsill to press her furry, orange-striped cheek against the glass and look down the side of the building toward the ruckus.

"Perhaps there's something wrong." Lucy stood. "Maybe Croft or Annette need something." Croft Barrow owned the bookstore on one side of the Honeybee, and Annette Lander managed the knitting store on the other side.

A pale face appeared at the window next to where Honeybee sat. Startled, she jumped from the sill and scooted to the corner, where she turned and directed baleful disapproval toward the interloper. A hand cupped the glass, and a young woman peered in at us beneath the half-drawn blind. She bobbed up and down slightly, and I guessed she was standing on tiptoe in order to see inside. Even with her hand shadowing her face, I could see her eyes were so wide, the whites showed all around the washed-out blue of her pupils. She shouted something, her palm on the glass now, fingers curling against the surface as if trying to dig through it.

Desperate.

A feeling of dread settled below my sternum as a shiver ran down my back. Mungo whined. I put him down on the sofa and approached the window.

Even with her shouts muddled by the thick pane, her lips mouthed words I gradually recognized. Over and over, she was yelling, "Katie Lightfoot! I need Katie Lightfoot!"

I ran to the front entrance without thinking, fumbling in the pocket of my shorts for the key to the deadlock. Aunt Lucy and Jaida joined me as I flung open the door. Humid heat instantly wrapped around us like a heavy blanket.

The woman turned at the sound and stumbled down the sidewalk toward us. Her knees buckled, and she threw out her hands, almost dropping a small leather purse. I grabbed her elbow to keep her from falling. She hardly weighed a thing, which didn't surprise me, given her stick-thin arms and the protruding collarbones evident through her thin T-shirt. Those wide eyes met mine, searching.

"Katie Lightfoot," she whispered. "I need her."

CHAPTER 2

"I'm Katie Lightfoot," I said, trying to keep the words brisk and reassuring — and utterly failing. Something was wrong, very wrong, and a big part of me didn't want to know what. The other part warred between curiosity and fear.

I'd expected her face to show relief when I identified myself, but instead her determination seemed to die a little. When she stumbled again, Jaida took her other arm. Lucy held the door open as we helped her inside the Honeybee, supporting her between us. Bianca and Cookie looked on wide-eyed as Mimsey bustled out of the kitchen with a glass of water.

She thrust it at the newcomer. "Poor darling. That heat is a bear, isn't it? Here. Drink this down, and you'll feel better."

Mimsey, I realized, had not heard the young woman's impassioned pleas for yours truly.

"Come sit down." I guided her toward one of the blue-and-chrome chairs by the nearest table; Jaida followed my lead. Mungo scurried under a nearby table, out of the way but available if needed.

Mimsey's eyes narrowed as she took in the stranger's slack jaw and frightened gaze.

"Sit down," I repeated in a soothing tone. "And tell me why you're looking for me."

She sank onto the seat. Her head turned, and she blinked up at me from beneath a thin fringe of dishwater-blond bangs. Slowly, she pulled her arm away from where Jaida still held it and reached her quivering hand toward my face. Her icy fingertips touched my cheek, and I barely managed not to flinch away. So cold, despite the fine sheen of perspiration that covered her freckled nose and cheeks.

". . . Said to come to you if I ever needed help," she said, so low I couldn't hear all the words.

I leaned closer. "Who? Help with what?"

"My uncle said," she murmured. Her head wobbled on her neck, and her eyelids fluttered for a moment before she seemed to right herself with an effort. She snagged me again with those eyes the color of faded denim.

"Honey, what's your name?" I asked,

reaching for the water Mimsey had brought over.

Her eyes rolled back, and she sagged in the chair. Lucy drew in a sharp breath as Jaida and I both reached for her. Together we got our shoulders under her arms and lifted her, no mean feat for Jaida, who still wore pumps with three-and-a-half-inch heels. Our guest was a featherweight, and we managed to get her to the sofa in the reading area. Bianca lifted her feet onto the cushion and removed her sandals while a worried-looking Lucy placed a pillow under her head.

Cookie watched it all with hands on her hips, then nodded decisively and announced, "I'll call 911." She reached for her oversized hobo bag and fished out her cell. None of us argued.

"Who is she?" Mimsey asked, sparing me a glance between feeling the newcomer's forehead with the back of her hand and checking her pulse.

"I have no idea."

"But she knows you," Jaida said.

I lifted my palms in bewilderment. "I've never met her. She said her uncle sent her." Who could she be talking about? Mentally, I ran through a roster of our regular customers, recent acquaintances, friends — anyone who might have sent this young woman to find me. To seek *me* out for help. Not a soul came to mind.

Behind us, Cookie murmured into her phone.

"Her heartbeat is dangerously slow," Mimsey said, forehead wrinkling.

I heard the sound of Cookie snapping her bag closed, and turned as she retrieved the glass of water Mimsey had set on the bistro table. She marched into the reading area and, without a word, tossed the contents in the unconscious woman's face.

"Cookie!" Lucy cried as my own mouth dropped open.

The woman on the sofa coughed, then whooped in a great breath and coughed again. Her eyes remained closed, and her breathing, though deeper, was still ragged. Mimsey grabbed her wrist, feeling for her pulse again.

"Gone," our guest muttered. The cords in her neck stood out with the effort of speaking. Her hair, now drenched, stuck to her face in thin streaks.

I lowered my face toward hers. "What's gone?" I asked.

Her eyes flew open, transfixing me. "Katie." It wasn't a question.

I put my hand on her bony shoulder. "Yes,

it's Katie."

She stared at me. Blinked twice. "It's gone. The gree gree." She grated out the last sentence in a rough whisper, and her eyelids did a little dance before closing again. "You must find it."

I leaned down and put my ear right by her lips.

"Savannah . . . voodoo queen . . . can tell you," she breathed before her head rocked gently to the side. She let out a long sigh.

Stunned, I rocked back on my heels, studying the young woman's face. "She's unconscious."

Mimsey patted her hand. "But her heart rate is up. I think the shock of that cold water may have actually helped."

I wanted to check for identification, but couldn't bring myself to invade the pockets of her cotton shorts.

"What did she say?" Cookie's voice was harsh.

Voodoo queen.

I looked up at her. "Something about a gree gree."

The blood drained from her face, leaving her olive complexion pasty and her lips pale pink.

"Cookie?" I rose to my feet. "What's the matter? Do you know what that is?"

She rubbed her forehead with a shaking hand.

"She has no pulse!" Mimsey said, pulling my attention back to the cryptic stranger on the sofa. She slapped the woman's cheek, not so gently.

There was no response.

"Here, let me," Bianca said. She elbowed her way past us and straddled the woman on the sofa, placing the heels of her palms on her chest. As she began compressions, we moved away to give her more space. My own heart beat hard and fast.

The sound of sirens whined through the windows, growing louder and louder until flashing lights out on Broughton Street painted the amber walls and high ceiling of the bakery in emergency tones.

I turned to wave them in, but stopped cold when I saw my aunt. Lucy had backed against the front wall and had both hands over her mouth as she watched Bianca work. Shocked compassion shone from her eyes before they filled with tears that spilled over and ran in twin runnels down her cheeks. I ran to the door and opened it, gesturing to the first responders, and then hurried to her side. As uniforms filled the room, I wrapped my arms around her. She held on tight, and I felt her shoulders hitch in silent sobs.

Poor Lucy. I'd had, what? Five close encounters with death in the past sixteen months? I'd also had more than one close call myself. But even though Lucy knew of my involvement with murder cases, she'd never actually seen any of the victims.

At least this time it isn't murder.

A dragonfly drifted in through the propped-open door. It flew around the bakery, pausing for a moment near Mungo, who was still hunkered out of the way under a table, and then zoomed up to my eye level. It hovered so close, I could see the dark veins in its iridescent lavender wings, the big round eyes that never blinked.

Then it suddenly left the way it had come in.

My heart sank. Dragonflies were my totem. They served as a kind of metaphysical tap on my shoulder, telling me to pay special attention. And I had a pretty good idea why this one had been so insistent.

Okay, maybe this is murder. Attempted *murder, that is. Because whoever she is, she's still alive.*

"Try to think positive thoughts," I murmured into Lucy's ear, as much to hear the words out loud as to comfort her.

One of the paramedics took over from

Bianca. I recognized him as Joe Nix, a friend and coworker of Declan's.

Lucy nodded against my shoulder, sniffed once, and took a step back as she wiped her eyes with an air of determination. "Of course, honey. You're so very right. *Intention.* We must unite in our good intentions for her." She reached down and clasped my hand in her right hand and held out the other one to Mimsey. The older witch took it and held out her hand to Cookie. Still visibly shaking, Cookie took it. One by one, we all joined together, Bianca grasping my fingers to complete the circle. Without a word we stood and watched as they loaded the young woman onto a gurney, sending her our combined healing energy.

A mask still covered her face, and an earnest EMT hurried alongside the moving gurney, pumping oxygen into her lungs with a handheld ventilator. I allowed a flicker of hope as they approached the spellbook club. Together, we moved aside, and they rushed through the door and out to the waiting ambulance.

Joe saw me, and recognition flashed in his eyes. After the woman was safely ensconced in the back of the van, he returned. Jaida pulled the door closed after him, muting the blare of the siren starting up as the ambulance drove away and shutting out the curiosity of the small crowd that had gathered on the sidewalk. In moments it was utterly quiet in the bakery; a silence made all the deeper by the suddenness with which the commotion had stopped.

I broke it. "Is she going to be okay?"

Joe shook head. "I'm sorry, Katie. I just don't know."

Mimsey's hand went to her chest. Cookie turned away.

"Try not to worry," Joe said. "They'll keep working on her, and Candler Hospital isn't far." He ran his hand through his blond buzz cut. "It would help if we knew what we're treating. What happened?"

I took a deep breath. "No idea. She showed up here and then collapsed. We got her to the sofa, and Mimsey here checked her pulse, which was quite slow. Cookie threw a glass of water in her face, and that seemed to bring her around until just before you got here, when her heartbeat stopped and Bianca started CPR."

His head jerked to Cookie when I mentioned the water, and she looked at the floor. A ghost of a smile crossed his face before he looked back at me. "What else can you tell me? Who is she? How can I get in touch with her family?"

29

I rubbed my hand over my face, feeling defeated. "I was going to ask you that," I said. "You didn't find any identification?"

He shook his head. "Not even a library card."

I sighed. "I've never seen her before."

"Well, if you think of anything else that might be helpful, give the hospital a call," Joe said.

I agreed, and he went outside to the fire truck waiting for him down the block.

We looked around at each other, stunned out of the easy camaraderie of the spellbook-club meeting. Mungo trotted to me, and I bent and picked him up. Honeybee came out from the corner where she'd been hiding and rubbed against my aunt's ankle. She picked up the cat and buried her nose in the orange fur of her neck. Heckle glided down to Mimsey's shoulder and tucked his head near her shoulder. She reached up to stroke his bright feathers. No doubt the others would have liked the comfort of their own familiars right then — Jaida's Great Dane, Anubis, and Puck, the ferret who'd found Bianca recently. The only one of us who didn't have a familiar was Cookie.

Cookie, in the reading area, quietly gathered her things to go.

30

I marched over to her. "Tell me."

Her head jerked up, but she didn't say anything. Her color had returned and she was no longer shaking. But there was something in her eyes. Sadness? Resignation? I couldn't tell.

"Gree gree," I said, trying to keep my voice gentle, even though I knew by asking I was starting something I might not be able to stop. "You know what that means."

She held my gaze for a long moment, then nodded. "Gris gris," she repeated, and her slight accent highlighted the word's French origin. "G-r-i-s. It's a talisman, of sorts." She took a deep breath. "A voodoo talisman of power."

My hand flew to the silver ring I wore on a chain around my neck under my workaday T-shirt. In my short stint as a witch I'd already learned a bit about the power a talisman could hold. Mungo nudged my hand with his wet nose. He knew a bit about power, too. "What does it do?" I asked.

One shoulder rose and fell. "It depends."

I paused, then plunged on. "Our visitor said something about a voodoo queen."

She looked away but didn't say anything.

"Any ideas?" I urged.

By now the others had crowded close to listen. Cookie still wouldn't meet my eyes, obviously eager to end the conversation.

But I couldn't let her, not yet.

"Please, Cookie. This poor woman comes banging on our door, asking for me, says her uncle sent her, and then babbles something about a voodoo queen and some lost talisman I'm supposed to find. I have no idea who this uncle might be, only that he may be involved with voodoo somehow. Or not."

Finally, she glanced my way. "So that's what she told you," she said, her tone speculative.

"Yes, and not much of anything else. So, what do you think?" My frustration leaked out around the words. I really wanted her advice.

She leveled a cool green gaze at me and picked up her bag. "I think I no longer practice the religion of my childhood. I think I don't engage in voodoo in any form."

"But —"

Cookie held up her hand. "I think you need to take your questions to someone else."

Lucy put her hand on my arm, and my next words died in my throat.

The door opened, and a strikingly handsome man entered. "Ready to go?" Oscar asked his new wife, glancing around at the rest of us with an expression that turned from mildly friendly to downright per-plexed. "Or am I breaking up the party?" He looked at his watch. "You said —"

"You're right on time." Cookie turned a dazzling smile on him. "There was a bit of excitement, which we're all recovering from. I'll tell you about it on the way home." Without meeting anyone's eyes, she hooked her arm through his, and they moved toward the exit.

"Bye!" Bianca called. The rest of us re-mained silent.

Cookie's hand rose in a gesture of farewell, but she didn't look back at us as they left.

I stared after her. "Well!" I said.

Lucy squeezed my arm once before let-ting go. "You know Cookie had some dif-ficult times in Haiti. And you know her father's death was related to him being a voodoo priest."

My shoulders slumped. "Of course. I wasn't trying to make her feel bad or bring up bad memories. It's just —"

"We know, Katie," Mimsey said, reaching for her purse. The energy in the room had definitely shifted.

Lucy went behind the espresso counter and retrieved a towel. She went to the sofa and began dabbing at the wet splotch left from the water Cookie had thrown in the woman's face. I watched as Honeybee followed her, leaping up on the coffee table and weaving between the half-full wineglasses without so much as touching a single one. The others began to wonder out loud about our visitor while at the same time moving to the Honeybee library to help clean up.

"She seemed pretty determined to find you, Katie," Jaida said.

I winced. "Determined. Desperate. Something. Lucy, have you ever seen her in the bakery before?"

My aunt looked up from her self-imposed task. "I'm sure I haven't, and I have a good memory for faces."

"You do," Bianca agreed, pulling the keys to her Jaguar out of her alligator clutch. "Katie, how did she know to find you here?"

"Well, it's not a secret that I spend a lot of time at work. Maybe the uncle who supposedly sent her is a Honeybee customer. But you're right — I'm not usually here this late." I frowned. "And I cannot, for the life of me, think of any of our regular customers who would fit the bill. It's not like I advertise that I'm a witch."

"Maybe the uncle isn't a customer." Lucy paused in wiping the top of the coffee table with a dish towel. She looked up at Mimsey. "Could he be one of the druids?"

I blinked. The spellbook club had a history with the Dragohs, a druid clan that had existed longer than Savannah had been a city.

Mimsey pursed her lips in thought. "It's possible, I suppose."

"I could check with Steve Dawes," I said. He was Declan's former rival and one of the Dragohs. We'd agreed to remain friends once I'd put the kibosh on romance, though that friendship came with a certain awkwardness. In fact, Steve's joining the druid clan was one of the reasons I'd chosen Declan over him. The other, of course, was that I fell for Declan's strength, gentleness, and humor. It also didn't hurt that he was handsome as all get-out. That man had eyes so blue, a girl could drown in them.

Never mind Steve's eyes, a deep, warm brown, accented by long eyelashes that —

Mungo broke in to my thoughts, wiggling in my arms to let me know he wanted me to set him down. Reluctantly, I complied. His little body felt solid and comforting in my arms.

Once on the floor, he ran under the table next to the entrance. As I watched, he nosed at something brown and rectangular tucked back against the wall. Curious, I approached and knelt down. He nosed the item toward me.

"Oh, my gosh," I said.

Everyone's head turned. Jaida, holding three empty wineglasses, paused on her way to the kitchen. "What is it?"

"Her purse," I said, stretching out on hands and knees in order to reach it. Mungo nudged it right into my palm. "Good boy! Thank you." I drew it out and straightened up.

Mungo wagged, *You're welcome.*

Lucy came over to join the others who had gathered around. I opened the metal clasp and peered inside.

Our visitor wasn't one of those women who kept everything including the kitchen sink in her bag. Unlike the ginormous tote bag I hauled around, which held everything from running clothes and a cell phone to my lunch and my dog, her purse was petite and had precise compartments. I was surprised there wasn't a phone. Other than a wallet, the purse contained only a thin notebook, pen, comb, and pale pink lip gloss.

I took the wallet out between my thumb and forefinger. Everyone's attention focused on the thin leather. I ducked my head and opened it. The stranger's pale face gazed out from behind the clear plastic window. She looked healthy, even happy, with a slight smile and friendly eyes that did not reflect any of the fear I'd witnessed within the past hour.

I squinted at the writing by the picture, hard to read through the cloudy plastic. I could tell it was a New York driver's license, but that was about it, so I removed the plastic card. My lips parted in surprise when I saw the name.

Lucy leaned over my shoulder. A moment later I heard her gasp.

"What is it?" Jaida asked, crowding close.

"Her name is Dawn." Dazed, I raised my head and looked around at the ladies. "Dawn Taite."

Mimsey's eyes sparkled. "Taite, as in T-a-i-t-e?"

I nodded and tried to work up some saliva in my suddenly dry mouth. "What do you want to bet her uncle's name is Franklin Taite?"

They exchanged glances, and I knew what they were thinking: *Here we go again.*

CHAPTER 3

Besides my family gift of hedgewitchery, which consisted primarily of garden and kitchen magic, the spellbook club had declared from the beginning that I was also a catalyst. That meant things sort of *happened* around me. Things like serendipity and coincidences.

And dead bodies.

Since I'd moved to Savannah, I'd been involved in four separate murder cases, and except for the first one, they all involved magic. Perhaps that one had, too — I was too new in the Craft to recognize whether Mavis Templeton was a witch or not, but she sure as heck had been evil.

Then I'd been told that in addition to being a catalyst, I was also a lightwitch. It had something to do with battling black magic, blah, blah, blah. I'd never really understood it completely because the man who'd informed me of this "calling" had disappeared soon afterward.

His name was Detective Franklin Taite.

Now, hearing his name, Lucy groped for the back of a chair and sank into it. Both Bianca and Mimsey looked shocked, while Jaida seemed to be considering the consequences of this news.

"Oh, my stars," Mimsey breathed.

Indeed. Because Franklin Taite had been dead for at least three months. Not that that was common knowledge. I knew only because he'd contacted me after he left Savannah, at least in a way. Granted, that way was through a psychic medium, who had, in turn, passed on a couple of irritatingly cryptic messages from the spirit world to me. But Ursula Banford channeled only the dead, ergo Franklin had to have crossed the veil by then. Which made a certain amount of sense, because I'd been unable to find hide nor hair of the man.

I had told Lucy first, and eventually the rest of the spellbook club. The last message the medium had given me was that Franklin was sorry he'd left before really explaining what being a lightwitch was all about, but that he would send someone to mentor me.

I'd kept that bit to myself. So far no one had suddenly appeared to explain to me just what I was, but now I wondered: Could Dawn be that mentor?

I shook my head, unable to wrap my mind around the notion. She'd been scared and desperate, apparently seeking *my* help, not offering any of her own. That didn't preclude her from being the person Franklin had promised to send, of course. Circumstances changed.

Boy, did they ever.

Bianca glanced at her watch. "Oh, Katie. I'm so sorry. It's after seven thirty, and Colette's at a friend's house. I need to pick her up." She looked at me. "This is all very strange, but don't you worry. We'll figure it out."

Jaida nodded. "We always do." She reached for her briefcase. "However, I'm meeting Gregory at Casbah for supper, and I'm already late."

I waved my hand. "Of course. Go on, you two. Enjoy the rest of your evening." I grimaced. "If you can."

Lucy stood and squared her shoulders. "I'll call the hospital. Let them know who they just took away in the ambulance."

"I'll swing by with her purse, if you want," Jaida said. "They might want it."

"Um, right. Of course." I stared down at the license still in my hand. Dawn Taite was an organ donor.

I slid the license back into the battered wallet and the wallet into the purse, then gave it to Jaida. She leaned in and gave me a hug, and I breathed in the scent of cinnamon I always associated with her. It wasn't until I felt the comfort exuding from her that I realized how badly I needed it. The adrenaline was beginning to wear off, and now a tremor shivered deep in my core whenever I thought of the despair in Dawn Taite's eyes, of how she'd looked like she would scratch right through the window glass to get to me.

What had Franklin been thinking when he sent her to me? When had he done it? And, for heaven's sake, how had she gotten mixed up with voodoo?

"Go home, Katie. Be with Declan," Jaida said.

I nodded. I, too, was going to be late for supper. After all that had just happened, I missed Declan like crazy, even though I'd seen him only that morning. "Good night."

Bianca and Jaida left together, and Mimsey helped Lucy and me with the last of the cleanup. The dishwasher was swishing away, and I had just texted Declan that I was on my way when the door to the bakery opened.

I cursed myself for not locking it behind Bianca and Jaida, until I saw who it was. Detective Peter Quinn paused on the threshold.

My phone pinged in my hand, and I read Declan's response to my text.

Quinn coming to see you. Should be there soon. No hurry.

"Hello, ladies," Quinn said. "When I stopped by Katie's house, Declan said she was still at work, but I didn't know I'd find you two here. Hey, Mungo."

Yip!

Honeybee and Heckle, not usually the best of friends, had both tucked themselves into unobtrusive nooks in the reading area.

At the mention of my boyfriend, I imagined him whipping up one of his patented firehouse recipes in the tiny kitchen of my carriage house. The thought made my stomach rumble, despite the recent drama.

Mimsey marched up to Quinn and took his arm. "Now, Detective, we don't need to cool the whole outdoors, do we?" she asked, tugging him inside and pushing the door closed behind him.

He looked sheepish. "Sorry."

"That's okay, darlin'." She beamed a big ol' Southern smile at him. "I'm sure you have a lot on your mind."

"Now, Mims," Lucy murmured. Then, "Peter, do sit down. It's always a pleasure to see you."

Except back when he was accusing Uncle Ben of murder. But there had been a lot of water under the bridge since then, and most of it was friendly enough.

Quinn's lips twitched with amusement as he settled at a table. He was tall, with neat, close-cropped hair far more salt than pepper, and a deep tan. As usual, he was dressed impeccably and looked cool as a glass of lemonade, despite the unseasonably high temperature.

I rose automatically, retrieved a plate, and put a mint julep blondie on it. "We don't have any coffee brewed right now . . ."

He waved off my budding apology. "I didn't come for food, Katie." He sniffed at the blondie. "Hmm. This smells awful good, though. Don't mind if I do." He took a big bite, and pleasure crossed his face.

Lucy surreptitiously slipped her copy of *Spells for Everyone* behind the counter. Mine, thankfully, was already in my tote. Mungo ambled over and sat down, placing his paws on Quinn's loafer. The detective reached down and scratched behind the terrier's ears, and Mungo squinted his eyes in doggy bliss.

43

"We're just finishing up our sp— er, book-club meeting after all that excitement!" Mimsey said, plopping onto the chair beside him with an expectant look on her face.

Quinn stopped with the blondie halfway to his lips. "Excitement?"

Disappointment wiped away Mimsey's smile. "You mean, you aren't here because of the girl who collapsed?"

His eyebrows raised. "Collapsed? When did this happen?"

"Just now!" Mimsey said, looking to Lucy and me for confirmation.

"I thought you were here because of that, too," I said. "But you went to my house first, so you were looking for me, right?" I seemed to be much sought after this Tuesday evening.

His lips pressed together. "I was. First tell me what happened. Who fainted?"

I took a deep breath. "A woman showed up a little after six. She was looking for me. We let her in, but she seemed woozy. Disoriented, you know? But also frightened. She lost consciousness. It didn't appear to be a delicate Southern swoon, Quinn. Anything but. Whatever knocked her out was serious."

He took another bite, interested, but, given his line of work, hardly shocked.

However, his eyes widened when I contin-

44

ued. "Her heartbeat stopped, and Bianca started CPR. The ambulance came and they took her to Candler. Joe Nix — one of the paramedics?"

He nodded. "I know him."

"Well, he told us she stopped breathing again before they left. So we don't even know if she's alive."

"She's a friend of yours?" he asked in a sympathetic tone.

"Nope. Never met her." I took a deep breath. "But I found her driver's license. Jaida is on her way to the hospital with it now. Quinn, her name is Dawn Taite."

Quinn's head jerked back in surprise.

"She mentioned her uncle sent her to see me," I went on. "Do you think she could be Franklin Taite's niece?"

Detective Franklin Taite had once been Peter Quinn's partner. I'd met Franklin over the body of a dead man Declan and I found when we were picnicking in Johnson Square.

Quinn dropped the last of his pastry onto the plate and glared at me. "Dawn *Taite*? Damn it, Lightfoot. I should have known you'd be involved somehow."

Mimsey and Lucy shared a glance.

I straightened my shoulders. "There's no need to swear at me."

He blinked, but his expression softened.

45

"Involved in what?" I wasn't sure I wanted to hear the answer.

"I just came from a rather, uh, mysterious *situation.*" He regarded Lucy and Mimsey, who were both leaning forward to catch his every word. "This is a bit unpleasant. Are you sure you ladies want to hear this, too?"

"Pffft!" Mimsey said with verve. "We're not wilting violets, Detective."

Lucy nodded her agreement, though with less enthusiasm.

A smile tugged at his lips. "All right, then." His attention returned to me. "A body was found in an empty warehouse out on Old Louisville Road. It didn't have ID. Fortunately, or perhaps unfortunately, I didn't need it."

Was that sorrow that flickered across his features before being replaced with his usual professional poker face? Or perhaps regret? Baffled, I waited.

"It was Frank Taite."

My jaw dropped. *"What?"* I felt the blood drain from my face. A shiver started at the base of my neck and ran down the length of my back. Intellectually, I'd already accepted that Franklin had crossed the veil, but hearing it like this came as a shock. The man I'd come to reluctantly consider one of my mentors was definitely dead.

"Oh, my," Mimsey muttered.

"But it couldn't be —" Lucy began then clamped her mouth shut.

Quinn ignored them. "When you were asking after him a few months ago, you mentioned that you tried to track him down but couldn't. I don't know why you wanted to talk to him . . ." Eyebrows raised, he waited for me to step in with an answer.

I remained silent.

He continued. "Anyway, he'd obviously returned to Savannah, though he didn't contact me. Or you." He waited for a moment, watching to see if I contradicted him, then said casually, "At any rate, I thought you might be interested that we found him."

He was baiting me, of course. Fishing. But at the moment I was more gobsmacked than anything else.

"He was murdered," I managed.

Quinn's lips turned down as he slowly shook his head. "It doesn't look like it. No obvious evidence of foul play. There were some slightly odd things near the body, I suppose, but easy enough to explain."

"Odd how?" I asked, instantly suspicious.

He shrugged. "Food remains — someone probably squatted there for a while. And there were some feathers, like a maybe cat killed a bird inside. There were a couple of broken windows low to the ground, so easy enough for animals to get inside. Even snakes."

I shuddered. *Snakes.* I was afraid of snakes to a spectacular degree. "How many snakes?"

"None, actually. Only bits of shed skin from one or two." He leaned back and laced his hands over his abdomen. "What I want to know is why Frank was there in the first place. To the best of my knowledge, he hadn't been in Savannah for more than a year, so why now? I contacted the New Orleans PD, and his lieutenant told me Frank left the department. There was some crazy case involving human sacrifice that compelled him to go out on his own as a private investigator last winter."

Human sacrifice. Yeah, that sounds like something that would have piqued Franklin's interest.

Quinn continued. "No idea why he was in that warehouse, though. The medical examiner said there was no obvious cause of death at the scene, but it could be a heart attack, an aneurysm, or any number of things. They'll know more in a few days."

"A heart attack," I repeated with skepticism. Instinctively, I didn't believe that, but I was still reeling from the idea that Franklin had been alive all this time. I could barely think straight. Unless . . . "Hang on." I raised a finger. "An empty warehouse?"

Quinn nodded. "Used to be owned by a lumber supplier, but they went out of business. It's been on the market for a couple of years."

Aha! Franklin has *been on the other side all this time!*

"So, the body had been there for a while." I leaned forward, elbows on the table.

Lucy's eyes widened. Mimsey patted her arm absently.

The detective looked curious. "How long is a while?"

"I don't know," I waffled. "Three months?"

His lips quirked in a half smile. "That's quite specific."

I shrugged.

"But no." He glanced at my companions. "From what I could tell, the body was, er, fresh."

"Oh!" I said in a small voice. *What the heck?*

Detective Quinn's eyes narrowed. "Three months, you say. And you were asking me if I'd heard anything from him, let's see . . . three months ago, give or take."

I tried to look innocent, but Quinn wasn't

buying. "I don't suppose you know anything about how or why my former partner, who was supposed to be in New Orleans, happens to be dead here in Savannah. Do you, Katie?"

I shook my head. "Nope. No idea."

He regarded me in silence for several beats.

"None," I said. "But his niece might be able to tell you something. If she's conscious."

If she's alive.

"Why was she looking for you?" he asked.

My shoulders rose and fell. "She passed out before she could really tell me." *Gris gris. You must find it.* I wasn't lying, not really. I still didn't know what Dawn Taite had been talking about. I needed a chance to think things through.

"Uh-huh." He rose to his feet. "I'll be in touch. And, Katie? If you change your mind and decide you might know something that would help me out? Call me. I mean it." He pointed at Lucy and Mimsey. "That goes for you two as well."

Lucy nodded, her eyes wide.

"Pshaw," Mimsey said. "You don't think we'd ever stand in the way of justice, do you?"

"No," he admitted. "God knows you and

your friends have helped the department's solve rate in the last year." He walked to the door. "I'll head over to the hospital now. Katie, I'll call you tomorrow."

"Okay," I agreed as he went out. He waved and strode away as the door closed behind him on its pneumatic hinge.

The three of us looked at each other.

"What the blazes is going on?" Mimsey demanded.

I rubbed both hands over my face. "I wish I knew." Dropping my hands to my lap, I distributed a long look between them. "But it isn't good."

CHAPTER 4

It was nearly dark when I pulled into my driveway. I paused after turning off my Bug, listening to the tick of the engine cooling and savoring the simple welcome of light shining from the windows of my small home. The soft, yellow glow gently outlined the dark leaves of the magnolia by the corner and cast the delicate ironwork of the porch railing into relief.

Declan's big pickup truck was parked in front. We'd been spending far more time at my place than his lately, partly because my air-conditioning worked better. We also spent many evenings, after the worst heat of the day had faded, working in the gardens. I was a bit proprietary about the herbs and certain other plants with magical uses, but Deck enthusiastically tended the vegetables and kept the lawn manicured, saying he missed having a yard since moving into his apartment. Now he was puttering around in my little kitchen, and I wanted nothing more than to settle in for supper and tell him about my weird, weird evening.

Mungo bounded to the ground as I gathered my tote bag from the passenger seat. As he gamboled across the grass, pausing to do his business, a half-dozen fireflies began to blink, gathering around him from all over the yard. I'd learned they were his totem, much like my dragonflies.

"Well, I'll be! Thought those lightning bugs were all done for this summer."

I turned to find Margie Coopersmith striding toward me from her house next door. Her towheaded five-year-old twins trailed behind, leading their wobbly baby brother between them.

"But they sure do love that little dog of yours." Margie's white teeth flashed in her summer-tan face. But when she got close enough for me to see in the light from the windows, she looked tired. Blond wisps straggled out of a sloppy ponytail, perspiration soaked her hairline, her cotton shirt was wrinkled, and her shorts had a mysterious mom stain by the hem. Behind her, the back hatch of the Coopersmiths' Subaru was open to show a couple of bags of groceries.

I set my tote bag on the grass and gave

her a big hug. "I haven't seen you around much these days. What have you all been up to?"

"Camp!" the twins shouted, their combined volume impressive. Mungo ran over, and they dropped to their knees to pet him.

Margie gave me a wan smile. "Like they said, camp. All of us, it turns out, which is not what I had in mind when I signed these little darlings up. But one of the leaders at Happy Hands Day Camp bailed on them at the last minute, so guess who's finger painting and Zumba dancing with a dozen five-year-olds instead of just two?"

"Holy cow," I said. "You are a saint."

"Saint Margie," she snorted. "You betcha." But she sounded so low, I wanted to hug her all over again.

"Is Redding gone?" I asked. Her husband was a long-haul truck driver for a national transport company, and was sometimes gone for over a week at a time.

She sighed as the kids reached us, then forced a smile as she looked down at them. "Daddy's on the road for another four days, huh, guys?"

Jonathan and Julia, known as the JJs, nodded as a single unit. "He calls us on the computer," Jonathan said, and Julia added, "Every night."

Margie looked down at her watch. "Lord, I didn't realize how late it is. He'll be calling any minute, and these two need to brush their teeth and get into their jammies before they talk to Daddy." The JJs pouted in response to her pronouncement, but she waved them toward their house. "Better hurry."

They took off at a run as she swooped Baby Bart up into her well-muscled arms. "Come on, big guy. You're due for a bath."

He giggled.

"Redding reads those two hellions to sleep every night he's on the road," she said, affection in her voice.

"He's a good man," I said. "I know it's hard sometimes, though, with him gone so much." Truthfully, I was in awe that Margie wrangled three kids by herself with such aplomb.

She allowed a small grimace to cross her face. "Well, heck. I did think I'd given myself a little break by unloading my kiddos at camp during the day, but it just didn't turn out that way." She shrugged and then straightened her shoulders. Bart regarded me with solemn blue eyes. "First-world problems, you know. We're lucky as anything, and we know it. They'll be in school pretty soon, and I'll probably miss them like the dickens." She turned toward her car, then paused. "You want to get together some night after bedtime? I sure wouldn't mind a real conversation with a grown-up."

"You bet! Let's set something up."

She opened her mouth to say something when a dramatic wail came from the interior of her house. Rolling her eyes, she started across her yard, yelling, "I'll call you," over her shoulder.

I waved my agreement and stooped to pick up my bag. The porch light flicked on as I strode toward the carriage house, Mungo trotting at my heel.

Declan met me on the threshold, along with a blast of cool air and so many scintillating scents that I couldn't identify them all. Shutting the door behind me, I breathed deeply. But before I could ask what was for supper, Declan cupped my chin in his palm and brought his mouth to mine. I ran my fingertips through his dark curls, and my body molded to his muscular frame. Everything flew out of my mind except the tart taste of apples on his lips and the intense safety I felt in the arms wrapped so firmly around me.

Then Mungo yipped his own greeting, so loud we started to laugh in the middle of our kiss. Declan stepped back and met my gaze with the half smile I found so sexy. I blinked, distracted by the cocktail of hormones rushing beneath my skin. Then the smells from the kitchen reached my brain again.

"What have you been cooking up, mister?"

"Well, hello to you, too."

"You can't expect me to stand on ceremony after a greeting like that," I said. "Now I am sorrier than ever to get home so late. I'm starving." *And not just for supper.*

He motioned toward the kitchen, to the left of the postage-stamp living room. "Then by all means, let's plate up."

Mungo trotted eagerly after him.

"I'll be right there," I said, reaching to close the shutters on the front windows. As I turned back, the sound of rattling dishes drifted from the kitchen. The fringed, vintage floor lamp illuminated my purple velvet fainting couch against the peach-colored back wall. Small wingback chairs faced it across the Civil War–era trunk that served as a coffee table. To my right, a built-in bookshelf held a few volumes and various knickknacks. Beside it, a tiny hallway led to the bedroom and three-quarter bath, and steps led from the main living area up to the dark loft above, where I kept a small television, a folding futon, and the secretary's desk that hid my altar from view.

As I walked across to the kitchen, my attention was drawn to the table on the covered patio outside the French doors. Declan had set it with a checked cloth, my mismatched Fiestaware dishes, candles, and a bottle of red wine, already open to breathe.

Come to think of it, I hadn't had a chance to drink any wine with the spellbook club before Dawn Taite had started pounding on the door. I just managed to stop myself from going out then and there and pouring a glass.

"Wow," I said, joining Declan. "Pretty fancy doin's for someone who likes to eat in front of the television with the game on."

He smiled and gestured toward the slow cooker on the kitchen counter. "Pork chops smothered in fried apples." Handing me a plate, he went on. "With savory corn pudding, tomato and cucumber salad dressed with feta and basil vinaigrette, and chilled watermelon grown by *moi*. In your garden, but still."

"You had me at *pork chops*. Holy mackerel, Deck. This is amazing!" I stepped over and lifted the lid of the slow cooker, inhaling the fragrant steam that curled up from the interior. "And a tablecloth? Candles?

How romantic."

He waggled his eyebrows à la Groucho Marx. "Glad you noticed."

I narrowed my eyes. "What did you do?" I teased.

Laughing, he started dishing tender pork, tart salad, and rich corn pudding onto plates — two dinner-sized and a small one for Mungo. "Grab the watermelon out of the fridge and open the door for me, woman."

Happily, I did as instructed.

As I walked by my tote bag, which I'd flung on the sofa, my cell began to ring. I opened one of the French doors for Declan and returned to put the bowl of cold watermelon down on the coffee table.

"Come on — do you really need to answer that?"

I glanced at the display, then up at him. "I'm sorry. It's Lucy."

He frowned, but took our plates outside.

I answered the call. "Lucy? Did you find anything out?" Before we left the bakery, she'd said she'd try to get an update from the hospital.

"Katie, honey, it doesn't sound good." I could hear the sadness in my aunt's voice.

My heart sank. "But she's still alive?"

Out of the corner of my eye, I saw Declan's head jerk up.

"So far," Lucy said.

"Did the hospital tell you anything more? Like what's wrong with her?"

"The hospital didn't tell me anything at all. You know how careful they are about patient information. But after I told Ben about what happened, he checked with Peter Quinn, who gave him the update." As Savannah's former fire chief, Uncle Ben had known and worked with Detective Quinn for several years — long before Quinn had wrongly suspected him of murder.

"Right," I said. "Well, thanks for letting me know."

"Are you all right?"

I shrugged, but she couldn't see that. "I don't know her. We did the best that we could tonight. But of course it bothers me."

Declan now stood in the doorway, blatantly listening.

"As for Franklin Taite, I already knew he was dead. Still, hearing it's actually true from Quinn is more upsetting than I expected."

His eyes widened at that. I tried a smile, but felt it slide off my face like warm butter.

"What are you going to do?" Lucy asked.

I sighed. "I don't know."

"Katie, it's pretty obvious you have to do

something."

"Just let me sleep on it, Luce. Okay?"

"Of course, honey. Say hello to Declan."

"Will do. Good night."

I hung up and joined Declan in the doorway. Together we moved to the patio, and he absently held out my chair. "Lucy says hi," I said, as he moved around to his own chair and sat down.

"That's not all she said." Leeriness and curiosity warred in his tone.

"Um, no."

"Katie! Spill! What happened at your book-club meeting?" Even though he knew full well what the spellbook club was, he refused to call them that. "Or does this have to do with why Detective Quinn wanted to talk to you?"

I'd taken a big bite of pork chop and had to wait until I swallowed to answer. "Both, actually." In between enjoying every morsel of the fabulous meal Declan had prepared, I filled him in on what had happened with Dawn Taite, about her cryptic message, and how Peter Quinn had shown up afterward with his own bombshell.

He ate slowly, listening. His face revealed little. When I was done, he said in a flat tone, "This has something to do with you being a lightwitch."

I took a swig of wine. A big one. The conversation was about to get sticky. "I suspect so," I admitted.

"Of course it does." The words came out harshly, but immediately Declan's expression turned tender. "I'm sorry. I didn't mean it to sound like that. I know this is what you do." We'd had a few difficult conversations since he'd learned I practiced spellcraft, but, for the most part, he was quite supportive — at least when it came to the hedgewitchery Lucy and I worked at the Honeybee. However, he wasn't too happy when I was drawn into murder cases that involved magic. I couldn't blame him.

"Well, it's only *part* of what I do," I protested. "It's not like being a lightwitch is my whole life." Or was it? How could I know for sure? I didn't even know for sure what being a lightwitch *was*. "And it's not something I chose, either." I didn't like how defensive it came out.

He smiled and reached over to squeeze my hand, which was resting on the tabletop next to my very empty supper plate. "I know. I get it. I'm on your side."

He was telling the truth about getting it, at least. He wasn't a witch and didn't practice any kind of magic, but he had his own unwanted "gift" to deal with. I ached to ask Declan about his uncle Connell, and whether he might be able to help. I held my tongue, however.

We didn't discuss Connell.

I'd tried a few times, after Declan declared he accepted that his uncle had taken over — taken over his body, that is. Connell was long dead, and there was some question in the Declan's family lore as to whether or not he had even been human. My boyfriend, Mr. I Think It's Cool That You're A Witch But It's Not My Bag, had had his mind suddenly wrenched into a different awareness when he had inadvertently, and most unwillingly, channeled his ancient ancestor during a séance.

Then it had happened again. Luckily, that time Connell had helped save our lives.

Declan said he was okay with it, but it turned out he wasn't — not really. Every time I brought it up, he got defensive, and that led to enough tension between us that we ended up arguing about something else entirely.

So I'd stopped trying.

Now as we spoke, he seemed to shrink into himself, growing somehow smaller and tentative. I saw something in those eyes I loved that saddened me: fear. My big, brave firefighter was downright scared of the paranormal aspect of my life — and now his. Or maybe it wasn't that. Maybe he was afraid of the not knowing, of the inevitable mystery of magic. I felt the same way sometimes. A lot of times. But I knew at least some of his trepidation had been sparked by the things he'd seen since getting involved with yours truly, as well as some pretty frightening stuff he'd experienced himself.

Like that time when I'd almost killed him. Anyway . . .

Then the fear was gone — or overcome — and my old Deck was back. Relief coursed through me as he stood and pulled me out of my chair. He drew me to him and held me close for several seconds in silence.

"It's just that I worry about you," he finally said, stepping back. "But I also love you and love who you are. The whole package. Got it?"

I felt my lip quiver and clamped it between my teeth. I nodded.

He grinned and ran his thumb along my cheek. "Okay. Now, what are you going to do to get to the bottom of this latest mess?"

"You really think I should get involved?" I wanted to hear him say it.

Declan laughed. "You were thinking you might just sit this one out?"

"It's closer to home than Quinn's other cases," I admitted. "And I want — no, I need — to understand what the heck is going on." I turned to gather the plates from the table. "After all, whether or not Taite was really dead when Ursula passed on his message to me — something I'm going to be calling her about, believe me — it seems that now he sent me another message, this time truly from beyond the grave, via his niece."

"The stuff about the talisman." Declan gathered the half-full bottle and wineglasses.

I nodded and started toward the kitchen with a stack of dirty dishes. "Apparently I'm supposed to find it, whatever it is. And it's not an ordinary talisman, like Lucy gave me when I first came to Savannah." *And later Steve Dawes,* I thought, mentally fingering the metal ring resting near the hollow of my throat. "It's a voodoo gris gris. And whatever *that* is seems to have upset Cookie."

"Voodoo." He put a lot of warning into the single word. "So, what's the first step, Detective Lightfoot?"

We'd reached the sink, and now I bumped his hip with my own. "Very funny. But without more information about what happened to Taite, I think the obvious thing to do is find the voodoo queen Dawn mentioned." I started loading dishes into the dishwasher.

He frowned. "I don't like that part of it. Not at all."

Straightening, I wiggled my fingers in the air like spider legs. "Spoooooky voooodoooo."

Declan grabbed my wrists without smiling. "Do not take it lightly. Just *don't*. You remember the fire on the Southside last year." A glimmer of that fear I'd seen during supper crossed his face again.

I sobered.

"A woman died in that fire, Katie, and in the end, the police proved it was a voodoo ritual that started it."

"I remember," I said. "But, honey, that fire wasn't started by voodoo. It was started by an overturned candle. An accident. Something like that could happen during one of the spellbook club's rituals."

His eyes narrowed.

"Or if the wind were to whip up right now? We left those tapers burning on the patio table."

"Oh!" His eyes widened, and he ran out of the room.

Of course the candles were fine. Mungo, who was still lounging in his patio bed, would have let us know if anything had gone even slightly awry during our few minutes inside. But it did speak volumes about my firefighting boyfriend's state of mind that he'd forgotten the basic rule to never leave a candle burning unattended.

Hopefully, my words would put his mind to rest. However, I wasn't taking anything about the voodoo element of this situation lightly. I didn't know much about that flavor of magic, but I'd seen the expression on Cookie's face, and remembered Lucy's admonition.

I don't know what happened to her father, but it had something to do with him being a voodoo priest.

Cookie's father had died when she was nine, right before the rest of his family had moved to Savannah.

CHAPTER 5

"Mmm. Those smell like a Caribbean vacation," Iris Grant said, leaning close to the macaroons I'd just removed from the oven. Her eyebrow ring glinted in the sunlight shining through the window that looked out on the alley.

"You just gave me a great idea," I said, glancing over at my aunt. She stood at another of the stainless-steel counters in the Honeybee kitchen, carefully slicing hummingbird sheet cake into luscious squares. "There's still some pineapple left, isn't there?" I could smell it in the still-warm cake, along with the scents of ripe bananas and vanilla bean. This morning the Honeybee really did smell like a tropical paradise.

Lucy looked up and nodded. "Quite a bit. You know Ben always buys things in cases."

"Yes, I do," my uncle called back to us from behind the register. "That's why you always send me to the bulk stores to stock up."

"You're right, Ben. Very efficient." I turned back to Iris. "Let's boil some of it down to make a nice, concentrated, sticky jam," I said.

"Like you did with the pomegranate juice yesterday?" Iris asked.

"Well, that's more of a jelly, but I want to use it for the same thing. You can see these macaroons are thumbprint cookies, as well. So we want to fill —"

"Macaroons?" Iris broke in. "Those don't look anything like the cookies my step-mother brought me last time she went to Atlanta."

"Ah." I held up a finger. "Little round sandwich cookies? Slightly crunchy and light as air?"

She nodded.

"Those are *macarons,*" I said, then spelled the word. "Though sometimes it's spelled the same as the coconut-based cookies we have here. *Macarons* don't typically have any coconut at all. The cookies themselves are delicate meringue stabilized with al-mond flour and sometimes an additional flavor to go with whatever filling you put inside."

Lucy laughed. "You sound like you should

open your own pastry school."

I blushed. "Sorry."

"No!" Iris said. "I want to know."

"Well, they can be a little tricky to get just right." I reached for a number-two can of pineapple. "I had an instructor who challenged us to come up with all kinds of crazy fillings."

Iris shifted position so I could reach the electric can opener. "What did you make?"

"Let's see." I thought back. "A sesame paste spiced with ginger, as I recall, and a curry cream with turmeric and chili. I seem to remember something with fennel, too."

"For *cookies*?" Iris almost looked offended.

I shrugged. "Savory cookies, yeah."

"Will you show me how to make *macarons* sometime?" Iris asked. "But filled with something chocolaty." She got a dreamy look. "Dark chocolate with raspberries. Or caramel. Or both."

Lucy put down her knife. "Sounds delicious, all right."

Laughing, I said, "We can make some for a daily special next week. But right now I'm going to finish up these coconut macaroons. We can fill half the thumbprints with the pomegranate jelly and the other half with pineapple jam. They'll taste like bite-sized piña coladas."

"I approve," Ben said, turning to face us. He'd recently changed his rimless glasses for a pair with brown frames that nicely complemented his ginger hair and neatly trimmed beard. At the moment there were no more customers waiting to be served, and the brightly lit kitchen was open to the rest of the bakery.

"A piña colada without rum?" Iris frowned.

I poked her tattooed shoulder gently. "What do you care? You can't legally drink for another three years, anyway."

She shrugged. "Whatever. So what's the deal with the pomegranate jelly?"

"You don't like it?" I asked.

"It's yummy," Iris said. "It's just that you made such a big thing about needing to use it in a recipe."

"Pomegranate is popular right now." I kept my tone mild, but my eyes cut to my aunt. I hadn't realized Iris had picked up on how strongly I felt about using the fruit in a recipe. The truth was, one of our patrons was a bestselling author who came in each morning for a muffin and green tea, and stayed until afternoon, typing away on his keyboard. Lately, Martin — though he published under another name — had shown up less frequently. When he did, he sat and stared at his laptop screen with a woeful, almost bewildered expression. Ben, who had a practiced knack for relating to customers, had finally teased it out of him: Our resident scribe was suffering from writer's block.

So Lucy and I had determined to do our best to help. We'd baked hazelnuts into moist fig muffins, a magical double whammy to increase his inspiration. We'd ordered bouquets of cornflowers and narcissus for the bistro tables from Mimsey's flower shop, Vase Value, because those two flowers held creative power. I'd even slipped up his tea order one day, giving him jasmine green tea instead of the plain variety, along with a few muttered words directing the flower's inspirational and intuitive powers to aid in overcoming his block. The pomegranate had been Lucy's idea; my twist was to concentrate the juice into jelly with the intention of concentrating its creative, generative power as well.

"And then you got really weird," Iris said, "standing over that steaming pot and talking to it."

My eyebrows shot up. I *really* hadn't intended for her to hear my incantations.

My incantations over a boiling cauldron. I

suppressed a smile at the thought, still avoiding her gaze.

"Hey, Iris, do you have a minute?" Ben asked. He didn't practice magic, but he knew what Lucy and I did in the Honeybee kitchen. Now he was trying his best to distract Iris from her current line of questioning.

"Um, sure," she said, finally catching my eye. Hers were full of curiosity, and, I realized, hope.

I smiled. "We'll talk about it later, okay?"

She grinned in return. "Yeah?"

I looked over at Lucy, who nodded her agreement. "Yeah."

"Cool!" She hurried out to where Ben had moved behind the espresso counter. "At your service, Mr. Eagel."

"Stop calling me that," he said. "If you don't start using my first name, I won't show you how to make a black eye," he said.

"A what?" came her puzzled response.

"One of our regulars orders it, so you need to know how to make it. Start with a cup of drip, and then make a double shot of espresso . . ."

I grabbed two of the macaroons, went to stand by Lucy, and handed her one as she began loading a display tray with the slices of cream cheese–frosted hummingbird cake.

"Are you sure she's ready?" Lucy asked in a hushed voice.

"More than I was." I also kept my tone low. "She has latent talent. We all agree on that."

She finished filling the tray and began to wipe down the counter. "Of course. All the members of the spellbook club have had a chance to meet her and . . . assess her potential. However, do you think she's really open to the idea of witchcraft?"

I pressed my lips together in thought. "How about if we start slowly? Rather than talking about the Craft, we could begin by introducing her to some of the qualities of herbs and spices. A lot of people know lavender is soothing and relaxing, and citrus is invigorating. What we do is simply introduce another level, or perhaps aspect, of what herbalists do when they use plants as medicine. Or how aromatherapists use essential oils."

Lucy gave a decisive nod. "I like it. We can gauge her reaction and go from there." She dropped the towel in the laundry hamper and put her hands on her hips. "Now, what are you going to do about Franklin Taite and his poor niece?"

I blinked at the abrupt change of subject, but we'd been busy ever since getting in that morning, and Iris had arrived early. This was the first chance my aunt and I'd had to talk about the Taites since she'd called me the previous evening. I glanced into the other room, then nodded toward the office. Lucy followed me in, and I shut the door behind us.

It was a small room lined with shelves. A computer desk and chair, one tall file cabinet, and the club chair where Mungo napped while I was working crowded most of the space where we performed the myriad of administrative tasks as necessary to running our business as the actual baking. I leaned my elbows on the file cabinet while Lucy sat in the desk chair, reaching over to stroke under Mungo's furry chin. He wagged his appreciation, looking between us with avid interest.

"I'm not sure how much I can do, actually," I said in answer to Lucy's question. "The whole thing is so strange. How could Franklin contact a medium when he wasn't even dead?"

"There's no doubt he died recently?" Lucy asked.

"You know as much as I do," I said. "Quinn hasn't told me anything you haven't heard."

"What does Declan think?" Lucy asked.

She knew he didn't care for how I got sucked into murder investigations, especially those that involved magic.

"He says he wants me to figure out what's going on."

I'd thought my aunt would be surprised, but she only nodded and said, "Of course he does. He's coming around. I told you he would."

"Well, when he channeled his uncle Connell, it did seem to change his mind about what's possible — and about what magic might really be about. He's been quite curious about my spell work since then, asking questions about things he used to avoid, or, even worse, marginalize."

"Hmm. Yes, I imagine having another consciousness speaking through one's lips might have that effect," she said.

"It frightened him, too. He doesn't like to talk about that, but I can tell."

"You've had your own share of frights," she said, her expression an invitation to open up.

I swallowed hard. "I just wish I knew what, exactly, I'm supposed to do as a light-witch. We don't know what kind of evil might have taken an interest in Franklin — or Dawn." And despite making light of it with Declan, delving into the world of voodoo was a big, scary unknown.

Lucy gazed at me with sympathy, but didn't offer any stellar advice.

I sighed. "So, here's the plan I came up with last night." Long after Declan had fallen asleep. "Such as it is. I'm going to call Quinn and see if he knows anything more about Franklin's death, especially whether they're considering it suspicious now. Then I'm going to see if I can track down Ursula Banford in case she can shed any light on how Franklin could have communicated with her from the spirit world when he was still alive on this plane."

My aunt nodded. "Both good ideas."

"Then I'm going to track down the voodoo queen Dawn Taite referred to. She said Savannah voodoo queen, so it has to be someone here in town, right?"

A frown creased Lucy's forehead. "Voodoo's not something to be taken lightly."

"No kidding. But at least I might have an in — or, rather, Cookie might have an in. I'm hoping she's still in contact with some locals who could help, even if she doesn't practice anymore."

Lucy stood and gave Mungo one last pat on the head before reaching for the doorknob. "She turned her back on her upbringing for a good reason. She might not be willing to get involved with some elements of her old community."

"All I can do is ask," I said. *Again.*

"That's true. She was in shock yesterday — we all were, of course. In the end, however, she's a member of our coven. And she likes you, Katie. A lot. If she can't — or won't — help, at least she might be willing to refer you to someone who can."

"I hope so," I said, as Lucy opened the door. The sound of murmuring voices punctuated by Ben's booming tone alerted us the Honeybee had gotten busy. We hurried out to help, and found the line to the register four deep.

My phone calls would have to wait for now.

When the rush was over, Lucy got to work restocking the display case beside the register, and Ben bundled up the garbage to take out to the alley. Our writer sat at a corner table, typing slowly, even hesitantly, but at least he was typing. Two women, similar enough in looks that they had to be related, sat at another table, lingering over sweating glasses of sweet tea and sharing a piece of Lucy's hummingbird cake. A young man sat across from a woman of similar age, both hunched over their laptops and in their own separate worlds, defined by whatever was playing through their earbuds. Both were swigging black coffee, and she was drumming her fingers on the tabletop. Given the textbooks piled by her computer, I guessed they were college students studying for summer finals. Another woman sat on the sofa by the bookshelves, engrossed in a hardback volume with a brightly colored dust jacket.

It looked like a small bomb had gone off in the reading area. Two chairs had been moved next to the front window; plates and cups littered the top of the coffee table. Even the windowsill where Lucy's Honeybee had been sitting last evening held dirty dishes. Apparently, the two self-bussing stations at each end of the bakery were invisible to our patrons. Still, business was business, and I wasn't going to complain about a rush or a little cleanup. I returned the chairs to their places and gathered crockery to take into the kitchen, happy to see the customers must have enjoyed their goodies; only crumbs remained on the plates.

I returned to the library to tidy the shelves of books. Our library was open to everyone who came into the Honeybee. Anyone could take a book or leave a book, but most of the volumes were supplied by the ladies of the spellbook club. They had started this practice before we'd even opened, and, in fact, had been loaded down with bags of books the very first time I'd met them.

They chose the books using whatever method worked for them. It was largely intuition, but Mimsey sometimes employed the use of her pink shew stone, and Jaida might check about the usefulness of a particular book using a tarot spread. However they chose them, the books in the Honeybee library were intended to help patrons in whatever way they could.

As a result, the collection was rather eclectic. Unsurprisingly, there were a large number of self-help books and a good-sized how-to section. There was also fiction — everything from contemporary and classic literature, to science fiction, romance, mystery, fantasy, and werewolf tales. There were memoirs and science books and cookbooks. You never knew how a book might benefit a customer, and it wasn't our job to guess. Only to supply the books. Whenever I saw someone leave with one of the books the ladies had supplied, I felt a flicker of satisfaction.

I picked up a copy of *How to Write Hit Country Songs* and tucked it into its proper place. Next I returned a copy of *Civil War*

Savannah to the shelf then picked up an old, dusty volume with the title *Herbal Practices Throughout the Ages.* Pausing, I took a look inside. It had been published in 1948. Still, the contents looked interesting, and the historical annotations could only add to the kind of kitchen magic I already practiced. It even had a section on using herbs to increase psychic powers. Grinning to myself, I tucked the book under my arm to take into the office. I'd have to ask the ladies which one of them had brought *me* a book this time.

Before I left, I turned to the woman on the couch. Her coffee mug and pastry plate were empty. I stooped to pick them up, saying, "How are you doing? Is there anything else I can get you?"

"Oh!" she squeaked. She slammed her book closed and blinked up at me with eyes so light brown, they were almost amber. "You startled me!"

"I'm sorry," I said.

She laughed and waved a well-manicured hand. "Oh, gosh. No, I'm sorry. I can just *lose* myself in a book sometimes." Now that she wasn't speaking in the high register of surprise, her voice was deep and silky, the round tones of the South smoothing the edges of her words.

I smiled in return. "I know exactly what you mean. It's actually rather wonderful, don't you think?"

She nodded, eyes lit in agreement. Her blond hair swung around her tanned shoulders in a smooth-as-satin blunt cut. Her summer halter dress was a breezy pink with a darker pink sash at the waist.

"I don't think I've seen you in here before," I said.

"This is my first time. I'm waiting for my boyfriend to meet me. He just went on and on and on about this place. I have to tell you, the fig muffins are to die for!"

"Thanks," I said. "My aunt Lucy came up with those."

"Well, you just tell her they are divine. I know I'm going to have to come back over and over again. There are simply too many yummy things to try. My boyfriend told me one of his favorite things to eat here are the Parmesan rosemary scones, but, you know" — she lowered her voice — "I simply had to have something sweet today."

"Sweet, savory, and sometimes a little of both. That's what we specialize in!" I turned to go. "And we certainly hope you do come visit us again." I had the distinct feeling she would.

"Why, thank you! What's your name?"

"I'm Katie Lightfoot. I own the Honeybee, along with my aunt Lucy and uncle Ben."

"Well, Katie, I am tickled pink to meet you. I'm Samantha."

"Nice to meet you, Samantha. I'd shake your hand, but —" I gestured toward my full tray. "Are you sure I can't bring you something else?"

"Oh, gosh, no. I'm full up. Is it okay if I just sit here for a while?"

"Of course."

She spared me one more smile before cracking her book open on her lap again. As she did, I saw the title: *How to Get What You Want . . . Every Time.*

Huh. I wondered which of the ladies had brought that one in.

The rubber soles of Iris' shoes squeaked on the tile floor as she spun and twirled through the usually mundane job of unloading the dishwasher.

"You seem awfully happy," I said, taking the clean muffin pan she offered me and putting it on the shelf beneath one of the counters.

She looked stricken. "Oh. Gosh, Katie. I'm sorry."

I looked up in surprise. "Why on earth would you be sorry for feeling happy?"

Lucy came out of the office in time to hear me. She stopped to listen.

Iris blinked heavily rimmed lids. "That woman who passed out in here and had to go to the hospital. That was, you know, *tragic.*"

My aunt smiled gently. "It was. But there's a lot of tragedy in the world, all the time. You still get to be happy."

A grin tugged at our protégée's lips. "Yeah?"

I nodded firmly. "Yeah."

The grin bloomed full force, and she twirled back to the open dishwasher to grab a bread pan. "I've been picking out my classes at SCAD. There are so many interesting things to choose from! I want to learn them all."

Lucy laughed. "Anything in particular appeal to you?"

"Oh, golly. There's fashion and graphic design and animation. I love the idea of animation, you know? Like, for the movies?" She waved the pan in the air to emphasize her point.

"Sounds like a good career," I ventured.

"Oh, but then there's filmmaking and jewelry design and all sorts of writing courses."

"Those sound good, too," I said.

"Heavens, all those choices would make my head spin," Lucy said.

Iris sashayed over to put the pan on an empty rack. "I know! Isn't it *wonderful*?"

"Well, let me know what you decide. In the meantime, I have some phone calls to make."

Back in the office, I grabbed my cell. For about two seconds I considered making my calls from the alley to ensure privacy, but it was too darn hot out — especially given the heat all the brick and asphalt soaked up. Last August, most highs had topped out in the eighties, but this year we'd hit a hundred three times already.

"Guess you're stuck with me," I said to Mungo as I closed the door.

His response was a long, disinterested yawn.

"I hope Iris doesn't wander in here while I'm questioning a psychic about dead people."

His ears perked up, and he sat back on his haunches to listen. At least the thrum of the air-conditioning system was louder in here, which would help to muffle my words out in the kitchen.

However, Ursula Banford didn't answer the number I had for her. Her outgoing voice mail message said she was working on set in Madagascar and would be checking messages infrequently. She was in high demand as a psychic — and personal trainer — in Hollywood, though, honestly, she hadn't done much good for me other than giving me messages from a supposedly dead Franklin Taite. Now I had to wonder if those particular messages had even been genuine. But I did think they had been. I knew she was the real deal — I'd had personal contact with her "posse" of spirit guides at a séance, and goddess knew she'd paved the way for Declan's deceased uncle to make his way across the veil.

But real deal or not, she sure wasn't going to be any help to me today.

CHAPTER 6

I called Quinn next. He answered on the third ring.

"Katie."

"Hi, Quinn."

"I believe I said I'd call you."

"Sorry! You want me to hang up, and you can call me back?"

Silence, then a small sound, and I realized he was laughing. I breathed a mental sigh of relief. Despite our frequent repartee and my willingness to push the envelope with him, I didn't want to get on his bad side.

"I was wondering how Dawn Taite is doing, and I know the hospital won't tell me anything directly," I said.

"Well, I can hardly blame you for being concerned," he said, apparently mollified by my motivation in calling. "She's in pretty bad shape."

I felt the muscles along my shoulders relax and realized I'd been bracing for worse news. "So she's still in the ICU?"

"Oh, yes. No change since she was admitted yesterday. She's in a deep coma, and the doctor who is treating her is baffled as to why. They've run a battery of tests on her so far, and there are more planned."

"Poor thing," I said. Mungo blinked up at me, concern shining from his gentle eyes. "Did you find out anything about her?"

His voice lowered. "She's Franklin's niece, all right. I talked with her mother up in Saratoga Springs. She told me Franklin was her husband's older brother, and after her husband died five years ago, Franklin hadn't been good about keeping in touch. Add in that Dawn and her mother have been more or less estranged ever since the girl dropped out of college. Mrs. Taite is on her way down to Savannah now."

"Did Dawn's mother say her daughter and Franklin were close?" I asked.

"Apparently, Frank asked Dawn to come work with him," he said. "That's why she quit school, but it's been a while since Dawn and her mother have spoken, so Mrs. Taite doesn't know what Dawn has been up to — with or without Franklin."

"So she was working with him," I said, deep in thought. Franklin had been on a quest against dark magic, and as a law offi-

88

cer he'd help utter strangers if they were in danger, whether the threat was secular or occult. Apparently, he'd roped his niece into joining him in the same mission.

Quinn took a deep breath before speaking with what I suspected was forced calm, "So? Are you going to finally tell me why you were trying to find Frank Taite back in May?"

I hesitated.

"Katie." Another measured inhalation. "Please. You know something about his death, don't you?"

"Um . . ."

"You've always been so helpful in the past." Disappointed now. Was he playing persuasive parent to my recalcitrant teenager? "Why on earth would you keep vital information to yourself?"

Oh, to heck with it. "It's not vital information, Quinn. I was trying to find Franklin to clarify something he said about . . . um, the way I help the police out sometimes." Granted, it was easier to talk about this stuff with Quinn over the phone than in person, but I wasn't about to start talking about lightwitches and magical callings. "The thing is," I rushed on. "I thought Franklin Taite had been dead for at least the last three months."

"Hmm. I wondered, given your questions yesterday. And you thought that because . . . ?" he prompted, almost managing to keep the impatience out of his voice.

I looked at Mungo and could have sworn he nodded at me. So I said, "You remember Ursula Banford? The psychic that worked on the set of *Love in Revolution*?"

"Mmm-hmm." Pure skepticism now.

"She gave me a message from Franklin. Back when they were shooting the movie here."

"A message?"

I barreled on. "From *beyond,* you know? The spirit world? Now, how could he possibly send a message through a medium unless he was already dead?"

"You have got to be kidding!" Quinn exploded. "You *believed* her?"

"She didn't know who Franklin was," I protested. "She had no idea what kind of message she was giving me. It didn't mean anything to her, only to me."

"Except he wasn't dead yet."

"Well, yeah. There's that."

"What was this message from beyond the fictional grave?" Quinn asked.

"That's not really any of your business. It certainly has no bearing on his death." At least, I didn't think so.

A sigh traveled through the wireless. "Good Lord, Katie. Don't you think you should leave that up to me? You usually seem so practical. Even, dare I say it, wise at times. Then you tell me something like this, and I have to wonder."

"Which is why I didn't tell you in the first place, and why I wish to heaven I hadn't now!"

Mungo made a warning noise low in his throat, and I realized I was practically shouting — at a homicide detective.

Quinn was silent. Then he said, "That's a valid point."

"Okay." I knew I sounded sullen. Maybe he hadn't been that far off the mark in treating me like a teenager. The thought did not fill me with pride.

"You and Frank shared an interest in the paranormal — that's for sure," he said.

If you only knew. "Does the medical examiner know what caused his death yet?"

"The preliminary report confirms heart failure, but it was caused by snake venom."

I moaned. "He was bitten?"

Quinn hesitated, then said, "They found the bite marks over his heart." I heard him take a breath. "Which is pretty weird. Still, it's possible he was already prone or even unconscious by the time he was bitten."

"You don't exactly sound convinced," I said.

He ignored that. "Katie, were you two that close? Frank left Chatham County PD right after last Halloween. I didn't even know you were . . . friends." It seemed to pain Quinn to say it, and I wondered what he was thinking.

"We weren't. Not friends, not close. I didn't have any contact with him after he left for New Orleans, either."

"I don't understand."

"Honestly, Quinn? Neither do I." In fact, the whole conversation made me feel more confused than ever. Mungo leaned over and nudged at my hand until I stroked his soft little ears, something he knew would comfort me as much as him.

"Is there anything else I should know?" Quinn asked. He sounded as defeated as I felt.

Should I tell him about the talisman Dawn had spoken of before losing consciousness? That I was supposed to find it? What about the voodoo queen?

No, absolutely not. If he reacts that way when I tell him about a message sent through a psychic, he's not going to take any talk about a gris gris or a voodoo queen seriously. It would be a waste of my time, and possibly he'd get in the way of what I knew I had to do.

So I answered, "Not that I can think of." I could always tell him later, if need be.

"Okay, then. I'll call you if there's an update on Dawn Taite."

"Or Franklin," I said. "Are you investigating his death as a homicide?"

He sighed. "As a suspicious death for now. Good-bye, Katie."

"Good —"

But he'd already hung up.

"Hellooooo!" The voice brought my head up from where I was rearranging the depleted platter of key lime tarts that were the day's special. It wasn't yet noon, and except for the two sisters sharing hummingbird cake, the same customers who'd been hanging out in the Honeybee before I'd ducked into the office were still staying cool inside.

"Mrs. Standish, how are you this morning?" Ben asked with a smile in his voice.

Brushing my hands off on a towel, I moved behind the register to stand by my uncle.

"Fine and dandy!" The rich, fruity tone of the words sounded like a Southern version of Julia Child. "Just had to stop by and see how y'all are today!" A few inches taller than Ben, she towered over me. She wore a white gauze tunic and slacks. Gold bangles clanked on her wrists as she gestured, and a gold chain that would have made an NFL player bling-proud shone from around her generous neck.

"Now, Edna," her companion said, moving out from where Mrs. Standish had eclipsed him. He wore his usual straw hat to protect his bald pate from the summer sun. His sunshine-yellow, short-sleeved button-down was tucked into festive Bermuda shorts that revealed bird-like legs and knobby knees. His dark eyes sparkled with good humor.

"Mr. Dean, it's good to see you," I said.

"Thought I'd come along to make sure Punkin here brought the éclairs back home."

She rolled her eyes at her beau. "As if I'd forget!"

He and I exchanged a brief look, and I suppressed a grin. He hadn't thought she'd forget; Mrs. Standish often returned to the Honeybee for more pastries because she'd eaten all the goodies from her first purchase before she arrived home.

However, Mr. Dean gazed up at her with obvious affection. And no wonder. The éclairs they'd come in for had been Lucy's idea when Mrs. Standish, a widow, had mentioned how lonely she was. Sure enough, the vanilla in the filling, along with extra oomph from my aunt's benevolent incantation, had opened up the possibilities for love. Mrs. Standish had netted the man she called Skipper Dean, and they'd been going strong ever since.

"It's just hot as *Hades* out there," Mrs. Standish declared, dramatically swiping the back of her hand across her brow. Hot or not, her iron-gray cap of hair was perfectly coiffed. "So we thought we'd take the ship out of port for a little runabout. Blow out the cobwebs, don't you know?" We all understood the "ship" in question was a twenty-three-foot motorboat.

The two students glared at her, no doubt because her loud voice cut right through their ear-budded privacy. I mentally shrugged. They'd just have to live with it. She and her date would be on their way soon enough, and Mrs. Standish had been one of the Honeybee's first customers ever. Loyal through and through, she'd encouraged Ben to join the Downtown Business Association before we'd opened and spread the word about our baked goods throughout Savannah. I loved every extreme thing about her.

"So, I hear you had some excitement here

last night!" she practically brayed. "Bless your little heart, Katie Lightfoot, you certainly have had a lot of tragedy here at the Honeybee!" Heads throughout the room turned to look at me.

Okay, *almost* every extreme thing about her. I wouldn't have minded a bit more discretion at the moment.

The door opened, and Steve Dawes came in. His eyes roved the room, lighting up when they met mine.

I smiled and lifted my chin in greeting, then returned my attention to Mrs. Standish. "I suppose that's so —" I began.

"I mean, first a murder before you're even officially open for business, and then having a killer attack you right here in the bakery! And don't think I haven't seen your name in the *Savannah Morning News,* my dear, more than once. You're practically famous!"

"Oh, I certainly hope not," I murmured.

Steve grinned at me over her shoulder, but he also looked puzzled.

"It's just so lucky you were here, it being after-hours and all, when that poor young thing *collapsed* like that!"

I pasted on a smile. "Is that in the paper already?"

"I haven't had a chance to look yet." She tapped her diamond-studded earlobe. "But

I do hear things, you know."

I knew. It seemed as if Mrs. Standish knew everyone in Savannah. It was one of the things that made her such a successful advocate for us — but, Lordy, I'd hate to get on her bad side.

"It really was lucky," I said. Steve had moved closer and was unapologetically listening. Then again, everyone in the whole place was listening, whether they wanted to or not.

"Who was she?" Mrs. Standish probed.

"I'm afraid she wasn't anyone I knew." Which was true, technically. "The ambulance took her to the hospital before we could find out her name." Also technically true.

Mrs. Standish frowned. "Well, we certainly hope the best for the poor dear." She brightened as I handed her a bakery box packed with a half-dozen vanilla éclairs. "Now we're cooking with gas, Skipper! Thank you so much, Katie. We'll see you soon!" She held out her arm to him, and with great dignity he thanked me and escorted her out to the street.

Steve shuffled up to the register. "What was that all about?" His honey blond hair was slicked back into the usual ponytail, but a frown ruined the line of his full lips. Serious brown eyes hooked my gaze and wouldn't let go. Ben moved behind the coffee counter.

I waved my hand. "Oh, you know Mrs. Standish."

Steve's eyes narrowed.

"What can I get you?" I asked.

"Parmesan rosemary scone. Dry cappuccino," he said without consulting the blackboard menu behind me. Now it was a challenge to see who would look away first. "Katie," he prompted. I heard Ben start the cappuccino. It was Steve's regular drink.

"I'm surprised you don't know already," I said, finally breaking eye contact with a sense of relief and reaching for a plate. "You always seem to know when stuff like this happens, sometimes even before I do." Steve had kept tabs on me ever since we'd become involved, and hadn't stopped when Declan and I got together. As a reporter and columnist for the *News,* not to mention druid and son of the powerful Heinrich Dawes, he had many sources of information.

But now he just shrugged one shoulder. "Sorry. Haven't been keeping up lately, I guess."

I was surprised to find that hurt a bit. *Don't be a ninny. It's good that he's not thinking about me all the time. Right?*

No one was standing behind him, so I lowered my voice and said, "A girl came here yesterday, looking for me. It was Franklin Taite's niece!"

His eyes widened. He knew my history with Detective Taite. We'd both thought he was a witch hunter at first.

"She passed out before I learned much," I said. "But she wanted me to find some kind of voodoo talisman."

The skin tightened on his face.

I handed him the scone, and he handed me a bill. "And right afterward? Peter Quinn dropped by to tell me they had discovered Franklin Taite dead yesterday — right here in Savannah!"

"Good God!" he exclaimed. "What have you gotten yourself into this time, Katie-girl?"

I glared.

"Sorry. I have been pretty good about not calling you that, though." He took a bite of scone.

The pretty blond from the sofa had gathered her things, including the book that had so thoroughly grabbed her attention. She approached now and asked, "Calling Katie what?"

Steve looked down at her, swallowing. "Nothing. I take it you two have met?"

"Just a little while ago." I smiled, genuine at first, and then felt it stiffen across my face. *I'm waiting for my boyfriend.* Was Steve Samantha's *boyfriend*? Good Lord, he hadn't dated anyone seriously since we'd stopped seeing each other.

Samantha wrapped one arm around his neck and pulled him toward her. She gave him a lingering kiss. "Mmm. You taste yummy!"

Oh, brother.

She turned her gaze to me, and something glinted in her eye that hadn't been there before. *Ownership.*

I continued to watch them, wanting to be gracious but steeped in my own awkwardness. I felt Lucy come up beside me.

"Well, hello, Steve. I see you've gone with an old standard today. And welcome to the Honeybee, dear." She directed this last at Steve's companion — er, girlfriend — with a true smile.

"Sam, this is Lucy Eagel, Katie's aunt. And this is her husband, Ben. Thanks," he said as he took the proffered coffee drink from my uncle. "And this is Samantha Hatfield."

Ben smiled, too, as he shook her hand. Yup, smiles all around. Of course, Ben was extra delighted. Declan was like a son to

100

him, so he'd never cared for Steve's interest in me.

Previous interest in me.

"Come on, lover," Samantha said, and I had to stop myself from gagging. "Let's take our yummies down to the riverfront."

First off, she had no yummies left except a book about how to get her own way. In fact, *yummies* struck me as vaguely obscene.

Second: *Yuck.*

"Sounds kind of hot," I said.

"Oh, we'll find some cool shade," she said, her smile not quite reaching her eyes when she looked at me.

"Okay, honey," Steve said. I grabbed his plate and put the rest of the scone in a bag so he could take it with him. I held it out to him at arm's length. He took it with barely a look of acknowledgment, set his half-full cappuccino back on the counter, and allowed her to lead him out the door before I could count his change.

I stared after them, trying to regulate my breathing.

"You knew it would happen sometime," Lucy said.

"Steve dating someone? Of course," I said. "I'm okay with that."

She looked skeptical.

"I am, honest. Just not her."

"And why not?" My aunt's voice was gentle.

"Because . . ." *Why indeed?* "Because I get a funny hit off of her. She wants something from him."

"I just bet she does," Ben said as he joined us. He waggled his eyebrows suggestively.

"Very funny," I said. I stalked back to the kitchen and began to take out the bread pans. There was sourdough sponge to mix.

CHAPTER 7

Determined to make a fresh start, I'd sold or given away almost everything I owned when I left Ohio to move to Savannah. I brought only my clothes and a few treasured pans, utensils and cookbooks, and a jar of sourdough starter. I'd made it on a lark while working as the assistant manager at a bakery in downtown Akron, a position that involved a lot more office work than actual baking, not to mention a boss with substandard business ethics. The starter never leavened a single loaf of commercial bread for his uninspired establishment, but I had used it extensively at home to make breads and biscuits, pancakes and waffles.

Some modern recipes for sourdough starter begin with store-bought yeast. More traditional methods often involve the skins of grapes, which naturally harbor some lovely wild yeasts. I'd done all of that in pastry school, but for this starter I'd used the simplest method ever: mix some flour and water together, put it in a corner open to the air (but covered with a thin screen of cheesecloth), feed it more flour and water each day for five days, and see what happens. There are wild yeasts in the air all around us. They're different according to location; the wild yeasts in San Francisco, for example, are particularly tasty, which is why sourdough bread from that region is so treasured.

The yeasts in Akron were pretty tasty, too — enough so that I tucked a jar of my homemade starter behind the driver's seat of the Bug and brought it south. It immediately became a staple at the Honeybee, and every afternoon I mixed up a new batch of sticky sourdough — in much larger quantities now, of course — and folded it into pans to slow rise overnight in the refrigerator. Each morning the Honeybee filled with the heady scent of baking bread, in addition to the sweet and savory smells of our other creations.

Over time, of course, Savannah had altered the flavor, adding her native varieties of airborne yeast to the mix and making it her own. In some ways I felt as though the city — and the people whom I'd met in my new home — had affected me in much the same way, infusing me with local lore and customs and changing something deep down in the core of who I was.

As I scooped the smooth dough out of the industrial mixer into pans and added more water and flour to the starter for the next batch, the tangy aroma teased my nose and made my mouth water. I realized I hadn't eaten anything since the yogurt and granola Mungo and I had shared that morning; Declan didn't generally tumble out of bed like I did at four a.m. My familiar, of course, had downed his second breakfast *and* lunch by now. I was more than due for some calories.

I sliced two pieces from one of the sourdough loaves baked that morning and slathered one with mashed avocado and the other with herbed cream cheese. Then I layered on Tasso ham, thinly sliced provolone, tomatoes, and fresh spinach. As Lucy came into the kitchen, I cut the sandwich in halves, put them on two plates, and handed her one.

She took it with a smile. "Mmm. Looks delish, honey. I'll grab us some mango sweet tea to go with."

Icy glasses of tea in hand, we settled in at a back counter in the kitchen, one of the few places in the open floor plan where the customers wouldn't see us, and dove in.

"Have you talked to Cookie about the voodoo queen yet?" my aunt asked around a bite of bread.

I shook my head. "I'd like to do it in person."

Lucy grinned. "Too easy for her to get away from you on the phone."

I grimaced. "Something like that. But that means I'll have to run by her condo tonight after work, and I'd rather not wait that long."

"We can handle things here," Lucy said. "It won't be that busy, and Iris will be here until close."

"I might take you up on that."

"You should call Cookie's office to see if she's going to be there." Lucy took a sip of tea. "It sounds like she's out working with clients an awful lot."

I nodded my agreement as a voice out front caught my attention. I stood quickly, wiping my mouth with a paper towel grabbed right off the roll. "Or I might not have to." I hurried out to where Ben was helping someone at the register.

Not someone: Cookie herself, in a form-fitting white suit over a silk shell the same shade of green as her eyes. The small white flower tucked behind her ear added a festive note.

My uncle had placed something in a bag with the Honeybee logo on it and was starting to hand it to her. "Here you go. Hope Oscar enjoys —"

His eyes widened as she grabbed it out of his hand and thrust a bill at him. "Thanks. Must be going," she said, and spun toward the door as if she couldn't get away fast enough.

"Cookie!" I said.

She slowed, and I saw her shoulders slump.

She's trying to avoid me.

Too bad.

"Hey, can I talk to you for a sec?" I asked.

Her eyes met mine. "Oscar wanted me to pick up one of your blue-cheese scones."

Or you wouldn't have come in at all.

"I need to drop it off at his lab and then meet with a possible buyer." From what I understood, Oscar Sanchez tested samples from homes and businesses for an environmental safety laboratory. He'd found Cookie her current job in real estate through his connections at work.

"Please?" I asked.

"I'm already late."

I just looked at her. She was a terrible liar. Her eyes skittered away, and her mouth pulled back in a gesture of resignation. She slowly walked back toward the register. Ben looked between us without hiding his curiosity. No doubt he'd hightail it over to ask Lucy what was up as soon as he had a chance.

Cookie stopped in front of me. "Let's go in the office," I suggested.

She sighed. "Sure. Okay."

"Hi, Cookie!" Lucy greeted her from the sink where she was rinsing off our lunch dishes. Our friend raised her hand in greeting but didn't say anything. My aunt and I exchanged glances, hers wishing me good luck. Iris, who had followed us in from where she had been tending the espresso counter, peered after us with frank interest.

I closed the door behind us. "Mungo, mind making some room for Cookie?" He stood on the club chair and stretched before jumping down to check his food dish. "I'll get you some chicken salad in a few minutes."

His forehead wrinkled, but he didn't protest. Instead he watched us from beneath the chair with much the same expression Ben had shown. I moved the piece of sheepskin that served as his bed and gestured Cookie to the best seat in the house. She sat slowly, tugging at the hem of her skirt.

"I'm so sorry to have to bother you like this," I began. "I know you don't want anything to do with voodoo anymore."

Her lips pressed together.

"But you're the only person I know who understands it. I really and truly need your help."

She frowned, looking down at the floor. "Oscar disapproves of voodoo, as well. When he was a child in the Dominican Republic, a neighbor hired a shady priestess to curse his older sister. Luckily, another priestess was able to avert the curse, but he knows how I feel. He wouldn't like it if I were to become involved."

Stunned, I sank into the swivel desk chair. "I'm sorry he had a bad experience when he was young. I am. But I'm surprised you won't help me just because *Oscar* wouldn't like it."

She must have heard the disbelief in my voice, because her head jerked up, defiance in her eyes. "You know I'm more independent than that. Even though I'm married now, I am still my own woman."

"Of course you are. You didn't even change your last name."

A grimace flashed across her face. "Oscar didn't like that, either. He's a very traditional man." She held up a finger. "Do not think I'm cowed by that, however. It's simply that we're both learning about compromise as we . . . adjust . . . to being married." She took a deep breath. "Oscar was married before, but it's a very different situation for me."

No kidding. Cookie had always been known for going through boyfriends and jobs every three or four months. When she'd returned from Europe with a different man in tow than the one she'd left with, none of the spellbook club had been surprised. But the ring on her finger had thrown us all for a loop. It hadn't helped that Oscar had little interest in socializing with his new wife's friends. He still felt like a stranger to us.

And perhaps a bit to Cookie, too, I realized. "Is everything okay between you two?" I asked.

"Yes! Of course. It's just that I don't wish to introduce difficulty into our relationship."

I quirked an eyebrow. She sounded more stilted than usual. Stress?

"Also, my new job is very time-consuming," she said. But she looked away as she said it, and I could see her resolve crumbling. "Plus, I'm redecorating our condominium," she tried. "The former owners had terrible taste."

"Please?" I asked again. "Just help me find

someone else who might be able to answer my questions. That's all I ask — a foot in the door of the voodoo community here in Savannah."

Mungo stood and nudged at her leg, adding his encouragement.

She pressed a palm over her eyes. Mungo watched her intently, then sat back when she finally gave a fraction of a nod and said, "I can do that, I think." Another nod. "Yes. I'll contact someone I used to know to see if he would be willing to help." Her hand dropped and met my eyes. "I cannot guarantee he will, however."

"I appreciate anything you can do."

She stood and smoothed her skirt. "I know. We are sisters, of a sort, Katie. I wouldn't do this for anyone else."

I stood and hugged her. After a moment, she returned it. "Thank you," I said. "When do you think you'll know?"

Her eyes flared, and I realized how pushy I sounded.

I raised my palms to her. "It's just that this feels so urgent, you know? With Dawn Taite in the hospital and Franklin Taite dead."

She blanched. "Detective Taite is dead?"

"Oh! Oh, my God. No one told you? I assumed the spellbook grapevine . . . I mean . . . Oh!"

"Jaida told me the woman's identity, and that she might be related to your detective."

So I filled Cookie in on Quinn's visit after half the spellbook club had left. "Feel free to tell Bianca and Jaida if you see them," I finished. "I need all the help I can get with this one."

"And it's far more personal than I had believed," Cookie said. "I'll make a call right after I meet with my client, Katie. We'll find this voodoo queen and the missing gris gris."

Cookie was true to her word. An hour and a half later, the Honeybee phone rang. Ben picked it up, murmured something into the handset, and handed it to me with raised eyebrows and a knowing grin. I took it back to the office, where Mungo was snoozing on his sheepskin again. He cracked open an eye as I sat down at the desk, but it drifted shut a moment later.

"I called an old friend of my family's," Cookie said. "He is from Port-au-Prince, and came to America soon after my mother moved us here. They call him Poppa Jack."

"Wonderful! And? Will he help us?"

"I don't know yet." Was that nervousness in her voice?

"I don't understand," I said.

"He wants to meet you. To . . . see you in person. Before he's willing to talk to you at all about voodoo or any of its many manifestations." She inhaled. "Poppa Jack will determine whether you're worthy of his help after he sees you face-to-face."

"Okay . . ." I drew the word out, trying not to feel slighted. After all, I didn't know this Poppa Jack person, either, and I was the one asking for help. "When can I meet him?"

"I would normally pick Oscar up after work, but I can leave the car for him if you will drive." Cookie, usually willing to rely on public transportation, now regularly borrowed her husband's car for her job. They were shopping for a second vehicle but hadn't found anything they liked yet.

"You mean now?" I looked at my watch. It was a few minutes after two.

"Right now. I'm on my way to Oscar's laboratory."

Lucy had already assured me I could leave. "That should be fine. I'll be there in ten minutes."

I hung up and untied my paisley chef's apron. Mungo had come to his feet, wide awake, at the mention of my leaving. I leaned down and scratched behind his ears.

"Sorry, buddy. I don't know this voodoo friend of Cookie's, and he might not be into dogs."

Ar-arr-ar.

"Shh. I know, it's a drag. But I can't leave you in the car — it's just too hot out. So hang out here, and maybe Lucy or Iris will bring you a treat." I stepped back, eyeing his wee form. "Not that you need it after that chicken pecan salad."

He snorted his disdain for effect, but then blinked up at me with worried eyes.

"It'll be okay," I said. "I'm just going to ask a few questions — if this Poppa Jack guy gives me the chance, that is. Cookie will be with me."

He made a noise in the back of his throat, but allowed me to grab my tote bag and walk out of the office without further protest.

"Lucy," I called.

She hurried back from the front of the bakery. "Katie? Is everything all right?"

"Cookie came through," I said. "She wants me to meet a friend of her family's. Can you handle things if I take off now?"

She glanced at the wall clock. "Sure. Iris and I can handle the prep for tomorrow. Right?"

Iris, chopping dried apricots, nodded.

114

"Already started."

"Thanks," I said, rifling in my bag for my typically elusive car keys.

"Where are you going?" Iris asked.

"To see a man about something that's lost," I fudged.

She frowned.

Lucy waved me toward the door. "Go. Call me if you find out anything. Otherwise, I'll see you before closing. Or if I don't, come by and pick up Mungo at our place."

"You're the best." I stooped to give her a kiss on the cheek.

"Pshaw," she said. I could see the quiet strength in the set of her shoulders and the compassion shining from her face. My aunt would do everything she could to help me — and Dawn Taite. That knowledge not only made me feel warm, but also bolstered my own resolve.

Franklin must have believed in me, or he wouldn't have sent Dawn to find me. I'll track down that gris gris, whatever it is. And I'll figure out what happened to them both.

Cookie closed the passenger door, and the Bug filled with the sweet scent of gardenia. My nonna, who had died when I was nine years old, had always worn gardenia perfume. Now the scent usually indicated that she was nearby, and a few times she had even spoken to me. However, this time I was pretty sure it was just the flower in Cookie's hair.

She saw me glance at it and removed it from behind her ear. "Here," she said, putting it in the empty stem vase attached to the dash.

I started to protest, but thought better of it. Perhaps refusing her gift would be seen as an insult. So all I said was, "Thanks."

The tiny smile that tugged at the corner of her lips told me I'd made the right call.

"Go toward Abercorn Street," Cookie directed. "Then follow the extension. Poppa Jack lives on the Southside, on the other side of the Armstrong campus. Look for Windsor Road."

I checked traffic and pulled away from the curb. As I drove, I debated how to ask Cookie about voodoo. Heck, I wondered *what* to ask her about voodoo.

"It's not evil," she said.

My eyes cut to her. "You've taken up mind reading now?"

"It's not that difficult. You're on another case, Katie. I understand that you've been called again, as a lightwitch or . . . I don't know exactly. However, I do know, as a member of your coven, that it's my duty to aid you."

"Duty, huh? Sounds pretty . . ." I trailed off. I had been going to say *grudging,* but that was uncharitable. I knew I was asking a lot from her.

"Yet it's the truth. And in this case I'm the only one of the spellbook club who *can* assist you. So I shall, as I am able." Her speech pattern was becoming more formal, though her accent remained nearly undetectable. Like me, Cookie had the ability to use her Voice to infuse her words with power, but that wasn't what was happening here. I had a feeling she was remembering an earlier time, a time she had put behind her — and now I'd forced her to think about it.

There was no help for that, but the least I could do was get to the point and not make her linger in the painful past.

"So, voodoo isn't black magic," I prompted. From what the others had said, Cookie's tendency to practice a slightly darker magic than the rest of us was rooted in her voodoo background.

She surprised me with a laugh. "It is black. It's white. It's purple and green and red. You and the others always talk about gray magic, as if the only colors of magic can be found on some continuum between white and black. But magic is bigger, wider, deeper than that."

I nodded and flicked on my right-hand turn signal. "That makes sense."

"The spellbook club believes it's dark magic to try to bend anyone to your will. Even love spells are forbidden — though I do know you and your aunt open the way for such things in some of your kitchen spells."

Like the vanilla in Mrs. Standish's éclairs, which had opened the way for her to meet Skipper Dean. "True. But that's not the same as tricking — or forcing — someone into falling in love with you."

"Exactly. In voodoo that would not be considered evil, however. The very definitions of good, evil, dark, light — all are different," she said.

"Really?" On one hand, stepping outside the box of good and evil was enticing. On the other, it felt vaguely dangerous. "What about the Rule of Three?" I referred to the part of the Wiccan Rede that stated that anything you did would come back to you threefold — good or bad. It was kind of like the Golden Rule on steroids, and the members of the spellbook club all tried to adhere to it whenever possible.

Cookie took a deep breath. "I personally

believe in the Rule, of course, but it's not a part of voodoo tradition. This is really simplifying things, but you don't have the time to learn everything there is to know about voodoo. There's not even one voodoo to learn about. There is voodoo from Louisiana, and vodou from Haiti." She spelled each of the versions. "Vodou is the national religion in Haiti, a deep part of the culture originating with the slaves that rebelled there. Did you know Haiti was the first country where the slaves overcame their oppressors and freed themselves?"

I nodded, fascinated.

"And there's vodun, which originated in West Africa and holds the seeds of Haitian vodou. Each, er, branch may revere different spirits — the loa — but they all believe in and respect the spirits of ancestors. Then there are regional variations of hoodoo, which is more of a folk practice. There is a Gullah-based version here in the Low Country."

"Okay," I said. It was starting to sound pretty complicated. "So, what kind of voodoo queen are we looking for?"

She shrugged. "She could belong to any of the sects. There are also hybrid belief systems that have developed over time. Not to mention charlatans in it for the money."

"But none of the flavors of voodoo are evil, per se," I said, thinking out loud. "Why does voodoo have such a bad reputation, then?"

"Well, there are certainly those who practice left-handed magic, who seek to harm, and who will take money from those who wish to harm others. You could think of them as witch doctors. They can be very dangerous. Very powerful."

A shiver ran down my back, and I turned the air-conditioning down a notch.

Cookie gave me a skeptical look but continued. "Then there are those practitioners who are like you."

"Like me?"

"You're a hedgewitch. They're root doctors. The *grune hexe.* They use the power of plants and intention much as you do. Many are healers. You could think of them as medicine men and women."

"I like that." My father was nearly full-blooded Shawnee and descended from a long line of shamans and medicine men. Though hedgewitchery ran in my mother's family, much of my gift for magic came from him.

"I thought you might. So you see, there can be evil in voodoo as there can be in witchcraft or any other magic," Cookie said.

"At times it's a kind of tug-of-war. A man hires a witch doctor to curse his neighbor — like what happened to Oscar's sister. The neighbor learns of this and hires a medicine man — or woman — who is more powerful to protect him. He might also hire another witch doctor to curse the first man. And then the first man might hire a more powerful witch doctor to re-curse his neighbor."

"Sounds complex."

"On the contrary, it's very simple. Good or evil, the one with the most power wins."

We rode in silence for a minute. As I watched for the sign for Windsor Road, I let what she'd said sink in. People brought their own intentions into any kind of sorcery, including voodoo. The fact that there was a great deal of power there, and that people are not always the best stewards of power, upped the ante.

"My father," she began.

My breath caught in my throat. I hadn't been going to ask her about him, as it wasn't any of my business, and Cookie was a fairly private person. Still, I wanted to know.

"He was a priest," she said. "A *hougan*. He had an enemy who was very strong." She licked her lips. "Stronger than he was."

And my father lost. The unsaid words hung in the air between us.

I reached over and squeezed her arm. A quick glance at her face revealed eyes shiny with tears. I returned my attention to the road. "I'm so sorry, Cookie."

Her chin dipped. "As am I. This man we are going to see was a friend of his in Port-au-Prince."

I pushed my foot down on the accelerator.

CHAPTER 8

Cookie directed me to turn right onto a private drive. We passed under an iron archway with a large sign over it. I turned to her in surprise. "Magnolia Park Senior Care? Your friend works here?"

She smiled. "No. Though he probably *does* work here, now that you mention it. Poppa Jack will never stop working until his heart gives out, I suspect. He lives here."

Live oaks strewn with Spanish moss lined the winding driveway. We crested a hill, and a large, stately house came into view. It looked more like someone's elegant home than a senior-care facility, and I suspected Magnolia Park's historic origins had involved some kind of plantation. A gabled roof rose above the white-and-brick building. Iron trellises decorated — and protected — the lower half of the tall windows on each of three floors, some with ivy or roses climbing up them, others bare to reveal intricate scrolls and swoops of dark metal.

I parked next to a gray van in the small lot in front, and we exited the car. I glanced at my watch. Almost two-thirty. The smell of new-mown grass and hot asphalt infused the muggy afternoon. We made our way up the front walk, and I pushed the button that automatically opened the impressive wooden door. Side by side, we entered. I paused to blink in the comparative darkness, but Cookie whipped off her ginormous sunglasses and marched up to the reception desk.

As I joined her, the woman behind the desk — Gloria, according to her name tag — reached for a phone and punched in a few numbers. While she waited, her heavily mascaraed eyes assessed her manicure from behind blue-framed glasses. Her hair was twisted up into a French braid on the back of her head, and her matching cotton T-shirt and slacks were a light peach color. "Good afternoon, Jack. You have a visitor." Her gaze flicked to me. "Are you with her?" she whispered.

I nodded.

"Actually, it looks like you have two visitors," she said into the phone. "Ladies." A few seconds, and then she nodded. "Okey-doke." She replaced the receiver and pointed behind her. "Down that hallway, then turn left. Jack's room is on the right."

I thanked her, and we began walking the direction she'd indicated.

The inside of Magnolia Park was appointed with antiques and plush brocade draperies, but the floor was a dark Marmoleum; nice enough, but out of sync with the rest of the furnishings. Practical though. My thought was confirmed when a white-haired woman in a tailored track suit went whizzing by on a motorized scooter. A fifty-two-inch television took up part of the back wall of the room we were walking through, and the lobby morphed into a general living area. A group of five ladies and one gentleman sat on the sofas arranged in front of it, watching Judge Judy take someone to task. As we passed a doorway, I peered in to see the dining room. Tables laid with white cloths had already been reset for the evening meal, but the air still hinted at a savory lunch.

Cookie's heels clicked quickly down the hallway that the nurse at reception had directed us toward, and I hurried after her. She slowed at the end, where we were supposed to turn left, then stopped. I reached her side and put my hand on her arm.

"You okay?"

She shot me a look of defiance, but I could see the reluctance there, too. Sudden trepidation bloomed in my own chest. I was about to meet a voodoo priest, and I realized I had no idea what to expect.

"Is this Jack fellow an intimidating sort?" I asked.

Her cool green eyes regarded me. "It depends on whether he likes you or not."

"How can you tell if he does? Like you, I mean. Me, I mean." Good goddess, I was babbling like an eight-year-old on the first day of school.

A humorless smile quirked her lips. "Oh, you'll know soon enough." Taking a deep breath, she stepped around the corner.

Paused, staring.

I rounded the corner, too, as a wide smile broke out on her face. "Oh, Poppa Jack!" And she was running down the hallway, arms open to embrace the man standing in the doorway of a room on the right. She flung her arms around him, burying her face in his neck. He swayed at her impact, but caught himself with the cane he held in one hand and embraced her with his other arm.

"Cookie. It has been so long. *Far* too long." The way he said it made me feel warm and fuzzy. I'd never met any of Cookie's family. Her brother was several years older and lived in Florida, and her mother had left Savannah to live near him and her grandchildren. But this man had *family* written all over his face, in sentiment if not by blood.

"I'm sorry, Poppa. I should have called before." She stood back and beckoned to me.

Poppa Jack turned slowly as I approached. Despite the deep lines carved in his mahogany face and the gnarled fingers that gripped his cane, his back was straight and his gaze steady. A ruff of still mostly black hair ringed his shiny pate like a monk's tonsure. Close up, I saw that his eyes, though trained on me, were both filmed with cataracts.

He was not nearly as enthusiastic in his greeting to me. "This is the woman you told me about," he said. Not a question.

Cookie nodded. "Katie Lightfoot. She needs your help."

"We will see." His tone was mild but firm.

"You'll like her," she said.

"We will see," he said again.

I pasted a smile on my face and held out my hand. "It's a pleasure to meet you, Pop —"

Cookie shook her head, just once, and I brought myself up short. Apparently *Poppa*

127

was a title I, an outsider, was not supposed to use.

"Um, Mr. . . . I'm afraid I don't know your last name." My eyes cut to Cookie. Why hadn't she told me how to address him?

"Call me Jack," he said, turning toward the paned double doors at the end of the hallway. "Let's retire to the garden to talk."

"Outside?" I asked, instantly regretting it.

He turned and looked at me with cloudy eyes. "Yes. Outside. They keep it too damn cold in here for old bones like mine."

"The grounds here are beautiful," I said. "Lead the way."

Whether he detected my false enthusiasm for sitting out in the ninety-eight-degree heat in ninety-five percent humidity, he didn't say. He simply nodded and, with Cookie's hand on his arm, went outside.

I followed behind, thoughts as to what to tell this man about Franklin and Dawn Taite already racing through my mind.

The back door opened into a courtyard, charming in its simplicity and lush with the sun-warmed scents of lavender, sage, basil, and jasmine. Cookie and I exchanged glances as we realized it was laid out in the shape of a five-pointed star, a classic witch's pentacle. Each of the points was devoted to plantings, while the center was paved with smooth stones, upon which wicker furniture clustered in an intimate seating arrangement. With increasing curiosity, I took in the plants, realizing as I did so that they were grouped much as I had arranged the beds in back of my carriage house.

In one section, savory herbs offered their leaves. In another, roses and lavender circled around a five-foot stone obelisk. Pink flowering jasmine climbed toward the point, all surrounded by sweet woodruff and the spent leaves of fragrant lily of the valley. A fountain formed of stacked, spherical marble burbled in another triangle, with lotus leaves floating along the edge and King Tut grasses reaching fuzzy flower heads six feet into the sky. But most interesting to me was the grouping of angelica, elderberry, and fluffy, golden Saint-John's-wort — all traditional magical plants with multiple uses. I turned to see that Jack had settled onto the cushion of one of the chairs and was considering me with those misted eyes.

He could see me. I knew that somehow. And as I had the thought, I felt a little *nudge,* an extremely subtle inquiry at the edge of my consciousness. I tilted my head to let him know I felt it, and he raised his eyebrows a fraction before the feeling of mild interrogation vanished.

Maybe Jack couldn't read my mind, but, like I was sometimes able to do, he could direct his intuition, focus it, and get very real information that way. He was probably a lot better at it than I was, though.

"This is a beautiful garden," I said, sitting next to Cookie on the willow love seat across from his chair.

"I enjoy it," he said. "A good friend who is a resident here planted it and cares for it almost daily. It gives her great peace to work out here."

"I imagine," I said.

"She practices magic," he said.

I kept my expression neutral.

"Of the old-school variety," he went on. "Like the old village witches used to practice. From what Cookie told me on the telephone, you know what I mean."

I hesitated for a second before nodding. "I know exactly what you mean." Of course Cookie had told her old family friend I was a hedgewitch. He needed to know who he was dealing with. After all, I was about to ask him questions about his own magic. Or was it a religion? Like Wicca, voodoo was apparently both.

"Are you any good?" he asked.

I blinked. "What?"

"At working with plants. Roots. In voodoo, we call your kind *grune hexe.*"

That was the term Cookie had used. I leaned back against the woven wicker, and heard it creak. "My kind, being those who practice garden and kitchen magic."

He shrugged. "For the most part." He settled further into the chair like a cat in front of a comfortable, warm fire, as I felt a trickle of perspiration run down my temple.

"I'm still learning about my gift," I said, trying for modest. "And I have a long way to go."

That nudge at the edge of my mind again.

I nudged back. "But I have hereditary power from both my mother and my father, and I'm doing my best to learn quickly — from anyone who is willing to teach me."

"Is that so?" A small smile tugged at one side of his mouth. "Is that why you're here?"

I looked at Cookie. She dipped her chin, encouraging me.

"Not exactly," I said, leaning forward. "I need information about voodoo queens in Savannah, and Cookie says you're the man to talk to." This was not a time to play games. Jack would know if I kept anything back and would probably refuse to help.

So I told him everything. I started with Franklin telling me I was a lightwitch —

that raised a speculative eyebrow — then gave him the play-by-play on Dawn showing up at the Honeybee, her muttered message and subsequent collapse, and ended with Quinn telling me Franklin was dead. "I still don't understand how that could be," I said. "How could he contact me through a psychic if he was still alive?"

Jack sat for a long time, looking at the garden with his veiled eyes. I could practically hear his thoughts clicking away — and then clicking into place.

"It is possible," he began, then stopped, frowning with indecision.

We waited. My temples throbbed, and I realized I was holding my breath.

In the silence, a shiny purple dragonfly winged into the garden, zooming from star point to star point, and out of the corner of my eye, I saw it pause at the fountain to drink. If this was one of those taps on the shoulder from the universe telling me to pay attention, it was a bit late. I was already focused like a laser on Jack and what he was about to say.

Then the dragonfly flew to me, landing on the back of my hand. I sat perfectly still, watching it flex its pairs of iridescent wings, wondering at its appearance. Coincidence? Suddenly it took off again and went toward

Jack. It landed on the handle of his cane, which leaned against the arm of the chair. He examined the insect, face impassive, the smooth skin of his head reflecting the sunlight like a sacred orb. A second dragonfly, this time a dark, glistening red, landed beside the first.

Without warning, he threw his head back and laughed. "Well! I guess I have my answer." This time when he trained his misty gaze upon me, it felt open. Maybe even welcoming.

"It is possible," he said, this time with no hesitation. "That your Detective Taite was suffering from a curse — a curse that put him in a coma like his niece is in now. Deeply unconscious but not dead. From such a place he could perhaps contact this medium you spoke of."

I blinked. "Really? Is that normal?"

He waved a hand in the air. "What is normal? But it is possible, I think. It would have to be a powerful curse, from a powerful priest or priestess." He pointed at me. "You would do well to steer clear of anyone like that. To be in such a comatose state would be very unpleasant."

I felt myself blanch. "Unpleasant how?"

"Imagine wanting to awaken but being unable to. Being trapped in your own con-

133

sciousness."

A chill ran down my back despite the blazing heat of the day. I felt Cookie looking at me.

"Katie? We can go now if you want." She sounded worried. "You can drop the whole thing."

I squared my shoulders and shook my head. "There's a reason why Franklin contacted me, whether he was dead or alive. Now his niece is in the hospital, and no one knows what's wrong with her. She could be under the same kind of curse you describe, Jack. That's horrible."

Jack dipped his chin in approval. "So, you will continue to seek the gris gris."

I held up my palms. "I don't have any real choice, do I?"

His eyes smiled, but I also saw regret etch his features. "The fact that you don't think you have a choice indicates that perhaps for you there is not one."

I chose to ignore that. It sounded a little too much like Franklin Taite telling me that lightwitches were incapable of dark magic. "So?" I asked. "Can you tell me who Dawn Taite might have meant when she talked about a voodoo queen here in Savannah?"

He tapped his a finger on his knee, looking thoughtful. "Three women in this city come to mind. They are all very different, but all could be considered voodoo queens."

I leaned forward in anticipation.

"Do you have something to write with?"

I reached into the tote bag by my feet and extracted pen and paper.

"The first one is a traditional vodou practitioner, a woman I knew in Port-au-Prince. There she was a mambo, or high priestess. Here in the United States she has eschewed the title and is only known as Marie LaFevre. She has a shop in Midtown. It is tucked away in a strip mall, easy to overlook. The name is Esoterique."

"Thank you," I said, scribbling away.

"Take Cookie with you," he said. "Otherwise, Marie may not talk to you at all."

I looked up. "Why not?"

"You're Caucasian," he said simply. "Voodoo is not your history, not part of your culture."

Technically I had a good dose of Shawnee Indian running through my veins from my father's side of the family, but Jack wasn't wrong about the rest. My heart sank. How was I going to get the information I needed to help Dawn Taite if no one would talk to me?

"Having said that, Mambo Jeni isn't African-American, and she calls herself a mambo," Jack said. "She's a fairly recent transplant to town, but I keep track of all the major practitioners. She is a business-woman, and I don't know if she was ever ordained. She'll probably talk to you, but it might cost you a few dollars. I also don't know whether she'll be able help you. She works out of her home." He gave me an address from memory.

"The third woman, Eulora Scanlon, has lived here in Savannah for twenty years. She is from Louisiana originally, where she learned from an older mambo and grew into her power in New Orleans. She does not call herself a priestess or a mambo, however, only a spiritualist. As such, she is known as Mother Eulora."

New Orleans again.

"Unfortunately, she is semiretired. However, she is well-known in the city, and has many former clients." He gave me another address.

"Thank you," I said, tucking my notebook back into my tote bag. Sitting back, I regarded the old gentleman.

"You have another question, Katie Light-foot," he said. "What is it?"

"Well . . ."

"Spit it out."

I couldn't help a smile, but it dropped

away as I asked, "Do you have any idea what the gris gris might be for? What kind of power it might have? And why Dawn wanted me to find it?"

He shrugged with one shoulder, then pushed himself to his feet with the aid of his cane. Cookie rose and hurried to take his other arm.

"A gris gris is usually a charm bag filled with herbs and other items specific to its intended use. Most often it is worn for protection. But like many voodoo spells, a gris gris' power can be reversed. If so, a protective gris gris can do harm instead."

I followed them back into the building, shivering in the refrigerated air after acclimating to the garden.

"Thank you," Cookie said when we reached his doorway.

"Yes, thank you, Jack." I held out my hand.

His palm was dry and warm in mine. "Poppa Jack to you, Katie. It has been an honor to make your acquaintance." He turned to Cookie. "And you, young lady. You must promise to come see me often. We could use some of your bright light around here."

"I promise," she said, warmth shining from her eyes.

"Katie," he said as we turned to go.

I paused.

"The gris gris might not be for protection. It could be for anything. It might only be lost." He looked grave. "Or it might be taken. If it is taken, you must be very careful. There is only one reason somebody takes another's talisman, and it is not to do good."

CHAPTER 9

In the parking lot of Magnolia Park Senior Care, I leaned my tush against the side of the Bug and examined the addresses Poppa Jack had given us. Cookie opened the passenger door but didn't get in. "You want to visit them immediately, don't you?" she asked.

"Well, this Mambo Jeni person's address is on the way back to the bakery. Do you mind stopping by there on the way? It's just after three."

"Of course." Cookie got in the car, and as I went around to the other side, I heard her mutter, "Apparently, I have to visit all the mambos with you."

In the car, I gave her a grateful smile and started the engine.

A few minutes later, we turned onto Davidson Avenue. My eye was immediately drawn to the one-story rambler in the middle of the block. Unlike its more sedate

neighbors, it was painted a brilliant periwinkle with a purple undertone that popped
right into my retina, thanks to the summer
sun. As I steered closer, it became apparent
that the house number would prove to be
the one Poppa Jack had given us. The red
neon sign in the front window blinked the
words PALM READINGS — PAST LIFE RE-
GRESSIONS — VOODOO SPELLS.

As I pulled to the curb, Cookie's lip curled
in distaste. "I don't know what Poppa Jack
was thinking, sending us here."

I shrugged. "He said voodoo queens come
in many forms. This one appears to be in
the form of a Jackie-of-all-trades."

She sniffed and reached for the door
handle. "Or a charlatan. I'm surprised she
doesn't sell Tupperware and Amway."

"Maybe she does. I could use some new
refrigerator dishes for the Honeybee."

Cookie gave me a look.

I grinned.

The lawn needed to be mowed, and the
leaves on the verbena and ferns in the pots
on each side of the front door were curling
from neglect and lack of water. The paint
on the doorframe had begun to crack and
peel. I reached for the doorbell, hesitated
when I saw it was in the shape of an elaborate eye, then went ahead and gave the dark

pupil a push.

The sound of rapid footsteps approached, and the door was flung open. A large woman regarded us through the screen door before pushing it open and gesturing us inside with a huge smile.

"Welcome, ladies!" She looked to be around fifty and was dressed in a skirt, flowery smocked top, and flip-flops. She wore no makeup, and her skin was the kind of pale you'd expect from a teenage boy who played video games and swigged cola in the basement all day. As she blinked at us in the light of the doorway, I wondered if she ever ventured out into the sunlight. When she turned, I saw that her iron-gray dreadlocks reached almost to her waist.

"Please, come inside," she invited. "I'm Mambo Jeni. And you are?"

We entered as requested. I glanced over at Cookie in time to see her school her expression to neutrality, then turned my attention to the mambo.

"I'm Katie," I said, "and this is —"

"Elaine," Cookie cut in.

I raised an eyebrow as Jeni nodded and waved for us to follow her toward the back of the house. As we walked through the living room, I took in the sagging turquoise sofa, the big-screen television that took up a chunk of wall space opposite it, the chair with reading lamp, and the bookcase full of videos and CDs. A gas fireplace was set into one wall, and framed movie posters decorated another. It was clean and uncluttered, but had an air of college rental — or, I realized, starting afresh with little money. My bet was that Jeni was either divorced or widowed. A picture on the slim mantle showed a dark-haired boy and girl in their teens, so she was probably a single mom, too.

With a flourish, the mambo opened a pair of heavy wooden doors to reveal what had once been the formal dining area of her home. A thick, elaborately patterned rug covered the dark hardwood in the middle of the room, and centered on that was a round table large enough to seat four people. A black silk cloth had been draped over it, the abundance of material pooling artfully on the red-hued rug beneath. The walls and ceiling were the color of roasted red peppers, and brass sconces hung at four-foot intervals, unlit. A tapestry covered with black and red runes cascaded down the center of the rear wall, and I could envision the sliding glass door it covered, no doubt leading out to a suburban backyard. The only other art on the walls were three black-

and-white enlargements of foggy hands —
each open as if in supplication.

Creepy.

Mambo Jeni closed the doors, and we
were plunged into darkness. I heard Cookie's surprised intake of breath beside me,
then the sound of a light switch being
flipped, and the room bloomed back into
view. Low light emanated from the sconces
now, just enough to define the perimeters
of the room and call out the weird hand
photos. A recessed spotlight shone down on
the center of the black-clad table, a golden
pool that cast the rest of the space deeper
into shadow. No light leaked in from the
outdoors, and if I hadn't just walked in from
the bright sunshine, I wouldn't be able to
tell whether it was day or night. The air
smelled of day-old sandalwood incense.

"Sit down, please," Jeni said.

We sat.

"Now, Katie, Elaine, what can I do for
you today? Are you here for one or both of
you?"

Cookie and I exchanged glances. "Er," I
said. "For me, I guess. Or both."

Jeni sat back in her chair, laced her hands
on the table, and smiled. "I see. Are you
visiting Savannah?"

"Noooo," I answered slowly, wondering

how much to tell her. *Play it by ear.* "We live here. We were told by a friend you might be able to help us."

She nodded. "Ah, word of mouth. Excellent. Who, if I might ask, is your friend?"

I looked at Cookie, and she nodded. "Poppa Jack," I said.

Mambo Jeni blinked. "I see." She considered us. "Or perhaps I don't. If you went to see Poppa, then you must be in the market for a bit of voodoo magic. However, there is, frankly, nothing I could give you that he couldn't. So . . . ?"

"We're in the market for information," Cookie said. "We were told a voodoo queen would be able to help us. Yours is one of the names Poppa Jack gave us."

Jeni looked amused. "A voodoo queen, you say. Well, I am flattered that Poppa would see me as one."

"You aren't?"

A slight lifting of her shoulders. "I am a mambo *sur point* — a certified junior voodoo priestess. I also do palm readings and past-life —"

"We saw the sign," Cookie said.

The mambo lifted an eyebrow. "Hmm. And you obviously disapprove."

Cookie didn't say anything.

"Well, no matter. A woman has to make a

living, and the economy isn't what it used to be. Before my divorce, I practiced the same things I do now, but once I was on my own, I had to up my marketing. A sign and a few ads don't take away from my power," she added.

"Plus, I bet you get a bit more of the tourist trade," I said. I could tell she had real ability. It hummed around her like a subtle electrical current. No doubt she would have been willing to help out Franklin as long as the price was right.

Jeni nodded. "Even this far away from the historic district." Shifting in her chair, she said eagerly, "Now, what is this information you're looking for? I'd love to help!"

Cookie remained silent, so I dove in. "Do you know a man named Franklin Taite?"

The older woman smiled broadly, and my hopes soared. Then her brow knit, and she said, "Hmm. Gosh. I don't think I've ever had the pleasure." Her disappointment in having to disappoint us was palpable.

Still, so much for this being our voodoo queen.

"Do you offer magical talismans to your clients?" Cookie asked.

"Oh, yes!" Jeni exclaimed.

A door at one end of the room opened. I hadn't noticed it in the dimness because it was painted the same color as the walls. Now bright light blasted in, and we could see a refrigerator and sink from our vantage point. The scents of burnt coffee and over-ripe bananas overlaid the dusty-incense aroma.

"Robert! I'm with clients!" Mambo Jeni called, clearly irritated.

The silhouette of a young man filled the doorway. "Whatevs, Mom. We're out of milk." His hair stood up on one side in a classic case of bed head, and he still wore pajama pants. No shirt.

"So get off your lazy butt, put some clothes on, and go get some," Jeni grated out. "And *shut that door.*"

"God. Bite my head off." The door closed with a force that made me jump.

Jeni took a deep breath and let it out slowly. "I'm so very sorry. My son should know better." She ducked her head and rubbed the back of her neck. "Now, where were we? Oh, yes — you wanted a gris gris."

Cookie held up her hand. "Not really. We want to know if you're aware of a missing gris gris."

"Missing? From where?"

I sighed. "We don't really know."

"Well, what was this gris gris for?" Jeni asked, leaning forward with curiosity now.

"Protection? To attract money? Birth control?"

"We don't know that, either," I said. "Wait — birth control? Really?"

"Sure. Interested?"

"Er, no, thank you."

Cookie bit her lip to tame her smile.

"So, if you don't know where it's missing from or what it was for, why are you looking for it?" Mambo Jeni asked.

"Well," I said, feeling foolish. "I think it's important."

"Important to whom? You?"

"To a dead man and his comatose niece."

She frowned. "I don't understand."

"That's okay," I said, standing. "We need to be going, anyway. Thanks for your help."

Mambo Jeni bolted to her feet. "Wait. I'm sure I really can help you somehow. Cast a hex, maybe a love potion? Those are my specialty."

Cookie looked at me and shook her head.

"No, thank you," I said as politely as I could.

"Please."

I didn't think she meant to say it, partly because when she heard herself practically begging for our business, her mouth clamped tight. Her shoulders straightened as she donned her pride.

Cookie was already at the door to the living room, no doubt as anxious to get out of there as I was.

"Wait," I said.

Eagerness brightened the woman's eyes. Maybe I could offer her some business after all.

"Mambo, can you contact the dead?" I asked.

"I . . . Like a medium, you mean?"

I nodded. "Can you reach across the veil like that?"

She hesitated, and then her shoulders slumped. "No. I'm sorry. I can't do that."

"I'm sorry, too. Thank you for being honest."

Her chin lifted. "I'm a lot of things, but dishonest isn't one of them." She strode past me and opened the door for the waiting Cookie.

Mambo Jeni's son was lounging on the sofa, eating dry cereal out of a bowl with his fingers. He looked even more disheveled in the light.

She went to the front door and opened it. Turning to Cookie, she grabbed her left hand, and before Cookie could pull it back, peered intently at her palm. Jeni raised her head and snagged my friend's gaze. "You have had many lovers and fall in love easily.

Your heart line tells the tale."

Cookie's eyes flicked to mine, full of alarm.

Good thing Oscar isn't hearing this.

"Ah, but here in your life line, there is a change in lifestyle. Recently?"

Cookie glared at her and tried to pull her hand back.

But Mambo Jeni wasn't having it and returned to scanning her hand. "Emotional trauma, early in your life, but resilient now." She looked up. "You must not let yourself be controlled by external influences. By men, especially. This is very important to your future happiness."

Cookie yanked her hand out of the other woman's grasp and started down the front step. "I'm not one to be controlled."

The mambo raised one eyebrow. "So you say."

I smiled as I passed her. "Thanks, anyway."

"That will be thirty dollars."

"What?" Cookie whirled on the sidewalk.

"It's what I charge for a palm reading," Mambo Jeni said.

My friend made a rude noise and turned on her heel. I regarded the woman on the step. "You were telling the truth?"

"I always tell the truth."

149

I fished in my tote bag and pulled out my wallet. Gave her two bills.

She gave me a dignified nod. "Thank you." As the door closed behind her, the sound of the television from inside drifted out to where I stood.

"What were you thinking?" Cookie demanded once we were in the car. "That woman didn't tell me anything I didn't already know, did not ask my permission to read my lines, and didn't help with your investigation at all."

"I know," I said quietly. "But she needs the money. Just chalk that thirty dollars up to karma, okay?"

Cookie rolled her eyes but didn't protest. I put the key into the ignition and pulled onto the street.

CHAPTER 10

The visit to Mambo Jeni had taken only half an hour of our time, but I was still surprised when Cookie suggested stopping by Marie LaFevre's shop.

"Might as well get as much of this done as possible before Oscar expects me," she said with a shrug.

Esoterique was tucked between a shoe-repair place and a furniture upholsterer in a tiny strip mall on the border of Savannah's Southside and Midtown. I must have driven by it dozens of times and never noticed it. Even with the GPS on Cookie's phone directing us, I'd nearly missed it.

"Cloaking spell of some kind?" I asked.

Cookie tipped her head to the side. "Perhaps. More likely simple discretion. This Marie LaFevre isn't trying to entice the tourist trade like the mambo we just visited." This seemed to cheer her.

Nonetheless, I felt more apprehension

than anything else as I locked the car and turned toward the narrow doorway. The iron bars on it didn't exactly make it feel welcoming.

We were ten feet away when the door opened and a tall figure filled the frame. All three of us stopped in our tracks.

He was over six feet tall and African-American, and after the surprise passed, he continued toward us, moving slowly and deliberately, as if with age. His face said he wasn't yet fifty, despite his halting step. His thin frame accented his height, and even in August he wore a Windbreaker over a white button-down shirt and blue jeans. He slipped the small paper bag he carried into the pocket.

He stopped, looking between us.

I smiled. "We're looking for Marie La-Fevre. Is this the place?"

"Ah. Marie."

I nodded once. "Yes. We were hoping to talk to her."

He eyed me with suspicion. "First time here?"

"Yes," Cookie said. "We have not met the mambo."

He snorted. "Best not let her hear you call her that. That mambo talk don't sit well with her. Don't know why, though. She sure knows her stuff." He fingered the packet in his pocket, and I wondered what it contained. A gris gris, perhaps?

This really might be the woman who can tell us what Dawn Taite was talking about. The thought gave me a little shiver, and hope flickered again as I thought of Franklin's niece lying in her hospital bed in the ICU.

He turned toward an older Chevy parked nearby. "Good luck, ladies."

Cookie and I exchanged glances as he slowly moved away, muttering, " 'Cuz you're gonna need it."

"What's that supposed to mean?" I asked.

She didn't answer, but her lips pressed together as she stalked toward the barred door. Despite her hurry, I had the feeling it was more about getting the encounter over with than making the acquaintance of Marie LaFevre.

A sisal mat sat in front of the door. Cookie thoroughly wiped her feet on it, though there couldn't have been more than dust on her shoes. Her hand faltered as she reached for the handle. I stepped up, yanked it open, and stepped inside.

Brightly lit display cases marched down each side of a narrow aisle, and though the recessed lighting overhead was directed on the shelves that lined the walls, the space didn't feel dark or cramped, like I'd expected. I heard Cookie behind me, and the door swooshed shut on its pneumatic hinge. Slowly, I walked down the aisle, drinking in the items on offer.

Candles of every imaginable color, as well as multi-hued combinations. Many were simple pillars; others were in the shape of people or animals or things I didn't recognize. Crystals reflected prisms against white cloth; tiny cloth bags awaited magical contents. Books lined a few shelves, and I wondered if any would be good selections for the spellbook club. Sewn dolls filled a basket. Their eyes didn't match, and they looked hastily stitched.

"Do you really stick pins in those things?" I whispered. We'd used a felted wool poppet in a spell to great effect once. These didn't look nearly as sweet as that one had.

"Shh," Cookie hissed.

There were tarot decks and teas, herbs and roots and oils, packets of glitter and mysterious powders. Spell kits, bath salts and soaps, jewelry, incense, and framed art were also available for purchase. Feathers and sticks; smudge bundles and smudge pots. A display of obviously rubber chickens and snakes made me suppress a smile. One case stopped me cold, the various bones it contained shining white and gray against deep blue velvet. On the lower shelf, small jars of what appeared to be soil or ash stood in tidy rows. I leaned down to examine them and saw the labels: BONAVENTURE, COLONIAL PARK, LINCOLN, LAUREL GROVE, BELMONT, AND DRAYTON HILLS. All cemeteries, and the last one I knew had been closed to the public for years.

Graveyard dirt.

I looked up to find a woman at the rear of the store, watching me with narrowed eyes. A blue dress draped across her shoulders, brushing the floor and the red-painted toes of her bare feet. A bright blue-and-green head wrap wound above her arched eyebrows and dark, glittering eyes. Her high cheekbones and long neck added to her regal bearing.

Queenlike bearing, if you would.

Multiple bangles clustered along both arms, and rings shone from her strangely long fingers.

"Marie LaFevre?" I asked.

She considered us long and hard. "Perhaps. Who are you?"

"Petitioners," Cookie said.

The woman stepped back, languidly waving at us to join her at the back of the shop.

155

There we found a sofa and three chairs. "Sit."

We sat. I looked to my right and saw the human skull sitting on an end table, leering at me with a stained grin. I quickly redirected my attention back to Marie LaFevre.

She lowered herself onto a chair across from us, her movements smooth and unhurried. "You heard of me from another? From a satisfied customer?"

"We're here at the suggestion of Poppa Jack," Cookie said. "He said you are the most powerful priestess in the city. That your amulets and gris gris can achieve anything."

Not exactly. But perhaps flattery would get us what we needed.

However, the voodoo queen's expression hardened, and her nostrils flared. "I doubt he said that. Yet here you are. Poppa Jack is free with information about me, whatever he told you. Too free."

"Ms. LaFevre," I broke in.

"What do you want?" Her tone was harsh, with an underlying current like electricity. With a start, I realized she was using her Voice on me! Or at least trying to.

Well, I could play that game, too. "Information," I said, putting some oomph into the word. "You see, there's a woman in a

156

coma, and a dead detective and a missing gris gris, and we were hoping you might be able —"

Marie LaFevre stood in one fluid motion. "Leave."

Cookie scrambled to her feet.

I gaped up at Marie. "What?"

She pointed at the door. "Leave. I will have nothing to do with whatever evil you have brought upon yourselves."

"The police found a man dead yesterday, and I only want to know if he came to see you when he was alive."

"No!" she shouted. Fear flashed from her eyes. "I don't know anything about a dead cop."

I held up my palms in supplication. "Please. No one thinks you did anything wrong."

At least not yet.

She shook her head vehemently and raised her hands as if to ward us off.

"Just tell me if you knew a man named Franklin Taite or a woman named Dawn Taite." I pushed harder with my own Voice, well aware that skill had seriously backfired on me more than once.

"Do not try your magic on me, girl!" Her glare held real fury. I felt myself blanch. She took a breath, obviously struggling for calm.

"I do not know this man," she said, and I felt the truth in her words. "Now you will go, or I will *make* you go."

Cookie grabbed my arm and started backing toward the door. "Come *on,* Katie."

I let her pull me out to the parking lot. The priestess paced after us, her long blue dress swirling around each step like a tide. Once we were outside, she slammed the door shut behind us. The sound of the lock turning was loud in the sunny afternoon air.

"Whew!" I saw Cookie was visibly trembling. "Oh, honey, it's okay." I put my arm around her shoulders and started walking her toward the car. "She wasn't going to —"

"You don't know that, Katie! Marie La-Fevre would be a formidable foe. I only hope you didn't anger her too much," Cookie said, pulling away. "You felt her ability?"

My steps faltered as I remembered the little sewn dolls. "Of course I did." My voice was quiet, and I felt a little shaky myself — not to mention disappointed. "Come on. Let's get back to the bakery. I'll buy you a zucchini basil muffin."

She patted her tiny waist. "Perhaps that would be a good idea. A little food might settle my stomach."

I gave her a smile, not mentioning the protective properties of basil. It might be a good time to recharge the other protective measures Lucy and I had taken at the Honeybee, too — as well as at my carriage house.

As much as I wanted to check out the third name on Poppa Jack's list, it was getting close to five o'clock and Cookie was obviously still upset about Marie LaFevre, even after downing a muffin and a glass of mango sweet tea. I offered to take her home, as we'd originally planned, but she insisted on calling Oscar to come get her at the Honeybee. In the meantime, she offered to help out with the final prep for the next morning's baking.

We hardly needed the help, but I took her up on the offer, anyway, to keep her from stewing about our encounters with the two voodoo queens. Lucy set Iris to cleaning up around the espresso counter while she began running the register tape, and Ben stopped by to chat with Martin. Usually the author was long gone by now, but he looked relaxed and satisfied, and as he put his laptop into its case, he invited Ben to sit down.

Oscar came in, dark eyes lighting with affection as soon as he saw his bride. She beamed a joyful smile that made me happy just to see. No wonder she'd wanted him to pick her up.

She waved to him. "Be right there."

"No hurry, love." He settled in at an empty table. Then she leaned close and murmured in my ear. "Please don't mention what we did today. Oscar thinks we were shopping."

I sighed. "I hate that you feel you have to keep this from him."

"It's better like this."

"But you're lying to your husband."

She gave me a look. "I'm keeping the peace."

"Okay, fine. It's your marriage."

"Thank you."

"Where are your bags?" I asked.

She looked confused for a moment, but then her face cleared. "Ah. My purchases. We only window-shopped. Better for a newlywed's budget, you know."

I laughed.

"I'll be by tomorrow morning, however, so we can go visit the spiritualist." Her eyes darted to the left, and I saw Oscar approaching. Iris watched him with wide, appreciative eyes.

"At ten?" she whispered quickly.

I nodded.

"Are you thinking of coming back to work here?" Oscar teased.

Cookie giggled. "No, silly man." She turned to me. "However, I'll take two scones for our breakfast."

"Be my guest," I said. "And here — take a loaf of bread, too."

"And some cookies," Lucy said, bustling toward the office safe with a bank bag in her hand. Martin had left, and Ben was tidying the coffee counter.

Loaded up with tasty baked goods, Cookie and Oscar left. Ben locked the door behind them and returned to his task.

I sidled up beside Iris, who was still staring after Cookie's handsome husband with wide, dreamy eyes. "He's gone. You can blink now."

Startled, she flushed a deep magenta. "Was I obvious?"

"Nah," I lied. "But he's some pretty sweet eye candy, I must agree."

"Mmm," she sighed.

Laughing, I went back to the office to retrieve Mungo and head for home — and Declan.

On the way, I couldn't help driving by the address Poppa Jack had given me for

Eulora Scanlon. *Just so Cookie and I can find it easily tomorrow morning,* I told myself as I slowed to a crawl, drinking in the small home and wondering about its inhabitant.

I looked down at Mungo, firmly belted into the passenger seat inside my tote bag. "Maybe I should stop —"

He interrupted me with a noise in the back of his throat.

"No?"

A car honked behind me, making me jump. I tromped on the accelerator, and we shot forward. "Yeah, I should wait for Cookie. Besides, it doesn't look like anyone is home right now."

Yip!

When I was halfway home, the old-fashioned jangle of my cell's ringtone sounded from the outside pocket of my bag. Mungo made a disgruntled sound and shifted in the seat.

"Sorry, buddy," I said, retrieving the vibrating phone. I generally ignored calls when I was driving, but when I saw who it was my curiosity won out.

"Hello?"

"Katie!" Steve said. "I'm glad I caught you. Not interrupting anything, am I?"

Translation: *Are you with Declan?*

"I'm just driving home from the Honeybee."

"Long day?"

"They all are. You know I'm there by five most mornings."

"Right." His cheerfulness sounded a tiny bit forced.

I waited.

Not for long. "So, this whole thing about Detective Taite and his niece? It's crazy that he showed up dead, and the whole voodoo thing is, well, worrisome, to say the least. Just because Sam is in my life doesn't mean . . . well. I want you to know you can count on me to help any way I can."

Relief flickered through me. Steve had been on my side since I'd moved to Savannah. I'd wondered if his having a new girlfriend meant that would have to change.

"Thanks," I said. "I don't suppose you know anyone in the voodoo community."

"Not really. Sorry."

I thought about asking if his father might know someone who could help find the missing gris gris, but discarded the idea. Best to avoid owing a debt to Heinrich Dawes if at all possible.

Steve spoke again. "Okay, listen. I also called because I was worried about you meeting Sam in the Honeybee like that."

Then why did you set it up like that?

"Worried? Why?"

He exhaled. "Oh, good. I thought maybe it was awkward."

Um, yeah. A little.

"You like her, then?" His tone was casual, but I had the feeling he really wanted my approval.

"Gosh," I said carefully. "I only talked to her for a second, but she seems nice enough." *If you're into chicks who read books about how to get what they want and refer to muffins as yummies.* "But the important thing is that *you* like her. Which you obviously do."

Mungo's dark eyes studied me as he listened.

"Oh, I do." Relief threaded his voice. "I really do, Katie. She's wonderful. Smart, and you saw how pretty she is. Funny, too. She's even charmed Father."

I felt my eyebrows climb my forehead. "Heinrich? Wow. Impressive." Steve's dad and I had eventually reached a state of mutual respect, but I would never say I'd charmed him. I was pretty sure he didn't even like me all that much.

"I know, right? I met her at the club a few weeks ago — she moved here from Hilton Head, the only child of a dot-com success story — and she's right at home with Father's muckety-muck friends, whether they're discussing stocks or golf or literature. Samantha can talk to anyone about anything!"

Well, isn't she wonderful!

I firmly tamped down the green-eyed monster who had, surprisingly, made itself at home in my solar plexus. It took more effort than I liked to admit.

"It's great that you found someone who fits so well into your social circle," I said.

He was silent.

Darn it.

"Katie, you're not angry, are you?"

"Of course not. I'm happy for you."

I knew I sounded lame. All I wanted was to get off the phone. I pulled into my driveway and turned off the engine. Declan's truck was parked out in front, and he was inside waiting for me. "Listen, I'm home —"

"You know I feel the same way. About you and Declan, even if he . . . Well, you know."

"Mmm-hmm." Declan and Steve had a bitter history long before I'd entered the picture. I got out and went around to the other side of the Bug.

Mungo jumped to the ground but didn't race toward the door like usual. He sat and watched me gather my things and close the door.

"And, Katie? I really do want to help if I can."

Declan came across the lawn and reached down to give Mungo a hello scratch. My phone call forgotten, Mungo flipped on his back and wiggled with delight as my boyfriend rubbed his belly.

"I'll let you know if I need anything," I said.

"Okay. I'll let you go. But don't forget."

"I won't. And, Steve?"

Declan's head jerked up when he heard who I was talking to. "I'm truly happy about you and Sam."

"Thanks. It means a lot to me."

We said good-bye, and I ended the call. Declan abandoned Mungo and put his arm around me as we walked across the yard. He kissed my temple. "Who's Sam?"

"Samantha. Steve has a new girlfriend."

A grin split Declan's face as he turned to me in the doorway. "That is awesome!"

"I knew you'd be happy for him," I said wryly.

"Who cares about him? I'm happy he'll stop bugging you."

"He doesn't bug me," I protested.

Declan ignored me. "But wait. Why was

he calling you just now, then?"

"To offer his help in finding the talisman. And to see if I like Sam. I met her today at the bakery."

"Oh, brother. He needs your approval? At least you gave it."

I rolled my eyes.

Declan frowned. "But I heard you."

I dumped my tote on the couch and headed for the kitchen. Declan had burgers formed and waiting for my little hibachi, and the makings for a garden salad took up most of the tiny table. I grabbed a carrot and a vegetable peeler as he filled the doorway to the living room.

"I heard you," he said again.

I shrugged and started peeling. "There's something off about her. I mean, she's cute. Awfully girly, likes pink apparently. She's nice enough. But —" I paused, thinking. Then I turned and looked at him. "I think she might be a gold digger, you know? After the Dawes fortune."

He laughed.

"Seriously. She was reading this book —"

Declan came up and put his arms around me from behind, pressing me up against the sink. "Katie, I wouldn't cue up the wedding march quite yet."

"Ha. Yeah, you're right. They haven't been

involved for very long."

"Are you sure you're not just jealous of her?" he asked.

I turned to face him. "You know I love you."

"Yep. Sure do. But Steve Dawes has been waiting and hoping for you all this time. That has to be nice for a girl's ego."

"Don't be ridiculous."

He put his hands on my shoulders. "Well, I can tell you one thing — you don't need to worry about the Dawes fortune. That family is not stupid, and no matter how smitten Steve might be with his new cutie, Heinrich would never allow a gold digger to get her hands on any of his money."

Of course he was right. I put Steve and Miss Samantha out of my head while we made supper together. To my relief, the heat wave seemed to be abating as we ate out on the patio. Mungo sprawled under the table after emptying his plate. Hand in hand, we were watching the sky turn and the clouds color, the remains of our burgers and salad scattered on the table in front of us, when Declan said, "You know, Dawes isn't the only one willing to help you find the talisman." There was an edge of bitterness to the words.

My eyes cut to him. "What do you mean?"

He continued to gaze skyward. "I've come to a decision. If you want me to, of course. And I don't know if it will work." Now he just sounded earnest.

"Declan, what are you talking about?"

"It's possible Franklin Taite can help you find this mysterious talisman his niece told you about, right?"

I stared at him.

"Well, maybe I can help you find Franklin Taite."

CHAPTER 11

I'd asked Declan once before to try contacting Franklin directly, as I'd hoped he could channel the dead detective like he'd channeled his uncle Connell. The request had angered him then, and I'd let the matter drop. So I knew his offer to attempt to reach Franklin now wasn't made lightly. It made me love him all the more.

"So, um, how do I do this?" Declan asked. I sat on the purple fainting couch while he paced in front of me, a bundle of nerves. Now he paused and blinked down at me expectantly.

Like I know how to contact the dead. Well, there is *Nonna. But she always contacts me, not the other way around.* My gardenia-wearing grandmother had made her presence known to me a few times, which was always comforting. But, heck on a biscuit, why did the dead have to be so darn cryptic all the time? Did dying make you a tease, or just a terrible communicator?

"What was it like last time Connell came to you?" I asked. "No, wait. Not the last time. The first time. During the séance."

One side of his mouth quirked up in an expression of chagrin. "I don't remember, really. It just *happened.* One second I'm sitting there, wondering whether the medium was some kind of fake, looking for hidden wires and floating tabletops, and the next I'm somewhere on the sidelines in my own mind, watching a stranger make my body move and talking with my mouth." He licked his lips. "It felt like I was going crazy."

"Oh, Deck. Are you sure you want to try this?"

He squared his shoulders. "If it'll help you. It's the least I can do."

"You do a lot," I said quietly.

He waved that off and started pacing again. "You know what I mean. It's the only thing I can do that's like magic. If I can pull it off, that is."

I stood and grabbed his hand to make him stop moving long enough for me to give him a sincere kiss. "I just had a thought. Let me check something."

Quickly, I climbed to the loft and went to the bookshelf above the secretary's desk that housed my altar. There it was: *Herbal Prac-*

tices Throughout the Ages. The book I'd found in the Honeybee library.

"What are you doing up there?" Declan asked.

"Looking for some help on how to get started." Flipping on a wall sconce, I leafed through the pages until I found the section on using herbs to increase psychic awareness. This wasn't a spellbook, so I didn't expect any actual incantations, but, lo and behold, there was a list of suggestions for sending a message to the dead.

And if you could send one, I was pretty sure you could receive one.

I clambered back down to where Declan waited, his toe tapping on the bottom step. He grabbed me as I descended and swung me to the floor beside him. I held up the book.

"What's that?"

"It's a start. Now gather up those three tapers left over from dinner the other night and bring them outside. We'll set up in the gazebo. I already work out there, and the energy will have a higher vibration for what we're trying to do. I'll meet you out there. Mungo, you're with me."

Declan looked after me with a bewildered expression but went into the kitchen to retrieve the half-burnt candles. I grabbed a pair of scissors and opened the French doors.

Cooling air molded around my limbs as I marched down to the herb garden. There, in the faint light from the kitchen window, I cut sprigs of lavender and parsley and braided the stems together loosely. I climbed the steps into the gazebo and set the bundle of herbs on the small circular table that sat in the middle of the purple-and-white five-pointed star painted on the floor. Mungo trundled after me as I returned to the rear of the yard, where a small stream cut katty-wampus across the corner by the fence. I'd not known I was a witch when I bought the carriage house, but it turned out that having my own source of natural, moving water had been a boon for the spells I worked at home.

Tall plumes of red amaranth were silhouetted against the fence in the sparse light. I cut a single plume and brought it back to the gazebo with Mungo trotting by my left foot the whole way. His dark gaze glinted up at me, and I knew he was ready to help however he could.

Declan waited for me inside the small gazebo. A slight breeze blew through, bringing the temperature down a few more degrees before dropping away.

"Shall I light the candles?" His voice shook.

"You sure you want to do this?" I asked again.

He nodded. "Yes." The word was terse. I had to stop second-guessing him. This was hard enough for him already.

"Okay. Go ahead and light the candles." I placed the amaranth over the bundle of lavender and parsley. "Put them equidistant around these herbs."

He peered at the small pile of plant matter. "Is that lavender and . . . parsley? Seriously?"

I tamped down a sigh. "All plants have magical energies. Among their other uses, these increase psychic awareness. The number three seems to be important, too." Four elements, four directions, four archangels for spells, but three candles and three herbs to contact the dead. It made me think of the Rule of Three the spellbook club lived by.

I shook my head. *Concentrate, Katie.*

"Okay, we have three candles and three energetic herbs, and we *should* have three people in order to have a real séance."

His shoulders slumped. "Well, so much for that." But he seemed a little relieved.

"Mungo?" I asked.

174

The little dog jumped up to one of the mismatched chairs that sat around the table.

Yip!

I grinned at Declan.

"You're kidding," he said.

"Nope. He's adorable and a real snuggle bunny, but at heart he's a wolf. Believe me — he's ready to help." I patted my familiar on the head. "Besides, it's not like we really have a choice."

Mungo whined.

"Sorry," I said.

"Oh, brother," Declan said, but didn't protest when I pulled away all but three chairs from the table. We both sat down.

"Okay, now hold hands." I glanced down at Mungo, who was standing on the chair on his hind legs, front paws on the table. "Or, you know . . ."

Declan rolled his eyes. I took his hand firmly in mine and curled my fingers around Mungo's tiny paw. He blinked up at me, almost seeming to nod. With obvious reluctance, my boyfriend mirrored my actions. However ridiculous he felt, at least his nervousness appeared to have abated.

"Now we have to chant."

"*Chant?* God."

"Remember at Ursula's séance? How we chanted for the murder victim to come to us from beyond?"

"Hrm. Yeah. Okay."

"How about something like, 'We call upon the spirit of Franklin Taite to move among us. We beckon you with the light of this world, and ask you to grace us with your presence.' "

We practiced a few times, until Declan had memorized my off-the-cuff summons to Franklin Taite.

"I think we're set," I said, watching him carefully. "If you want to stop, we can at any point. Just break contact."

His nervousness had returned, but he murmured, "Okay," and closed his eyes.

I exchanged a look with Mungo before following suit. Quickly, I ran through the most burning questions I had for Franklin.

Has Dawn been cursed?

How can I help her?

Where is the gris gris, and what do I need to do with it?

I also wanted to know why Franklin had been killed and by whom, not to mention getting more information about being a lightwitch. But first things first. Dawn was still alive, and therefore my priority.

As Declan cleared his throat to start chanting, I decided I'd just have to play it by ear.

"We call upon the spirit of Franklin Taite to move among us," I murmured, and Declan joined in, also keeping his voice low. "We beckon you with the light of this world, and ask you to grace us with your presence."

As we repeated the call to Franklin's spirit, I reached out mentally and immediately sensed the regal canine presence that was Mungo. Then there was the *something* that Declan projected, unlike the power current I usually associated with magic. It was subtle and mysterious, and I found it downright sexy in the split second it took to recognize it. Then I moved on, reaching out with my intuition and intention to welcome Franklin Taite's spirit.

Something stirred in my consciousness. Was that Franklin? I felt my blood zinging through my veins, my heartbeat concentrating in my temples. Mungo stirred beside me, and I cracked an eye to take a look. His eyes were wide open and trained on Declan.

My boyfriend's eyes were clamped shut in concentration as he muttered the chant, now under his breath. The cords in his neck stood out, and everything about his body language screamed determination in the face of fear: shoulders hunched forward, brow furrowed, teeth clenched.

Relax. Allow. But I didn't want to say

177

anything out loud, break his concentration.

Whatever had fluttered at the edge of my senses veered away. I couldn't say why, but I didn't think it had been Franklin. It could have been anyone — anything, really — once Declan had opened to the other side. The thought speared alarm through my solar plexus.

What have I asked Declan to do?

I let go of his hand.

His eyes flew open, bleary and unfocused. For a second he didn't seem to be home in his own body. But then he blinked and looked at me with clear, if confused, eyes.

"What did you do that for?" he asked.

"Did you feel him? Did I ruin it?" I leaned forward as Mungo slid his paws away from us and dropped down to sit on his chair with a look of mild disgust at our human antics.

But Declan shook his head. "I don't think so. I tried to concentrate as much as I could."

"I know, honey. Thank you for —"

"Hellooo!" Margie's voice came floating over the fence. "That you, Katie?"

Instinctively, I blew out the candles, but we weren't doing anything that would look suspicious. Well, maybe the bunch of herbs on the table were odd, but she probably wouldn't even have noticed that.

"Of course it's me," I said. "Who else did you expect would be hanging out in my gazebo?"

She laughed, and her face appeared above the four-foot fence that separated our backyards. "I thought you might want to come over for a drink. The kiddos are in bed and . . . Oh, is that Declan?" I could tell she was trying to keep the disappointment out of her voice. "I'm so sorry. You two are having a nice, intimate evening, and I come barreling over to interrupt. Please forgive me!"

"We're just sitting out here," I said, directing an apologetic look at Declan, who still looked a little shaken despite our evident failure in summoning Franklin's spirit. "You're welcome to join us."

"Well, thank you kindly, really. That is just so sweet. But I don't want to be a third thumb, and, besides, I don't want to be that far from the kids, especially Bart. You know?"

"Of course," I said. "Maybe I could come by tomorrow night? Or the next? Deck here is going on his forty-eight-hour shift tomorrow morning, and I'll be at loose ends for a couple evenings after work."

"Oh!" Her tone turned upbeat again.

"Well, I don't want you to get lonely. How about in two days? I have a church thing after camp tomorrow."

"It's a date," I said.

"All righty, then. I'll just leave you two alone. There's an *Everybody Loves Raymond* marathon I wanted to catch tonight, anyway."

"Good night, Margie," Declan called.

"G'night," she responded, already halfway back to her house. "See you soon, Katie."

"See you," I said with a wave.

"She's lonely, isn't she?" Declan said.

"When Redding is gone," I said.

"I'm glad I don't have to leave you to your own devices for that long," he said. Then he took my hand in his own again. "I'm sorry I couldn't contact Franklin. I tried, but there was just nothing. Nada. Zilch."

Not quite, I thought as I squeezed his fingers. "No worries. It was a long shot, anyway. It was very sweet of you to try." I could feel the disappointment coming off him in the dark. He felt like he'd let me down. "Really," I said. "And it's okay with me if you never think about trying to contact anyone who has crossed the veil again. Connell was a fluke. Let's just leave it at that."

He made a sound of agreement.

I suddenly yawned so wide, I thought I'd crack my jaw. Quickly covering my mouth with my hand, I let the weariness of a day that felt chock-full of failure wash over me. "Time for bed," I said.

"Really?" Declan asked with surprise. Because I required so little sleep, I rarely went to bed before he did and was always up well before dawn.

I nodded. "Yeah. I'm exhausted. Long day at work, not to mention trying to track down a voodoo queen. I'm about to fall asleep."

"Okay," he said. "I'll be in a little later, if you don't mind."

"You okay?" I asked as I rose to my feet. Mungo jumped to the floor with a little *thump*.

"Sure. I just . . . want to think a few things through, is all," he said.

I leaned over and kissed his forehead. "All right. I'll be inside if you need me."

He didn't smile. He didn't give me a squeeze or kiss me back, either. But, hey, we all need our space sometimes, and no doubt he really did have some introspection to wade through.

Inside, I shed my workaday clothes, which I felt like I'd been wearing for days, took a quick shower, and donned my version of pajamas: yoga shorts and a spaghetti-strap tank. In the dark kitchen, I drew a glass of water from the tap and looked out at the gazebo. Declan was sitting in the same chair, thinking goddess knew what.

Perhaps he'd tell me in the morning, before he went into the firehouse and I left for the Honeybee. In the meantime, I was going to get some shut-eye.

Yip!

Mungo's bark brought me wide awake, heart pounding, hand reaching for Declan beside me in bed.

He wasn't there.

Mungo barked again, bouncing on the bed and facing the doorway to the hallway on quivering legs.

A tall figure was outlined in the dark rectangular space.

"Deck?" I asked in a small voice, already feeling foolish. Who else would it be? But what the heck was wrong with Mungo?

But when he didn't answer, I started to get scared. I reached for the bedside lamp and switched it on.

"Declan! Are you trying to scare the living daylights out of me?" I slumped back against the headboard, blinking in the bright light. "Mungo, *hush.*"

My familiar turned and glared at me. He bounded up on my stomach.

"Ooph. What is wrong with you?"

He got right in my face. *Yip!*

I jerked back, scared all over again, and looked up at Deck. "What the . . ." The words died on my tongue. The man looking down at me was my boyfriend.

Only, *not.*

"Deck . . . ?"

A knowing smile broke out on his handsome face, and one eyebrow rose suggestively as his eyes ran up and down my prone and barely clad form. "Aye," he said.

Even a single word was enough to alert me to what had happened. I grabbed the sheet and covered myself. "Connell, you stop that!"

Mild disappointment mixed with amusement across the clean-cut features of the man I loved. "Ah, lassie. Don't yer know how long 'tis been since I've seen anythin' so grand?" The heavy Irish brogue made his words seem playful, but I wasn't so sure.

"What are you going to do?" I asked in a small voice.

"Do? Och, Katie darlin'. 'Ave I managed ter frighten you again, and in so wee time? I'm only lookin'. Wouldn't 'urt yer for the world." He sighed, examining the sheet draped around me as if he could see right through it. "Oh, but it's not a sin to look, now, is it? Most lassies would be flattered by the attention."

I narrowed my eyes. "I have quite enough attention, thank you very much. And from the man who you've displaced from his own body."

He actually looked a little sheepish.

Throwing off the sheet, I reached for my robe and cinched it tightly around my waist. Connell watched with appreciative eyes the whole time, but I ignored him. I'd be damned if I was going to cower, half-naked, in bed while some dead jerk possessed my boyfriend.

I turned to him and put my fists on my hips. "Now, why are you here?

He considered me, then moved across the room. I ducked out of his reach, still not trusting his motives. He lifted the curtain, and looked out onto the street. "Things 'ave changed so since me day." Looking back at where I now hovered by the doorway, ready to run out and go to Margie's if I needed to, he added, "I do see the world from where I am, t'be sure. Watchin' and guardin' yer man here. Trust himself ter choose work that can git a man killed. Admirable, t'be sure. Foolish, as well."

"Why are you here?" I asked again. "And what do you mean 'from where I am'? Where are you when you're not" — I waved my hand — "inhabiting your family member's body? And do you know how hard it is on Deck when you show up like this? How utterly awful it feels for him?"

He smiled a sad smile and folded his arms over his chest. "In answer to yer last query, I wasn't tinkin' o' that, I must admit. 'Tis only that —" He waved his hand. "You don't know how lucky yer are ter be corporeal." He looked so sad when he said it, but then Declan's face lit up with another of Connell's oversized grins. "An' in answer to your first question, 'twas yer who opened 'is psyche up ter me. A wide-open invitation, if yer will. Candles an' parsley and the like. Now tell me, how could I refuse ter come for a nice visit?"

"So when Declan tried to get in touch with Franklin Taite to help me, he opened himself to the other side, and you stepped through."

He made a face. "Not exacly ter the other side, as yer put it. Only ter the place I inhabit."

Which brought me to my second question: "Are you saying you're not dead?"

"Hmm. Not so much. But not alive,

185

either, Miss Katie."

He smiled at the confusion that must have been on my face. " 'Tis a purgatory of sorts. An in-between place. Me kind don' exactly die."

CHAPTER 12

I remembered the picture of Connell that Declan had shown me in the McCarthy family album. The man who was old when he married his young bride, the man who looked exactly the same as she grew older in the photos, down to the buckled jacket, jaunty hat, and high riding boots. The man who had left after his love's death, never to be heard from again.

The man who had been rumored to be . . . nah.

They're magically delicious singsonged in my mind. I shook my head to dislodge the earworm.

"It can't be," I muttered.

His eyes widened in surprise, and his laugh boomed forth before ending in a kind of cackle. Good thing the windows were closed, because I would have a hard time explaining to Margie the loud Irish guy in my bedroom in the middle of the night.

"Begorra! What is it yer thinkin', then?"

"What kind of guardian are you if you don't know your own legend in the McCarthy family?" I asked.

He laughed again. "And Declan 'ere passed it on ter you. Well, then. Let us jist say I'm 'uman enough ter be almost killed, but not enough ter die."

I squinted at him in the dim light. "Who else is there in this purgatory of yours?" Could it be the same place a cursed soul in a coma on this plane might visit?

But sorrow crossed his features again. "I couldn't tell you, lass. 'Tis a lonely existence — that's for sure." He brightened. "Which is why I so enjoy the company of the livin'! I choose me favorite from each generation of the McCarthys. A fella, t'be sure — I wouldn't ken what to do with a girl child. Declan 'as been a bit of a challenge, don't you know, what with all the fighting fires and romancin' a witch."

I tipped my head, considering him. "Can Declan contact the dead, then?"

"Och, no. Only me. 'Cause I chose himself, you see."

"So, you can't help us find Franklin Taite's spirit," I said.

Slowly he shook his head. "Sorry, Miss Katie."

"You have to leave Declan, you know. You've already taken him over for longer than the other times." A horrible thought occurred to me then: Was it possible that Connell could take over Declan indefinitely? I imagined him there in the back of Connell's mind, off to the sideline in his own body, trapped and terrified.

"Connell!" I said. "Let him go! He didn't mean to let you through. It was a mistake."

Connell/Declan's face fell. I actually thought I saw tears forming. "Well, now. T'be sure, I can't stay," he said, shoulders slumped. "It was pure nice spendin' a bit o' time with you, though, Miss Katie. Yer one in a million, and me fella has the luck of Eire ter know ye." He closed his eyes, and I knew he was about to leave Declan's body.

"Wait," I said.

He opened his eyes, that eyebrow lifting in a gesture of wonder and possibly hope.

"Is there anything we can do here, on this plane, to help you get out of your in-between place?"

He looked down at the wooden floor of the bedroom. "That is a kind offer — a kind offer indeed." He lifted his hands perpendicular to his sides. "I think I'd take you up on it, no matter which side I went ter, but there's nothin' you can do. At least not that

I've knowledge of."

"I'm sorry," I said, and meant it.

"Tanks. Let me offer you something for your kindness."

I waited, eyes wide.

"Ach. This voodoo is foreign an' frightenin' ter me. All I know is the object yer seekin' is hidden between layers of magic."

"The talisman? You can see it? Sense it?" The words tumbled out of me, and for a second I forgot this man was squatting in Declan's body and had been about to leave.

"The talisman," he confirmed, and closed his eyes again. Anxiously, I waited for Declan to come back to me, whole and true. Connell's eyes popped open again. "Beware of someone new ter you, as well."

I opened my mouth to reply, but then he was gone, and dear Declan stood looking at me in bewilderment, those gorgeous blue eyes reflecting the soul I'd already come to know and love so well.

I rushed to him and threw my arms around him. "Are you okay?"

He embraced me absently, muttering in wonder, "That was weird — really weird."

I pulled my head back and looked at him. "And scary. I know. I shouldn't have talked to him for so long."

"Hmm. Scary, yes. But not as bad as it

was before. Maybe I'm getting used to it?"

I stepped back now to stand by the bed. "Declan McCarthy, don't you dare start inviting your uncle to come visit. It was bad enough waking up to find him ogling me. I have no intention of going to bed with you and waking up with him."

He blanched. "I hadn't thought of that."

"Well, I sure did," I muttered as I got back under the covers.

I didn't sleep well, waking several times to check that it was really Declan snoring beside me. I was pretty sure he couldn't have faked that snore, though. At four o'clock, I finally dragged myself out of bed, dressed, and went for a run. The morning breeze soothed my skin, and soon endorphins were running though my veins, lifting my spirits. My feet pounded against pavement as I passed beneath streetlights with no traffic to distract me. I found my rhythm, and my thoughts began to sort from one big, confused jumble into distinct categories of confusion.

My boyfriend channeled his possibly-a-leprechaun, not-dead-but-not-alive great-great uncle. I'd had a night of tossing and turning to let that sink in, but my mind still shied away from accepting it. Even though

Declan's mother had heard stories about Connell's supernatural roots on a visit to track her relatives in Ireland, I'd never actually believed one of Deck's ancestors could really be a *leprechaun*. He hadn't, either, grinning as he told me the tale. He had also rightly pointed out that I couldn't arbitrarily draw the line regarding what was possible and what wasn't when I wanted *him* to believe in magic.

Okay, then. Uncle Connell, possibly immortal and in his personal purgatory, could possess Declan practically without warning. Check.

However, Connell hadn't been the only thing muddying my half-dozing thoughts. Dawn Taite was still in a mysterious coma. Franklin had been killed by a snake, possibly — no, make that *probably* — in some kind of sacrificial ritual. Dawn's sudden appearance at the Honeybee, begging for my help, had been too desperate and alarming — not to mention her current state of mysterious unconsciousness — for there not to be a cause.

A curse. Place by a person, Katie. Someone is behind all this. Connell said to beware someone new.

The missing voodoo talisman had something to do with his death, my gut insisted.

The image of Dawn's fingernails scrabbling on the window glass in the bakery kept returning to my mental movie screen, becoming clearer each time rather than fading as most memories do.

The gris gris is missing. You must find it.

Well, there was Cookie's friend, Poppa Jack. I didn't want to believe, for her sake, that he embraced the dark side of voodoo. It didn't make sense that he'd help me, either, by sending me to the voodoo queens.

Unless he was offering me a distraction from the truth.

Nah. We'd talked in that star-shaped garden at Magnolia Park. It was a sacred place, a witch's place, and he'd taken us there to determine whether I was worthy of his assistance. I was pretty sure I could trust Poppa Jack.

What about the voodoo queens he'd directed Cookie and me to? Marie LaFevre had certainly had some strange items on offer in her shop, and summarily turned us away. Because she had something to do with Franklin's death? Maybe. I hadn't thought she was lying, but, on the other hand, Ms. LaFevre possessed obvious power. Though I didn't like to admit it, her Voice could have worked on me after all — at least enough to make me think she was telling the truth.

Perhaps Franklin had her in his sights on his ongoing quest against evil. Even during our brief exchange, I suspected the woman would have little compunction about engaging with the darker side of voodoo.

Mambo Jeni was down and out, certainly, but evil? I couldn't discount it, but I didn't know what she'd have against Franklin and Dawn. Mostly I'd felt sorry for her. She might be willing to do just about anything to make a buck, though. So if Mambo Jeni was responsible for what had happened to the Taites, it was possible she was working for someone else. Talk about layers of magic. Ugh.

As for the third voodoo queen, Mother Eulora, I hoped to know more about her before the day was out.

Who else?

I grimaced as Oscar Sanchez came to mind. Cookie's husband was handsome as all get-out, and the spellbook club was delighted that Cookie appeared to be so deeply in love. He was a scientist and made a good living. She'd told me they planned to have children in a few years. He was polite and interesting to talk to. I didn't feel a terribly friendly connection to him, however. Perhaps it was his subtle disapproval of the spellbook club that I picked up on.

Oscar knew his new wife was a witch, but he didn't necessarily like it. And he definitely didn't like her being involved with voodoo.

Yet why would he be involved with Franklin's death? He'd been out of the country three months ago.

No, wait. Cookie had told the spellbook club that after she and Oscar got married in France, he'd come to Savannah to look for a job in May. She'd followed a couple of weeks later. How "new" had Connell meant? Because Oscar was not only new to me, but his own wife hadn't known him all that long.

Other people relatively new to my life included Iris and Skipper Dean. And, according to Steve, that girly-girl Samantha had elbowed her way into his life only a few weeks ago. Of course, she was new to his life, not mine. I sighed. I met dozens of new people at the Honeybee in the course of a day's work. Surely Connell hadn't meant any of them. And what about Dawn herself? Was I supposed to beware of her?

I began to mentally roll my eyes, then stopped. Literally stopped running on the sidewalk a block away from the carriage house.

What if Dawn herself is not who she appears to be?

The sun was beginning to lighten the sky when I opened the front door. Declan was already up and the smell of bacon was in the air, but only Mungo looked well rested.

I kissed the cook and hurried in to take a quick shower. Twenty minutes later, I was settled in at the kitchen table, a plate of bacon, eggs, and crispy hash browns in front of me. I dug in with gusto.

"I have to stop by my place before my shift," Declan said. He sat across from me, digging through the man-sized portions on his plate. Mungo stood over his place mat in the corner, eating his own breakfast. "And by the store — I'm going to make the guys at Five House Mexican steak sandwiches tonight."

"Mmm. Sounds fabulous. Mungo and I will work on those leftover pork chops."

Declan put his fork down. "Katie? Are you okay?"

I swallowed and looked up. "You mean about last night? Connell?"

He nodded.

"It was . . . weird. But I don't have to tell you that."

He shook his head.

"Um . . . do you think you can stop him from showing up like that? I mean, you opened to him during our little séance and all, but does he have ready access to, well, to —"

"To you?"

"Well, yeah."

He sat back. "I don't think so. I was there when he was talking to you, in the background. Unlike the other times he's shown up, I felt like I could have pushed my way forward. I wanted to hear what he had to say, though."

I lifted an eyebrow. "He had a few things to say about me."

"Come on, Katie. It's not like you were in the shower. Plenty of people have seen you in your sleep gear. It sure didn't seem to bother you when Steve did."

I ignored that. "So, your, er, relationship with Connell has changed?"

"It feels like it. Most of the time he's not around, but then he'll be there, in the background."

I felt the skin tighten across my face. "That doesn't sound good."

His head tipped to the side. "I don't know yet. But I sense that he's on my side, you know? He's watching over me — and over you, too. Like your nonna does."

I started to argue that it was completely different to have the spirit of your grandmother occasionally make contact than to

197

have a half-dead ancestor from the Old Country take over your physical being, but Declan looked at the watch on his wrist and suddenly stood.

"I've got to go, darlin'. I'll call you later, okay?"

Finished with breakfast, I stood, too. He swooped me into a big hug, laid a good-bye smacker on me, and then released me to grab his coat and head for the door.

Things were busy at the Honeybee that morning, but when Cookie showed up at ten o'clock, Lucy shooed us out the door. I drove right to Eulora Scanlon's house without consulting the address. Cookie didn't seem to notice, however, and I didn't mention I'd thought about visiting the voodoo queen — no, *spiritualist* — the evening before on my own.

It was a small, square house on Lincoln Street. The wooden siding was painted butter yellow; the trim, pale beige. The closer we got, the smaller it appeared, dwarfed by the homes that loomed on either side. The neatly trimmed lawn was set off from the street by an openwork, decorative iron railing. The gate swung open on well-oiled hinges, silent and smooth. I walked up the narrow tabby sidewalk that precisely bisected the front yard, with Cookie on my heel. On either side of the walkway, bright orange marigolds alternated with classic red geraniums. A small table flanked by two rocking chairs with worn but clean patchwork cushions took up most of the space on the covered porch. I didn't see a doorbell, so rapped on the dark wood of the door. And waited. Beside me, Cookie shifted her weight from one foot to the other, fidgeting with her bracelet.

I tried to quell my own nervousness. If this woman couldn't — or wouldn't — help us, I was back to square one. *Perhaps Poppa Jack knows of others,* I told myself. Or perhaps Quinn would come up with information about Franklin's death — or his life the past few months in Savannah. Neither possibility filled me with hope, however. I tried to center, to focus my intuition to mentally probe beyond the door, trying to get an idea of what to expect from the third of our voodoo queens.

Nothing.

There wasn't even a response to my knock. I looked to Cookie, who shrugged. Determined, I knocked again, then backed off the porch so I could see the windows. Gauzy curtains shut out the view of passersby. No lamps shone inside, but the windows were large and the light curtains would still let in the sunshine. Someone could be in there.

And avoiding us. Could Mambo Jeni or Marie LaFevre have alerted Eulora Scanlon that we might be visiting? I sighed at the thought. My bet was on the latter.

As I was getting ready to head back to the car in defeat, the door opened. I quick-stepped back up to the porch to find Cookie stammering out, "We are here to petition Mother Eulora for assistance."

"Petitioning" hadn't worked so well with Marie LaFevre. I pushed up beside her, peering through the screen door at the handsome woman regarding us from the other side.

"We need a spell," I said. "A . . . a spell to find something lost."

A perfectly shaped eyebrow arched in response.

"You are Eulora Scanlon," I said. "Aren't you?"

"I'm sorry," she said, her voice deep as a cave. "No spells. No magic here. Not anymore."

"Please," I began as she shut the door in my face. "Please, Ms. Scanlon!"

The latch clicked, and I heard footsteps walking away.

I stepped up and pounded on the door with my fist. "Mother Eulora," I yelled. "Just let us talk to you!"

Silence answered my plea. It was broken by only the distant sound of a megaphoned voice from a tour bus the next block over and a light breeze sighing through the cypress tree in the neighbor's yard.

My shoulders slumped, and I turned to Cookie. She leaned one slim hip against the porch railing, looking as if she had somehow failed.

I put my hand on her arm. "Thank you for trying. I know all this has been hard for you."

"I'm sorry there isn't more I can do. I suppose we could try finding someone online that could help. Or maybe the spellbook club . . . ?" She blinked hard, and I realized she was nearly in tears.

"Oh, Cookie! Please don't feel bad. We'll figure something out." I gave her a quick hug, and we turned and began walking slowly back to the street.

"Ladies!" a light, wavering voice called behind us.

We looked over our shoulders to see the screen door open and a short, round woman bustle forth. She had a deep butterscotch complexion and a puff of pure white hair.

She stopped on the top step and put her hands on her more-than-ample hips.

"I do believe you were looking for me."

I felt a grin break out on my face as Cookie and I hurried back.

CHAPTER 13

The woman was shaking her head, and a wide smile revealed teeth so even and white that I suspected they might not be her own. "That Tanna. She's a little overprotective. Doesn't like me to see clients anymore."

A fine web of wrinkles laced her face from forehead to neck. Her eyes flashed with amusement as she spoke — at least on the surface. They were brown, so dark as to almost appear purple, and as they searched my face, I felt her assessing me far beyond social niceties. Real power drifted from her in waves. Far more than from Marie La-Fevre.

Her eyebrows lifted, and her smile became more speculative. "However, I think you two are truly in need of my help."

"You're Eulora Scanlon?" I asked, trying to keep my eagerness under control. Of all the voodoo practitioners Cookie and I had met in the past twenty-four hours, this woman might really be able to help us.

Or hurt us. I suspected that Cheshire cat smile fronted more than cherubic goodwill — just like Mimsey's Southern charm. In fact, she reminded me a great deal of the senior member of our coven.

She dipped her chin. "I am Mother Eulora."

"Right. Sorry," I said. "Mother Eulora."

The hard-eyed woman who'd answered the door appeared behind her, stooping to murmur into the older woman's ear.

"Bah," the self-proclaimed spiritualist said. "I know you are looking out for me, dear. But I'm not on my deathbed yet."

When Tanna didn't respond, Mother Eulora turned to meet her gaze. They engaged in a silent battle of wills for several seconds before the younger woman looked away.

"Show them inside," she said to Tanna in a gentle voice, then gestured us forward. "Please." She went back inside.

We sidled past an unsmiling Tanna and found ourselves in a tidy living room. I took in the chintz sofa where someone had set aside a copy of the *Savannah Morning News,* the glass-topped coffee table decorated with a bowl of wooden apples and three copies of *Southern Living* magazine, the mauve-colored silk shades on the floor lamps book-ending the sofa, and a serious collection of figurines — all of which, I realized, were hedgehogs — on a long shelf over the television. Nowhere was there a hint of an altar or any kind of magical activity. Then again, no one would come into my home and think, *Oh, a witch lives here.* After Marie LaFevre's shop and the wacky dining room at Mambo Jeni's, it was refreshing.

"Real magic does not require trappings," the voodoo queen said, settling on the sofa. "In case that's what you were wondering."

I smiled. "You caught me."

"Please sit down. Tanna, would you please get us some tea?"

"Oh, that's okay," I said.

"Some people say you should never accept food from a voudon. That we cast spells that will bloom when you ingest them."

Cookie's swallow was audible, and I looked over to see her gazing wide-eyed at Mother Eulora. I wondered why my friend hadn't mentioned that to me. Given my own newbie knowledge of hedgewitchery, I was willing to believe it was true.

"I'm sure it would be fine, Mother Eulora," I said. "I'm not thirsty, though."

"Me neither," Cookie said in a small voice.

Mother Eulora grinned, flashing her perfect dentures. "Eulora is fine. Or Mother.

We have not met before."

I shook my head. "No, ma'am. My name is Katie Lightfoot, and this is, er —" I shot a look at Cookie. Did she want me to introduce her as Elaine, like at Mambo Jeni's?

But she stepped forward. "I'm Cookie Rios."

Tanna brought a tray with tall glasses of tea in from the kitchen. I jumped up and pushed the magazines on the coffee table to one side so she could set it down.

Eulora took the proffered glass without looking at her. "Cookie. I like that name. I have not heard it before. Rios, though. That is a name I recall. Dominic."

"Yes, ma'am," Cookie said.

"Dominic was your father?"

Tanna's gaze sharpened.

Cookie nodded.

"I heard about what happened to him in Haiti. I am sorry, my dear."

Cookie looked at the floor. "Thank you."

Then her gaze returned to me. "So, you are Katie Lightfoot. The candela."

All the air seemed to leave the room. I stared at her. *Candela* was another name for lightwitch. I'd never heard anyone besides one other person utter it.

"You knew him," I breathed. "Franklin Taite."

Tanna glared at me. I had no idea why, but I could feel my heart beat faster, and I struggled to slow my breathing.

Eulora scooted back on the sofa cushion. Now she could lean against the back, but her feet no longer touched the floor. "Oh, yes. I know him. I know him quite well. And through him, I know you. Better than you might care for, actually."

I licked my lips. "I don't understand."

"Soon enough." Eulora took a slow sip of tea. "I assume you heard of me from Franklin."

My eyes cut to Cookie, who frowned, then back to Eulora. "Not exactly."

Her brow furrowed. "Now I don't understand."

"Um." I took a deep breath.

"Poppa Jack gave us your name," Cookie broke in before I could continue.

Eulora laughed. "Poppa Jack! How is that old coot?"

Cookie seemed to relax. "He's at Magnolia Park now. But he's still going strong."

"Well, if you have to be in assisted living, that's not a bad place to be. It's nice out there. Fancy." Eulora reached up and patted Tanna's hand, which rested on the sofa behind her head. "But this is my apprentice, and I couldn't ask for better."

Tanna inclined her head. "And yet you fight me constantly."

"A workout for the willpower is all that is. Have to keep fit up here," she pointed to her forehead. "When the rest starts to go."

I opened my mouth to protest, but her smile dropped and she shook her head. "It is what it is. Now. Katie Lightfoot. If Franklin didn't send you, why are you here?"

"Well, I'm here about him," I said.

"You said you were looking for a spell." Tanna's tone was accusing. "A location spell."

Eulora shook her head. "Oh, Tanna. This one does not need us to cast a spell. She's perfectly capable of doing that herself."

"I lied," I said to Eulora's apprentice. "We've been to see two other voodoo queens, women Poppa Jack suggested. Being up front with what we're looking for didn't work out so well with them."

She looked down her nose at me, and her voice was harsh. "So, what do you really want here?"

Eulora cocked her head to the side in a silent echo of Tanna's question.

"How well do you know Franklin Taite?" I asked, feeling my way.

"Well enough that he told me about you and what you are," she said flatly. I sensed she was losing patience.

"Well enough to know he had left the New Orleans Police Department?"

She frowned. "Yes. He left to pursue his own path. He is determined to track down as much dark magic as possible in his lifetime. Seeking balance against evil, which he's seen more than his share of. He met you during one of his official cases that involved magic." She considered me for a few seconds. "You do not trust me. That is understandable. But I was Franklin's mentor in his ongoing quest to root out and defeat the darkness. You had not heard of me before Poppa Jack told you of me, yet here you are, and I suspect you need my help. Help Franklin cannot give you."

I pressed my lips together. Everything she said rang true. But Eulora was still talking about Franklin in the present tense. I needed to break the bad news.

"Franklin never helped me. He told me I was a lightwitch almost a year ago, and then up and left town for Louisiana. I haven't seen him since."

She looked surprised. "I hadn't realized."

"And now he won't ever be able to help me or anyone else. Ms. Scanlon — Eulora.

I'm sorry. So very sorry."

Realization began to dawn on Mother Eulora's face. "He's . . . passed?"

I nodded. "The police discovered him two days ago."

Her hand went to her throat. Her eyes glittered with wetness, and her breath came in small gasps. Tanna moved swiftly, sitting down beside her and chafing her wrists.

"Mother! Wait here. I'll get your pills."

I leapt to my feet. Cookie appeared frozen in her seat.

"No, Tanna." Eulora grabbed the woman's arm so she couldn't leave. "I'm all right. Hand me my tea, though, will you? Katie, please sit down."

Tanna obeyed with alacrity. Eulora took a sip and handed it back to her apprentice, who showed no inclination to leave her side. I sank back into my chair but perched on the edge, ready to reach for my phone and call 911 at a second's notice.

"How did he die?" Eulora asked.

"The police detective — Franklin's old partner — who told me about finding Franklin said he died from a snakebite," I said. "He was in a warehouse out on Old Louisville Road. It's been empty for a while, and Detective Quinn thinks the snake got in through a broken window."

Eulora closed her eyes. "I very much doubt that."

My stomach twisted. "Why?"

"He came to see me about four months ago. He wanted information about how human sacrifice is used in voodoo magic."

I heard Cookie suck in her breath. Hadn't Quinn mentioned something about a case in New Orleans that involved human sacrifice?

"What did you tell him?" I asked.

"That sacrifices are usually to appease a spirit or gain its favor. However, some believe it's possible to absorb the power of a life sacrificed — whether that life is animal or human."

I blinked. "Good heavens."

Her eyes were sad. "That's not a belief restricted to voodoo, of course. Everyone from ancient druids to the Aztecs have offered up the lives of others."

Could Franklin have been sacrificed? The thought made my heart stutter.

Cookie stood and went to the coffee table, taking one of the untouched glasses of tea and sipping from it. Letting Mother Eulora know she trusted her. She sat back down and placed the glass on a coaster. "Do you know anything about a gris gris, Mother?"

Eulora's eyes flashed a smoky purple.

"Franklin came to me when he first began his quest against darkness. He had seen too much as a policeman — more as a homicide detective — and had come to realize how often black magic was involved. I gave him a gris gris then, to help him."

"How?"

"It was charged with the ability to identify magic in the first place, and then to determine whether it was a threat. It could also be used to help defeat magic under certain circumstances."

I passed my hand over my face. "Franklin's niece sought me out only hours before I learned his body had been found." I brought my eyes back to hers. "She lost consciousness before she could tell me much. She's in the ICU at Candler Hospital right now, in a coma, and the doctors can't figure out why. But before she passed out, she told me to find a voodoo queen. I think that's you."

Eulora looked shaken at this new information but nodded. "Go on."

"She also told me the gris gris was gone. That I had to find it. Do you think she meant the one you gave Franklin?"

Eulora pushed herself to the edge of the sofa and put her feet on the floor. Tanna rushed to help her, but the older woman shrugged her off. She stood and walked to me, standing in front of my chair and looking deeply into my eyes. "It can be no other one. When Franklin came to see me last, he asked me to recharge it. He was going up against someone very powerful, he said. So I did." She put her hand on my shoulder, and it felt blazing hot even through the cotton of my shirt. "If it is gone, you must find it. You *must.*"

I put my hand on top of hers, mesmerized by her gaze. "Tell me why. And tell me how."

"In the wrong hands, the gris gris can be flipped. Reversed so the magic it holds can be used to augment black magic. If it was taken by whoever Franklin was challenging, that would be very bad news indeed."

I took a shaky breath and dared to blink. Her gaze softened, and she patted my shoulder twice before moving back to perch on the edge of the sofa. "But in your hands, Katie Lightfoot, it can tell you if Franklin was murdered — and who did it."

"How do I find it?" I breathed.

She shook her head. "I don't know." Then her face brightened. "I can show you what it looks like, though. Tanna, please bring my album."

Eulora's apprentice's mouth turned down in disapproval, but she left the room.

"This niece of Franklin's," Eulora said.

"Her name is Dawn," I said.

"Dawn." She tried the name out on her tongue, then nodded once. "How did she look when you saw her?"

I described her pale thinness, her fright.

"Hmm. Yes. I'm afraid she might be suffering from a curse," Eulora said thoughtfully.

"Poppa Jack thought the same thing. Can it be reversed?"

"Possibly. It would be best to have the gris gris in our hands first, though. Its absence is most alarming. I'd also need to know who cast the curse, and the reason."

Tanna returned with a large book bound in dark red leather. She handed it to Eulora, who pushed aside the bowl of apples and opened the book on the coffee table. She turned a few pages, then gestured for Cookie and me to come see. We got up and took seats on either side of her on the sofa. She pointed to a picture. "That's the gris gris I charged for Franklin."

"The exact one, or one like it?"

"The exact one. I keep track of all the powerful spells I've released."

I bent forward, drinking in the small details. It was not a bag filled with herbs and magical items like I had expected, but a pendant on a simple chain. It was a dark gray metal rectangle about one and a half inches by two. Figures and designs had been etched into the surface, some geometric, but others swirled like conch shells or like the petaled design nature carved on the backs of sand dollars. Tiny rivets of a different metal, possibly copper, were driven into the corners. White fringe had been tied into two holes drilled near the bottom.

Eulora fussed with the archival corners that held the picture in place. Tanna reached down, removed the photo, and gave it to her charge. Eulora handed it to me.

"Mother," her apprentice began. "Let me make a copy for her."

"No," Eulora said. "Katie needs this more than I do." Her eyes bored into mine. "She will return it when she's done with it."

I nodded my agreement. "Of course. Thank you." I could tell her energy was fading. I patted her hand and stood. Cookie followed suit. "We have to be going," I said. "But I'll be in touch."

"Wait. Tanna, get the box."

With a sour expression, Tanna went back down the hallway and came back with a simple wooden box with a hinged lid. Eulora opened it to reveal several compartments inside, each holding a small cloth bag or piece of jewelry. She selected a bracelet and handed it to me.

"If Franklin's niece is cursed, you must take great care. Wear this for protection."

"From . . ." I licked my lips. "From a voodoo curse?" I thought of Dawn's gaunt face, her frightened eyes, her breath stopping in her chest.

Mother Eulora just looked at me. After a second's hesitation, I took the bracelet with a trembling hand. It was a simple thing constructed of mother-of-pearl beads strung on a piece of waxed twine.

"Thank you," I said. "May I pay you?"

"Don't be ridiculous," she said. "Put it on, and don't take it off until this business is finished."

"I promise."

Eulora looked up at me but didn't stand. "Tell me if you find out anything about what happened to Franklin. Anything at all. Or if you find the gris gris. Or if his niece . . ."

"Absolutely," I said. "Thank you so much for your help, Mother Eulora." I took a few steps away, then paused. "Did Franklin happen to tell you where he was staying when you saw him?"

She nodded. "He rented a room not far from here, down toward the park." She waved her hand in the direction of Forsyth Park, which was only a few blocks away. "I don't know exactly where, though. And I don't know how long he stayed. He only came to visit me the one time on that trip to Savannah. I thought he'd left town in pursuit of more wicked sorcery."

He would have come more often if he could. How could anyone resist this amazing lady?

I thanked her again and joined Cookie at the door. Tanna hurried to show us out without bothering to hide her relief that we were leaving. Following us out to the porch, she stopped me.

"Mother is in poor health, Ms. Lightfoot. I don't care a whit for that Franklin Taite or for his niece, only for Mother Eulora. Do not tax her," she warned.

Cookie said, "She's lucky to have you, Miss Tanna. I assure you, we mean no harm to her."

Mollified, Tanna nodded at us and went inside, shutting the door firmly behind her.

"To quote Mimsey, 'Lord love a duck,' " I said, peering at the photo of the gris gris as we stood on the sidewalk. "We hit the jackpot with Mother Eulora."

A wide smile blossomed across Cookie's face.

"I never could have done it without you. Thank you!"

"It was my duty," Cookie said as we walked to the car.

I started to protest, then saw she was laughing.

"At least you were able to find the voodoo queen Franklin's niece told you about," Lucy said without looking up from where she vigorously stirred flour into hot butter and water on the stove. "That's certainly progress."

As soon as I'd returned to the Honeybee, I'd related everything Cookie and I had learned to both Lucy and Ben. They, in turn, had told me Detective Quinn had stopped by with news that Dawn Taite was still in intensive care. She remained in a coma, and the doctors remained baffled. Then a group of teenagers had come in, and Ben had returned to take their orders while Lucy and I went back to the kitchen. It was Iris' day off, so we could talk freely, as long as we kept our voices low.

"Mother Eulora must be the one Dawn meant," Lucy went on. "After all, she knew Franklin — and she knew about the talisman."

I peered over her shoulder. "Yeah. Spooky

what she said about the gris gris, though."

She reached for a bowl of grated cheese and dumped it into the flour mixture before glancing up at me from under her furrowed brow. "*Spooky* is a mild way of putting it. *Terrifying* is more like it. Whatever voodoo magic is at work here, the idea that someone could augment their dark magic with that talisman scares me half to death, Katie. And Franklin wanted you to get involved in a situation like that? What was he thinking?"

I grimaced. "I wish I'd had a chance to talk to Eulora more about that — and about being a lightwitch. I suspect she might be the one who can tell me what Franklin never did. But we wore her out with our visit as it was."

Still, I had every intention of going back and asking her. She had called me a candela, so surely she knew what that meant.

"*Gougères*?" I asked, eyeing the contents of the pan.

She shook her head. "*Pão de queijo.*"

"Ah," I said. Similar, but Brazilian rather than French, and gluten-free. *Pão de queijo* was made with tapioca flour, and the bite-sized puffs ended up crispy-chewy on the outside but tender and airy inside.

"Yum," I said. "We need to put those on the regular menu."

"These are a special order for Mrs. Standish," Lucy said. "Appetizer for a fundraising cocktail party she's hosting this evening. It's for the animal shelter, I believe." She scraped the smooth, shiny dough into one of the large standing mixers and reached for the eggs.

"Bless her for thinking of us," I said. "I hope there will be a few leftovers for us, though."

She smiled and cracked the first egg into a ramekin before transferring it to the mixing bowl. "Don't worry — I'm making a double batch." Once the first egg was blending into the dough, she turned to me, the next egg in her hand. "Seriously, what are you going to do about that talisman?"

"Try to find it — goddess knows how, though. Eulora gave me a picture of it. Cookie was going to ask her for a spell to find it, but Eulora said I didn't need a spell from her. Being a lightwitch and all."

Lucy raised an eyebrow. "Is that so? What about a spell from us? Or, rather, with us?"

"The spellbook club?"

"Of course!" She added another egg to the *pão de queijo*. "I can call the ladies as soon as I'm done here. We can meet here, right after we close. Remember the location spell we did for Mavis Templeton's murderer?"

"Yeah, that didn't really work very well . . ."

"Bah," she said and cracked another egg. "You were too inexperienced to help us then. Now you'll be in the circle with us, and heaven knows you add oomph to our spell work."

I reached for a stack of silicone baking mats and began placing them on metal sheets in preparation for the little cheese puffs. "I'd sure love to try. Getting a hold of that talisman would put the kibosh on someone using it for dark magic, but as important — at least to me — is that Eulora said it could help me figure out what happened to Franklin. And if I can find *that* out, I might be able to help Dawn."

"I hope so." Lucy flipped off the mixer. "Poor thing. You get these in the oven," she said, rinsing her hands in the sink. "And I'll start making phone calls."

"Make sure Mimsey brings her shew stone," I said.

CHAPTER 14

The evening was overcast, and the heat wave seemed to have broken. Mungo trotted happily beside me, his leash loose in my hand. Lucy was setting things up back at the Honeybee. She'd shooed me out for a walk, saying it would help clear my head for the location spell. Mungo hadn't been getting much exercise, either, so I'd brought him along.

As we walked along Bay Street, I dwelled on Dawn Taite, still lying unconscious in a hospital bed. *Beware of someone new.* Connell's warning, cryptic as anything. Even the not-quite-dead seemed determined to confuse the living.

Well, I certainly didn't suspect Mother Eulora of having any nefarious intentions toward Franklin or Dawn. Not only was she his mentor and the origin of the gris gris that helped him ferret out magic, but she had also been genuinely devastated to learn of his death.

Tanna, on the other hand, I just didn't like. That didn't mean she was evil, of course — I was unable to read her at all. Eulora obviously trusted her, and Tanna appeared devoted to her mistress. Could that be an act? Or could her worry about Eulora's health have caused her to dip into darker arts, and Franklin found out? She would have known him from his association with Mother Eulora, and indeed would have known much, if not everything, that her employer knew about him.

We strolled by Emmet Park. The Spanish moss hanging from the trees above waved in the slight breeze caused by a passing transit bus. Once the loud engine had faded into the distance, I detected another rumble to the east. A flash in my peripheral vision made me turn my head. Dark clouds piled on the horizon, and the still air buzzed with the subtle flavor of metal.

"Come on, buddy. Better head back before it starts to pour," I said. We took off at a light jog.

Mungo and I turned into the alley behind the bakery and entered through the unlocked back door. I heard Mimsey's excited voice, then Jaida's deeper tone. I unleashed Mungo, and he bounded around the corner.

I followed to find the two ladies helping Lucy to move a table in front of the espresso counter. The window blinds were already closed, and soft yellow light shone down from three ceiling-fan fixtures above.

"Hi! You're early. Or am I late?" I looked at my watch.

"We're a little early," Mimsey said, eyes twinkling. "I wanted to help set up. It's been far too long since we've cast together!"

Jaida grinned at the older woman's obvious delight. "Too bad we can't all be here."

Mimsey looked crestfallen. "Someone can't make it?"

My shoulders slumped, too. I wanted the power of the full coven for this spell.

"Cookie said she and Oscar have plans she can't break," Lucy said, looking at me with sympathy.

I rolled my eyes. *Oscar.* I was happy for Cookie — I really was — but her new husband sure threw a wrench into things.

"And Bianca couldn't get a sitter for Colette on such short notice," Lucy said.

"She should bring the little one with her," Mimsey said, her brow furrowed in frustration. "My daughter started learning the Craft before she was ten."

I muffled a flare of envy. My mother had done her best to shield me from any knowledge of magic, afraid of being ostracized in the small town of Fillmore, Ohio. I'd been twenty-eight before Lucy had stepped in and told me about my witchy heritage, and until then I'd felt like an outsider in every aspect of my life except baking.

"Colette is only seven, and it's Bianca's choice," Lucy said in a mild tone.

"Well, of course," Mimsey agreed, but she sounded pretty cranky, at least for Mimsey. I didn't blame her. Getting the spellbook club together in its entirety had been like herding cats lately.

Jaida unfolded a cloth of rich brown velvet. I hurried over and helped her spread it on the table.

Mimsey's face cleared, and she nodded in approval. "The perfect color for finding lost objects. Lucy, do you have the map?"

My aunt moved behind the counter and drew out a map of Savannah I recognized from the previous location spell we'd tried. She laid it on top of the brown velvet, and Mimsey reached into her capacious handbag and drew out a small bronze stand decorated with green stones. She set it on the map and retrieved her scrying stone from the bag. It was a smooth sphere of pink quartz crystal about five inches in diameter

— literally a crystal ball. She set it on the stand.

We pulled over four more bistro tables, arranging them at east, south, west, and north. Jaida set four black votives on them and actually pulled out a compass to make sure they were spot-on the four directions. Lucy added a drop of ginger oil to each wick, and the air filled with the potent, spicy scent. I went into the kitchen and came back with the canister of salt.

Jaida eyed the industrial-sized container. "Fancy."

I examined it, then looked up at her. "Not good enough, huh?"

Slowly, she shook her head. "Respect the elements, Katie, if you want them to work with you."

I went back into the kitchen, got out the marble bowl of the mortar and pestle set we used to grind herbs and spices. I debated whether to wash it, but decided the many incantations that Lucy and I had muttered over it would add magical energy rather than contaminate our good intentions. I wiped it thoroughly with a soft cloth and filled it carefully with salt.

The four of us moved within the perimeter of the tables, and Mungo tucked himself under the central table to be out of the way.

Normally, I would have asked him to stay outside the circle, but I didn't know what kind of magic the talisman might hold or whether it — or whoever had it — would resist being found. I wanted my little guy as protected as the rest of us, and the other witches didn't protest his presence.

Jaida had placed a tarot deck next to Mimsey's shew stone. Rather than the classic Rider-Waite cards, which she usually used for disposable spells like burning magic, this set depicted stylized dogs in vivid primary colors. The backs of the cards were all Great Danes. I smiled, since her familiar, Anubis, was a Great Dane who no doubt approved of his witch's choice.

Lucy laid a device I'd never seen before on the other side: a thick silver wire and another of copper, twisted together in the middle to create a kind of handle for the two prongs of a Y.

"What's that?" I asked.

Her lips curved in an easy smile. "My dowsing rod. I had Ben go home and get it this afternoon."

"I've never seen you use it," I said, fascinated.

"That's because I'm really bad at it." She laughed at the look on my face. "You know Mimsey is the only one of us who is any good at divination."

I glanced at Jaida, who shrugged. "It's true. I'll do a spread, but I'm pretty sure the cards aren't going to give us an address, if you know what I mean."

"Then why . . . ?" I asked Lucy.

That smile again. "Just because I'm not great with the dowsing rod doesn't mean it won't work for you. As I recall, you actually pulled off a location spell of sorts back when you were just learning."

"You'll show me how?" I asked, feeling a little nervous.

She nodded. "Of course. Shall we begin?"

I placed the picture of the gris gris Mother Eulora had given me on the corner of the map, off the grid of streets but propped up so we could all see it. My aunt turned off the overhead lights, and I moved to the eastern table to begin pouring a fine line of salt along the floor, moving deosil to the south, then west and north. Lucy followed, lighting the candles behind me as I defined the spell circle with the salt. As she touched flame to wick, she invoked the elements of air, fire, and water, and ended with earth. I closed the circle in the east and returned to where the others were already seated at the table. Mimsey was on the north, better to access the elemental power of earth as she gazed into her stone. I sat across from her with Lucy on my left and Jaida on the right. Mungo leaned against my ankle, warm comfort in the semidarkness.

I'd never cast a full circle like this with only a portion of the members of the spell-book club. It felt weird. Incomplete.

"Mimsey, you go first." I was itching to try Lucy's dowsing rod, but Mimsey was the eldest and most experienced. Plus, as my aunt had pointed out, she was better than the rest of us at divination.

She didn't argue. We all clasped hands, forming a circle within the circle. We closed our eyes, and Mimsey murmured, "We call upon the earth to reveal the location of Franklin Taite's voodoo gris gris."

Her words made me think of Declan trying to access Franklin's dead spirit. I'd talked to him at the firehouse earlier in the afternoon, filling him in on the visit to Mother Eulora but not mentioning my plans for the evening. He probably thought I was at home —

Lucy squeezed my hand. "Focus," she hissed.

I sent an apologetic look around the table and closed my eyes again, centering my attention back on the map, the gris gris, and my desire to find it. We joined in Mimsey's invocation three more times, then fell silent and opened our eyes. The older witch bent forward over her crystal, probing it with her physical gaze as well as a deeper vision.

The orb seemed to grow a little brighter, the pink quartz pinker, the crystalline structure within called out in sharp relief. I scanned the surface, tried to delve deeper, but all I managed was a slight throbbing behind my forehead. I turned my energy toward Mimsey's intention rather than my own. I felt the others doing the same, including a canine-flavored soupçon of energy from Mungo, still hunkered at my feet beneath the table.

From outside, the muffled sound of traffic. A horn honked, and a grumble of thunder echoed from far away. Mimsey's eyelids fluttered, and I saw her grip Jaida and Lucy's hands tighter as she leaned forward. I closed my eyes and imagined myself *inside* her shew stone, throwing out my senses in all directions, seeking the gris gris.

A confusion of images assaulted my mind's eye, as well as scent and tactile impressions. I felt myself gasp, but I no longer felt like I was in my own body. I drifted, increasingly untethered, floating . . .

Fog. Smoke. My own reflection. Mimsey's

twinkling blue eyes. A glimmer of red. A heavy feeling in my chest. The rasp of slithering snakeskin. Fear. Angry desire. Blades and bones and the smell of something rotting . . .

Hands tightened on mine, and I heard a voice calling my name. A whining, then a sharp pain on my ankle brought me back to myself, eyes popping open. Mimsey was looking at me, her eyes wide but also delighted. The others had also turned their attention from the crystal ball to me. Lucy's face was a picture of worry, while Jaida appeared more speculative.

"What?" I asked.

"So? Where's the talisman?" Mimsey asked in return.

I lifted one shoulder and let it drop. "I don't know."

"Well, what did you see, then?" she demanded.

"Nothing. What about you?"

"I saw *you* see something." She scowled.

I closed my eyes, trying to bring back the sensations. Finally, I shook my head. "I don't know how to describe it."

"But no gris gris," Jaida said.

I shook my head. Mungo jumped up and put his paws on my leg. I dropped Jaida's hand to stroke his head before reaching lower to rub my ankle where he'd nipped at it. "Thanks, little guy."

He cocked his head to the side and blinked up at me with brow furrowed.

"No, really," I said. "I think I could have gotten lost in that stone."

Lucy shuddered. "Sometimes I wish I'd never told you about your gift of magic."

I looked at her in surprise.

A small smile tugged at her lips. "Not really. But you scare the dickens out of me sometimes."

"Sorry," I said, ducking my head.

"Could the gris gris be shielded?" Jaida asked.

I gently extricated my fingers from Lucy's grip, thinking of Connell's warning that the talisman was hidden between layers of magic. Since Declan had been quite private about his previous experiences with his uncle, I hadn't shared his nocturnal visit with the others. Now I simply said, "I wouldn't be at all surprised. None of the impressions I got were of the talisman itself. Do you still want to try a tarot spread? That way, we'll at least know whether it's in the cards to keep looking."

Jaida pursed her lips, which were still bright ruby from her day at the office. "I don't think so."

I felt the blood drain from my face. "You

don't think we'll find it at all?

Jaida pointed at me. "That is exactly the kind of thinking we can't afford. *You* can't afford. As circumstances change, so do outcomes, but the cards will only capture now and the possibilities that exist now. That's fine in most circumstances, but I won't be responsible for putting any negative thoughts in your mind right now. Whatever the likelihood of your finding the talisman, you have to push forward."

"Why are you so anxious for me to find it?"

Jaida tapped the table with vermillion nails. "You aren't the only one who saw Dawn Taite collapse and almost die. I know you have a history with her uncle that the rest of us don't, but we all want to help her." She looked at Mimsey and Lucy, who both nodded. "And that means we help you, because you're the one who's going to find that talisman. You know that, right?"

I felt the weight that had settled across my neck ever since Dawn had shown up at the Honeybee increase by half again. It was one thing for me to feel like I needed to help Franklin's niece, but another altogether to carry the expectations of everyone else. Slowly, I said, "I guess so."

"Well, then, let's see you try this dowsing

rod," Lucy said with a smile in her voice.

Jaida nodded her encouragement. "Go on, Katie. If anyone can track down that talisman, you can."

"Yes, dear," Mimsey said. "We have faith in you."

Yip!

I had to laugh. "Thanks, Mungo."

Lucy held the dowsing rod with the copper wire in her right hand and the silver wire in her left. She balanced it across her fingers in a light grip, thumbs on top to prevent it from falling. Taking a deep breath, she said, "It's the same idea as pendulum scrying to find things on a map," she said. "You've done that a few times already."

I nodded. This whole divination thing was so darn iffy, though. Even after practically falling into Mimsey's shew stone, I didn't feel any closer to the truth. Discouragement settled in my chest, but I straightened my shoulders, anyway, determined to do my best.

My aunt inhaled again, and I knew she was centering herself. Her eyelids closed halfway as she held her arms over the map. The dowsing rod stuck straight out, parallel to her fingers. Slowly, she moved it around the map, turning her shoulders in order to keep her arms straight. Back and forth, back and forth across the street grid, all the way out to Tybee Island, then over to Garden City.

I hadn't eaten since Lucy had suggested this gathering of the spellbook club. In general, it was good not to eat before practicing magic, but I'd waited too long and now I felt a little light-headed, in addition to the noises my stomach was making.

Suddenly the rod dipped, and I stood to peer down at the map. But Lucy smiled and handed it to me. "That wasn't a magical revelation. My arms are just tired. You try."

I took the rod, happy to finally try dowsing, but still feeling defeated by all our failures so far. Either the gris gris didn't want to be found, or whoever had it was very good at hiding it. Besides, I was hungry.

Imitating Lucy, I held the rod out over the map, muttering, "Come on, voodoo gris gris. Mother Eulora told me all about you, gave me your picture. We need you. Where are you?" The mother-of-pearl bracelet grew suddenly warm against my wrist. I was still standing, so when the tip of the rod suddenly nosedived in my hands, the sign was more than clear. The twisted metal end whipped straight down, the force against my fingers strong enough that I almost dropped it. The tip touched the map, and

Jaida immediately leaned forward to note the location.

Mimsey clapped her hands, causing Mungo to run in tight circles around our feet. "Wonderful work, Katie! I knew you'd get the hang of divination one of these days."

Lucy beamed at me. "You did very well, honey. That dowsing rod is my gift to you."

"Yeah, nice job," Jaida said, leaning over and marking the map with her fingertip. "But I wish we had a larger map. This is a whole block."

I put the rod aside and leaned over to look. "It would help if we had some light. I can hardly make out the street names."

"Let's open the circle," Lucy said. "And turn on the overheads."

She and Mimsey made short work of it, going from east to north and around, widdershins this time. They thanked the elements, blew out the candles, and moved the tables aside. Lucy flipped on the overheads.

Together we clustered around the large table again, and Lucy marked the spot Jaida had been holding. It was a block on Lincoln, in the historic district and not far from the bakery. Quite close to Mother Eulora's house, in fact — and in exactly the direction she'd pointed when she'd told us where

Franklin had rented a room.

"I think Franklin may have lived there," I said. "Either the talisman is still with his things, or he hid it nearby."

Jaida's skeptical look didn't surprise me. "That might mean it isn't really gone. Do you think he cloaked it, then? But why?"

"To hide it from the wrong people?" I wondered. "But Dawn said it was gone."

"Maybe she didn't know her uncle had hidden it," Mimsey said, and Lucy made a sound of agreement.

"We have to go down there." Jaida looked at her watch. "But it's too late to start banging on doors. We'll have better luck in the morning. I'll be by around nine-thirty, and we'll go together. Will that work?"

I looked at Lucy, who smiled. "Of course. Iris is working tomorrow morning."

Mimsey nodded her approval. "I'm glad you're going with Katie," she said to Jaida. "The talisman may help her, or it may be dangerous. I won't trust it until I see it for myself."

CHAPTER 15

The rain fell across the Bug's windshield in heavy sheets as I drove home. Mungo couldn't have cared less about the weather outside; he'd hunkered down in my tote bag and gone to sleep before I even got past Oglethorpe Square. I tried to keep my attention firmly on the road, but I couldn't help going back to my thoughts from my run that morning, and then again as I'd walked Mungo earlier that evening.

Both Quinn and Mother Eulora had mentioned that Franklin had been working on a case that involved human sacrifice.

That had to be some serious evil.

Let's see, then. There were Poppa Jack, Marie LaFevre, Mambo Jeni, Mother Eulora, and Tanna. I already trusted that Mother Eulora was on my side, and felt the same about Poppa Jack, if only because of how he treated Cookie. The other two voodoo queens and Tanna were unknown quantities. But what about the other "new" people I'd met? I was fairly sure our young Goth employee wasn't a secret voodoo practitioner who was into human sacrifice. Steve's fancy new girlfriend from Hilton Head, though irritating, was also an unlikely suspect. But what about Oscar? He sure seemed to be a bossy pants with Cookie, but she said he disapproved of voodoo because of the curse placed on his sister. However, I didn't know him well enough to be able to judge his motives or beliefs. Could he be lying to Cookie?

Human sacrifice, though? Seriously? All I knew was that Cookie felt she had to hide things from him, and that made me wonder what he was really like.

Margie's house was dark when I pulled into my driveway, and I remembered her mention of a church function. Mungo and I rushed through the downpour from the car to the front door. Inside I turned on lights, closed the shutters, and headed for the kitchen.

I sighed with contentment after finishing up the leftover pork chops and corn pudding. The food brought me back to earth after the spell work. Mungo dozed in the doorway to the bathroom while I took a long, hot shower to further ground my energies. Then I donned my nighttime garb and snuggled under the patchwork coverlet on the bed, with a cup of chamomile tea. Before diving into the new John Sandford mystery, I checked in with Declan via text. His terse reply that he'd been called out to an accident on Interstate 16 wasn't personal, I knew. At least he wasn't fighting some huge conflagration. Car wrecks could be hard on the responders, but at least they weren't as dangerous as fire. I sent good thoughts to whomever had been involved in the crash and placed my phone on the nightstand.

In the meantime, I was going to escape into a tale of murder and mayhem that had nothing to do with my real life. Mungo settled in next to me with a contented groan and promptly began sleeping off his pork chops. Three hours later, I was doing the same thing.

"What's all this on the floor?" Iris asked. She was sweeping up around the espresso counter and now bent over to examine the small pile of white crystals her broom had gathered. The bakery would open in five minutes.

From where I was stocking the display case, I could see it was salt. Lucy shot me a look and scrambled down from the step-stool where she'd been updating some of our menu items on the blackboard behind the counter. Wiping chalk dust on her calico apron, she said, "Someone must have spilled something. I'll get you the dustpan."

Iris straightened. "The tables are re-arranged, too. Did you do that yesterday?"

Lucy and I exchanged a glance. "Um," I said.

Iris pointed her finger at me. "Wait a minute . . ." She turned and walked around the area in front of the register, eyes intent on the floor. "I know what this is! I've read about it in that book I found in the reading area! *Spells and Charms and Magic — Oh, My.*"

Which enterprising witch put that there? I reminded myself to ask at the next spellbook-club meeting.

Iris whirled. "It's salt, isn't it?"

I gave a slow nod, and Lucy watched her with gentle curiosity.

"You cast a circle last night?" Her hands were on her hips now, her tone triumphant. "I *knew* it."

Lucy moved to her and took both of Iris' hands in her own. "We did. We were trying to find something to help Katie."

"Help Katie?" Iris asked. "What's wrong?"

Now worry knitted her brow.

"Nothing's the matter with me," I said. "I'm trying to find out what happened to the woman who collapsed in here on Tuesday evening."

"I can't believe that happened during your book-club meeting," Iris said.

"Weeelll . . ." Lucy drew out the word, and looked over her shoulder at me. I dipped my chin in encouragement, figuring it was now or never. "It's not just a book club," she said in a soft voice. "It's a *spellbook* club."

Iris stared at my aunt, then at me, then back at Lucy, who was still holding her hands. Then she let out a whoop of laughter. "You're witches! Like, really! That's *awesome*!" She gave Lucy a quick hug, then backed away with a big grin on her face and did a little two-step. "I work with witches," she sang, then stopped. "Oh, my God. Can you actually curse people and change the weather and things?"

"Erm," Lucy said in a wry voice. "Not exactly."

Iris' face fell.

"Well, we might be able to," Lucy acquiesced with an amused expression. We had certainly cast some powerful magic as a group. "But that's not the kind of magic we do. Katie and I are hedgewitches."

Iris brightened again.

"For us, it's a family thing. Our great-great-great grandmothers and beyond have been village healers. For generations upon generations. They lived on the outskirts, near the hedges that surrounded most towns back then, barriers of vine and leaf that people believed kept them safe from outsiders. Hedgewitches ventured beyond those natural walls to enter the fields and forests to gather their herbs and plants, which they brought back to heal their communities."

"That is so cool!"

Lucy couldn't help but smile. "The knowledge of how to use plants, herbs, and spices is in our genes, though we don't need to cross any literal hedges now. Some people might consider us green witches, or call us natural witches. We use the elements of nature and direct the natural energies of plants and herbs to help others."

Realization dawned on Iris' face. "You do it here, don't you? You cast spells here in the bakery."

"We . . ." Lucy faltered then squared her shoulders. "Yes. To help our customers."

Iris pointed her finger at me. Again. "The pomegranate jelly."

I nodded. "Yup. To help Martin with his writer's block."

She stared down at the floor, not seeing it, but nodding vigorously to herself as she processed what we'd told her. Then she looked back up at us. "You said you'd teach me about using herbs and spices in baking."

"Yes," Lucy said.

"Will you teach me what you do? Or do I have to be in your family?"

My aunt and I laughed. I said, "And here we were worried she wouldn't be interested." I locked eyes with Iris. "You don't have to be in our family to learn kitchen magic. Anyone can learn how to direct their attention and intention to affect the world around them, but I knew the minute I met you at the cheese shop that you had an affinity for magic. It's one of the reasons I invited you to fill out a job application here."

"Really?" She clamped her hand over her mouth, blinking at me with eyes that shone with excitement. And something else, something I recognized from when I finally came to believe what Lucy had told me about our family's magical heritage: belonging.

Our little Goth girl had found herself a home.

"Come on," Lucy said. "I'll show you the spell I showed to Katie first. Let's whip up some cheddar sage scones."

I laughed and went to open the Honeybee for business.

I drove by Mother Eulora's, pointing out her tidy house to Jaida.

"Cute."

"Down to the collection of hedgehogs in her living room," I said, turning the Bug toward Forsyth Park and going another block before slowing to a crawl. "She said Franklin rented a place a few blocks away, in the direction of the park, but she didn't know exactly where. This is the block where the dowsing rod touched down. Keep your eyes peeled for possibilities."

"Gotcha," Jaida said, her attention glued to the buildings we passed. In the backseat, Mungo stood on his back legs and peered out, too, smearing doggy nose prints on the glass.

Large single-family homes lined the street, and since we were still in the historic district, almost all were quite old, if not actually constructed before the Civil War. Mother Eulora had said he'd rented a room, and that could have been in any one of them. I squeezed the steering wheel in frustration. Even assuming the location spell had narrowed the search this far, there were still so many possibilities

"There." Jaida pointed to a three-story house. "You can tell by the balconies it's been broken up into apartments."

She was right. Each of the iron-railed balconies had window boxes, but there was nothing consistent in the plantings, and some were empty. A lower one held a bike, the one above it a small bistro set, and two had grills. Cheered, I pulled into an empty spot in front, and we got out. Mungo jumped into my tote bag in the backseat, and I slung it over my shoulder.

A dozen buzzers set into the brick of the front alcove confirmed Jaida's conclusion. Knocking on the oak front door netted us nothing. None of the names by the buzzers identified Franklin Taite as a resident, but there was one that said MANAGER. I pushed it.

We heard the sound of footsteps on a hard surface. The door swung open to reveal a white-bearded man wearing dark-framed glasses, khakis, and a short-sleeved chambray shirt.

"Help you?"

"I'm Katie Lightfoot." I stuck out my hand. "And this is Jaida French."

He shook briefly. "I'm afraid we're full up right now, ladies." A nod toward where

Mungo leaned out of my tote. "And we don't allow pets."

"Oh, we're not interested in renting an apartment," I said.

A wry expression settled on his face, and he pointed to the NO SOLICITING sign by the bank of buzzers. "I guess you didn't see that." He stepped back and started to shut the door.

"Wait. We're not selling anything," Jaida said.

I took a step forward. "We're looking for one of your tenants."

The apartment manager paused, looking doubtful. "I'm sorry. I don't think —"

"He's not a current tenant," Jaida said.

"Franklin Taite," I said. "Do you know him?"

He looked relieved, and for a moment I thought we'd found the right place. Then he shook his head, and I realized the relief wasn't because he could help us, but because he was off the hook.

"Sorry. Never heard of him."

I glanced over at Jaida, unwilling to give up. "He might have been using another name."

The manager's eyes widened, and I rushed on. "He's shorter than me, in his late forties or early fifties, a little overweight, thinning

247

light brown hair —"

He held his hand up. "No one here like that. Seriously. I've had the same tenants for the past six months, and most are students or young couples." His hand tightened on the door. "I really can't help you."

"Wait," I said this time.

He stopped closing the door, the irritation on his face blooming into anger.

"I'm sorry," I said. "We know he lived in this area, but not exactly where. Are there any other converted apartments on this block?"

His head tipped to the side in thought. "Cozie Temmons lets out rooms in her home. Like a boarding house, you know? Mostly single men rent from her. She's a great cook, and that's part of the deal." He gestured with his chin. "It's the second house in from the corner on the other side."

I felt a grin spread across my face. "Thank you. Thank you so much."

He nodded and shut the door. I turned to Jaida. "That's got to be the place, don't you think?"

She smiled. "Let's go find out."

We left the car parked where it was and hoofed it down toward the corner. Mungo's head bounced up and down next to my elbow in time with my stride. We paused in the shade of the live oaks in front of our destination. It was a smaller version of a plantation-style home, complete with double-decker wraparound porches and terraced landscaping stepping up from the low wrought-iron fence to the brick foundation. The house was a mellow cream color, accented with dark green shutters and corner trim. We opened the gate and started up the gray brick steps, moving between the boxwood hedges, shiny azaleas, and green and white hydrangeas. The porch was painted classic haint blue, a Southern tradition meant to protect the home from spirits. Another NO SOLICITING placard, this one brass, hung from the porch railing. Next to it was another sign, this one announcing ROOM FOR RENT.

Bingo.

I raised my eyebrows. "Do you feel anything? Power that could come from a talisman or anything else?"

Jaida shook her head.

"Me neither." There was history in this spot, no doubt, and I felt sure a number of spirits were packed into the homes of this area, but if the talisman was here, it wasn't broadcasting its presence.

This time knocking brought an immediate

response. The woman who answered had short brown hair, brown eyes, and a full-lipped, welcoming smile that revealed a slight overbite. She wore shorts and a T-shirt and held a wooden spoon in one hand. The smell of bacon and onions drifted out to the porch, making my mouth water.

"Hi there! Come on in. It's hot as pepper out there." She stepped back, waving us in, and we obeyed with alacrity.

Shutting the door behind us, she said, "Now, who are you here to see?"

"Um, are you Cozie Temmons?"

"Oh, you want to see me." She laughed and looked between us. "I only have the one room available, though, and it's very small. Come on in the kitchen. We can talk while I finish up the potato salad for tonight's supper."

We followed her through the comfortably furnished parlor into a large, welcoming room redolent with the smells from the front porch, plus the added tang of vinegar and spices waiting to be tossed with warm potatoes. The steam still rose from a big bowl of them, fogging the window over the enameled sink. On another counter, a platter of chicken pieces dripping with buttermilk waited by a deep, wide skillet. Classic fried chicken with German potato salad and goddess knew what else. Cozie's boarders were lucky indeed. I looked down to see Mungo's nostrils flaring — and was that a bit of drool? I patted him on the head, and with a small sigh, he hunkered down in the bag.

Pouring the dressing in the bowl with the potatoes, Cozie began to gently fold it all together. "Sit down," she said.

Jaida and I sank into two of the red vinyl chairs.

"You're not here about a room, are you?"

I shook my head. "How did you know?"

She shrugged. "Most of my boarders are men, some of whom have been with me for years and years. The others are, to a man, recently divorced, don't know how to do their own laundry, and can't cook a lick." She laughed. "They're good guys, though. And they pay handsomely for my domestic prowess."

I grinned. "Plus, you can always kick them out."

She pointed the spoon at me. "That's right." Turning back to set the bowl down, she said, "Only had to do that a couple times in almost fifteen years, but it is nice to have as an option." She turned and leaned back against the edge of the sink. "So, what can I help you with?"

"Franklin Taite."

Her eyebrows rose in surprise. "Now, that was a man who didn't fall into either of the usual categories. Are you here to pay his back rent?"

I looked at Jaida and wrinkled my nose. "He owes rent?"

"Lord, yes. He just up and left without a word a few months ago. Never came back."

"Did you report him missing?"

She snorted. "He wasn't missing. He was running out on his rent. I didn't find a suitcase."

Beside me, Jaida's shoulders slumped. I felt the same way. "How long ago was that?"

"Let's see." Her gaze drifted up and to the left as she remembered. "About three months."

"Did he leave anything here?" I asked.

"A few things. After he'd been gone for a few weeks, I boxed them up, cleaned up the room, and rented it to a nice gentleman who moved here from Nashville after his wife passed away."

"Can we see his things?" I asked. "The stuff you boxed up?"

Her brow wrinkled. "Listen, I appreciate you listening to me complain about Frankie, but I have no idea who the heck you are. Why would I give his stuff to you?"

"How much rent does he owe?" I asked.

Jaida nudged me with her foot.

Cozie looked torn. "Are you his daughter or something? Do you know where he is?"

"Nooo." I drew the word out, scrambling for a good story. Should I lie? Her clear eyes regarded me with an openness that made me decide against it. "I'm a friend. And he's not coming back."

She blinked.

"His body was discovered a few days ago." Leaving out that it had been right here in Savannah, and, as Quinn put it, *fresh.* I stifled a shudder.

Her hand covered her mouth, and her face grew pale.

"I've been trying to find where he lived here in town," I said. "We were . . . friends, like I said."

"Oh, Lordy be. I can't believe it. And here I thought he'd stiffed me." She sank into one of the kitchen chairs and put her elbows on the Formica tabletop, guilt written all over her face. "I just can't believe it," she repeated.

"I'm sorry to deliver the bad news," I said. "But do you think we might have his belongings?"

Jaida nudged my foot again, and I realized that in my eagerness to find the gris gris I'd managed to sound pretty cold about Franklin's death. "His niece is here in town," she cut in with her best soothing tone. "No doubt she'll want to see them."

"Well . . ." Cozie's fingers tapped on the tabletop, her face a mask of bewildered sorrow. But when she looked up at me, her gaze cleared. "If he has a niece, don't you think it might be better to give them to her?" Her voice was worried and kind, but there was steel there, too.

"We'll be happy to take them off your hands," I said. "And maybe I could pay at least part of his back rent." I didn't think I could pay all of it. Baking was a joy and kept me solvent, but I didn't have a lot of disposable cash laying around, either.

Cozie's eyes narrowed, though. "That's starting to sound a bit like a bribe. You sure seem to want his stuff, for someone who's just a friend."

"I didn't mean —"

"Sorry, but we had a break-in last night, and I'm not feeling my usual trusting self." She sat back in her chair and crossed her arms over her chest. "I'll wait for the niece. And she'd better have ID —"

"You had a break-in last night?" I cut in.

"Yes. With all the men who live here, and all the coming and goings, I don't know how. But the lock on the back door was jimmied sometime during the night. I found it wide open this morning." Cozie looked toward the door in question, now sporting a bright and shiny new dead bolt. "Luckily, the locksmith could come right away. It won't happen again with that lock."

"Did the burglar get away with much?" I asked with sympathy.

She sat up. "You know, that the funny thing. I don't think they took a thing."

Jaida and I exchanged a look.

Cozie shrugged. "Maybe they just wanted a bite to eat, or maybe one of my boarders scared them off without realizing it. The police took my statement and left. There wasn't much elsc they could do." She shook her head. "Anyway, about Frankie's niece."

"I'm afraid she's somewhat indisposed right now," I began.

Jaida shot me a look of warning.

I paused, regrouping. "What about giving his possessions to the police?" I asked. "Would that be okay? You see, Franklin Taite was a homicide detective right here in Savannah for a while. I assure you we have good intentions, but if it would make you feel better, I'll ask his former partner, Detective Peter Quinn, to stop by and talk with you."

"A *homicide* detective? Heavens, I had no idea. Yes." She stood, and we followed suit. "Yes, that would be fine. Thank you for understanding. You just can't be too careful these days, you know? I'll wait to hear from Detective . . . Quinn, did you say?"

Nodding, I took one last sniff of the divine kitchen smells, and we said our good-byes.

CHAPTER 16

"What do you think?" I asked Jaida as we walked back to the car.

She made a face. "The timing of that break-in is pretty suspicious. I wonder if she would even notice if someone took 'Frankie's' stuff."

"No kidding. I almost asked her to go check, but she was already suspicious enough."

"Will Quinn follow through?" Jaida asked.

"I don't see why not. He wants to know more about his old partner's death, too. And he asked me to call if I had any information that might help."

She looked at me curiously. "Have you told him about Dawn's message? About the gris gris?"

"Not yet. After all, what could he do? He doesn't even believe in magic." We'd reached the car, and I hit the keyless entry.

"Are you sure?" she asked.

I responded with a humorless laugh. "He yelled at me about believing a psychic, Jaida. Finds what he sees as my preoccupation with the paranormal somewhat amusing. I'm pretty sure he's not going to help when it comes to voodoo curses."

She shrugged. "You're probably right."

"He'll want to know Franklin left with a suitcase. He's been someplace else for the past three months. Possibly in a coma."

"Detective Quinn might be able to find out where," Jaida said, stopping at my car.

"Exactly what I was thinking," I said, and stepped off the curb. "Though I'll have to convince him why it's a possibility, and I'm not sure how to do that."

A car drove by as I was opening the driver's door, and I looked up to see Steve's black Land Rover. I smiled and raised my hand to wave, then dropped it when I saw the blond locks winging out the open window were a much lighter shade than Steve's smooth, honeyed hair.

And, wouldn't you know it, tied with a pretty pink ribbon.

Tamping down the instant irritation that flared when I realized Samantha Whatshername — Hatfield? — was driving Steve's car, I deposited Mungo into the backseat and slammed the door. Steve let other people drive his car all the time. His dad. His lawyer.

Not me, though. Not once.

But I hadn't needed to borrow his car. Maybe his girlfriend's Porsche, or whatever she drove, was in the shop. Steve was a generous guy, after all. It was a perfectly reasonable explanation. Still, I couldn't help watching the vehicle turn at the corner, showing Sam's cute, ski-jump nose in profile.

"Get in," I said to Jaida. "Quick."

"What?" But she slid into the seat and shut the door. I started the engine and pulled away from the curb, tromping on the accelerator.

Jaida reached for the seat belt. "Where are we going now?"

"I'm just curious about something. Bear with me."

Jaida settled back in the seat. I felt her eyes on me as I turned onto Park.

A movement caught my eye, and Tanna rounded the corner on foot, heading away from Mother Eulora's with a large shopping bag in her hand. Her head came up, and she saw me watching. Her expression hardened in recognition, and her eyes narrowed into a glare as we passed.

I saw the Land Rover ahead, and slowed

to keep a Prius between it and the Bug. My car wasn't ostentatious, but it was memorable enough. Not that Samantha knew what I drove.

"Why are we following Steve?" Jaida asked.

"We're not. We're following his girlfriend."

"Oh. Well, that makes perfect sense, then."

I glanced over at her. She wore an amused expression. "There's something off about that woman," I said.

"You're going to feel a little foolish when she pulls into Whole Foods."

"Yeah. Probably." But some intuition had told me to follow her, and more and more I was learning to pay attention to those feelings. If I made a fool of myself in front of Jaida, so be it.

Samantha drove through Midtown, apparently without noticing the celery-green Volkswagen hanging back behind. We drove by Esoterique, and I pointed out Marie LaFevre's shop to Jaida. Then, when we reached the Southside, I started to get a funny feeling of familiarity. It was confirmed as the Land Rover turned onto Davidson Avenue. I slowed to a crawl just before the street sign.

Jaida leaned forward. "You're going to lose her."

Mungo chimed in from the backseat. *Yip!*

I snorted. "Funny how interested you are all of a sudden."

She spared me a sarcastic look.

I guided the car around the corner. By the time we reached the periwinkle house belonging to Mambo Jeni, we were going the speed limit. The Land Rover was parked in front, and Samantha was walking up the sidewalk to the door. She didn't even look around as we passed.

Jaida wrinkled her nose. "Do you think she lives there?"

I shook my head. "No. But that's where one of the other voodoo queens lives."

Her eyebrows shot up. "Oh, really?"

Now I nodded. "Mambo Jeni. And you know what? She told Cookie and me that love potions are one of her specialties."

When we got back to the Honeybee, Jaida grabbed a coffee drink and headed off to her office. My call to Detective Quinn about Cozie Temmons went to voice mail, so I left a message for him to call me, and hurried out to the kitchen. The lunch rush was just starting, and I spent a solid hour and a half constructing custom sandwiches on fresh sourdough bread and croissants. We'd recently expanded our menu from eleven to one-thirty to accommodate downtown businesspeople on the run, as well as visitors to Savannah on their midday tourist march. It had increased our traffic by at least ten percent during those hours.

In the middle of it all, Declan stopped by with Joe Nix and two other firefighters I knew from Five House. I made them all giant grilled-cheese sandwiches with layers of Tasso ham, thinly sliced pears, and a hefty slather of mango chutney tucked between the slabs of sourdough bread. Before they left, I managed to pull Deck aside long enough to update him on what Jaida and I had found out from Cozie Temmons. Then the guys were off, and I was back on more sandwich duty.

Things wound down, and I policed the emptying tables. As I took a bin of dishes from the bussing area into the kitchen, the bell over the door rang. Cookie marched in. She spied me and threaded her way toward the kitchen. She must not have been working, because she wore cutoff denim shorts that showed off her leggy beauty and a casual top.

"Hi!" I called, opening the dishwasher.

She came in and stood at the counter. Her eyes flashed.

I paused in reaching for a dish. "Is something wrong?"

"Did you tell him?"

"Tell who what?" But I had a notion.

"Oscar!" She planted her fists on her hips. "He knows we didn't go shopping yesterday."

"Huh. Well, I sure didn't tell him."

She glared at me. Iris came into the kitchen, took one look at us, turned around, and left.

I lifted my palms. "Oh, come on, Cookie. When would I have even talked to him? And you asked me not to say anything about the" — I lowered my voice — "voodoo stuff, so I wouldn't." I turned away and started stacking dishes in the rack again. "Not that I think it's a great idea to lie to your husband, but as you pointed out, your marriage isn't really my business."

She was quiet. When I turned back, I saw her anger replaced with tearful hurt.

"He's very angry with me, Katie."

I hid a sigh and gestured her toward the office. "Come in here, where we can have some privacy."

Mungo jumped down the second he saw Cookie. "Thank you, little man," she said. "But I don't need to sit down."

"Well, I do." I sank into the desk chair. She leaned against the file cabinet, searching her fingernails as if they held the secret to the universe.

"What happened?" I prompted.

"He accused me of lying about what I was doing yesterday afternoon. I think he's more jealous than I believed."

"Oh . . ." That didn't sound good.

"I assured him I was with you, and when he didn't believe me — after all, you work here all day, and he knows that — I admitted that you asked me to help find a mambo here in Savannah." She licked her lips and looked away. "He didn't seem that surprised, so I wondered if you'd already told him."

"Well, I didn't."

She sighed. "I know. I'm sorry. But he was so angry."

I jumped up. "Why? You can do whatever you want to, Cookie!" I held up my hand in a traffic cop gesture. "Not that you wanted to help me in the first place. I get that. But you decided to in the end, and that's *your* decision, not his!"

She sighed and slumped down in Mungo's chair, anyway, right on top of his fuzzy sheepskin bed. "I shouldn't have lied. You were right about that. It hurt his feelings."

"Yet he still got angry when you told him the truth."

"Yes." Her dark green gaze rose to mine. "As I mentioned, he has his own past with voodoo, in Santo Domingo, where he was raised before he left for school in Barcelona. It's something we have in common, you see, and now he feels I have betrayed him by reengaging with the community."

"Honey, I'm sorry." I bent over and gave her a hug. "I never thought your helping me would trigger such difficulty with Oscar."

She stood and gave me a proper hug in return. "It's not your fault. You're my coven sister. He has to understand that."

I stepped back and searched her face. "Does he? Or is practicing the Craft the same to him as practicing voodoo? Is this irreparable?"

Cookie blew out a breath and lifted one shoulder. "It'll be all right, I think. I'll give him some time, then try to explain again." She gave a tiny wince. "I wasn't terribly tactful during our conversation."

I couldn't help but laugh. "You are as fiery as they come, darlin'. I'm glad to hear falling in love hasn't tamed you too much."

A grin split her face. "Ha! No, you're right. I'll make this all right with my husband — whether he likes it or not!"

■ ■ ■ ■

As much as I hated hearing about the tension between Cookie and Oscar, I'd been wondering how to tell her I wanted to go see Mother Eulora without her. She probably wouldn't have minded; she hadn't exactly been over the moon about our visits to the various voodoo queens, and now her husband was angry at her. At least she'd had the chance to reconnect with Poppa Jack. I hoped they would stay in touch; perhaps he might help to fill the void her father had left behind.

However, what with all the talk of Franklin, dark magic, voodoo curses, and the power of the gris gris, I hadn't been able to ask Mother Eulora about being a lightwitch. I'd come to Franklin's mentor in a roundabout way, and under downright awful circumstances, yet I felt sure Eulora was the person he'd promised would tell me more about my apparent gift. Or calling. Or whatever. That was the point — to find out just what being a lightwitch was all about. I didn't really want to have that discussion with anyone else around. Even Cookie. Certainly not Tanna.

"I'd better call first," I said to Mungo,

who stood and stretched on the club chair. However, 411 didn't have a listing for either Eulora Scanlon or Mother Eulora.

"Dang it. She probably has a cell phone. I should have asked for her number. I wonder if Poppa Jack would have it."

I could have sworn Mungo rolled his eyes.

"Well, how would you know? You haven't met any of the players in the voodoo world."

He jumped to the floor and climbed into my tote bag, which was leaning against the file cabinet.

I couldn't help but grin. "I take it you want to meet Mother Eulora?"

Yip!

I laughed. "Okay. Let me check in with Lucy, and we'll head over there. The worst thing that can happen is she's not there." I considered. "Or that Tanna won't leave us alone to talk." Yes, that was a real possibility, especially given the look she'd given me earlier. "Or that she doesn't like dogs."

Rrrr?

"Well, it's possible. Some people don't." I picked up the tote and slid my cell phone into an outside pocket. "Not our kind of people, of course. But one thing at a time."

He gave a doggy snort and, as I picked up the tote, settled into the bottom of the bag so even his ears couldn't be seen.

Ben was being Mr. Social with a group of Savannah business owners who'd stopped in for sweet tea and macaroons, and Lucy and Iris were in the kitchen, talking in low tones with their heads close together. Seeing them, I thought of Lucy teaching me about hedgewitchery and was surprised to feel a flicker of jealousy. It was short-lived, however. Having another willing student, as well as an employee who knew what we did so that we didn't have to hide our kitchen spells, was an unqualified good thing. I really liked Iris, too.

When I saw Lucy put her hand on the teen's shoulder, I realized something else. Lucy and Ben were madly in love even after a dozen years of marriage, but they'd met later in life and didn't have any children. Iris' mother had passed, and her stepmother was a perfectly nice woman who owned the cheese shop down the block. Still, I knew they weren't particularly close.

And, really — can you have too many mothers?

Smiling to myself, I untied my gingham half apron and hung it on the wall with the rest of my vintage collection. "You mind if I take off for a couple hours?" I asked my aunt.

"Of course not," she said, then stopped

and gave me a sharp look. "Where are you going?"

"Mother E.'s," I said, keeping it casual. "I'll be back right after."

She squinted at me but didn't ask questions, understanding that I didn't want to elaborate with Iris standing right there. Iris herself watched me with sharp curiosity.

"Okay, honey," Lucy said in a mild tone and turned back to the jar of dried herbs she held in her hand. She said to her new apprentice, "Now, this is thyme. It allows one to access the courage we all carry deep inside."

Setting my bag — and Mungo — down behind the register counter, I quickly filled a bag sporting the Honeybee logo of an orange kitty with muffins, macaroons, oatmeal chocolate-chunk cookies, and an assortment of scones.

With a friendly nod at Ben and his friends, I exited by the front door. The weather had taken a pleasant turn overnight, and the early afternoon was only in the eighties.

"Shall we walk?" I asked Mungo, who had raised his head and was taking in the sights.

Yip!

"Do you want down to walk?"

His head ducked back down.

"Lazy bones," I muttered, but hoisted the

tote strap higher on my shoulder and set off on foot for Mother Eulora's little house, the bag of pastries in my other hand.

As I turned the corner, movement on the porch alerted me that someone was home. Approaching, I saw two figures in the chairs there. One was Mother Eulora, and the other was a girl of about twelve or thirteen. Thin and animated, she was chatting a million miles a minute and kicking her heels against the porch to keep the rocker going at a pace to match her words. She wore white shorts and a T-shirt advertising a band called Midnight Red. Her hair was pulled back with a purple scrunchie. She stopped talking for a moment to take a drink from a tall glass on the table between them, then dove back in to her story.

Eulora turned her head, saw me coming up the street, and waved. I waved back, relieved at her welcome. Opening the gate, I skirted the bicycle laid down on the front walk, went up to the bottom step, and stopped.

"Katie," Eulora said before I could speak. "I would like for you to meet my great-granddaughter, Cecelia Scanlon. Honey, this is Katie Lightfoot. She's a new friend."

"Hi, Cecelia," I said, and went up the steps to the small porch.

Cecelia rose to her feet and stuck out her hand. "It's very nice to make your acquaintance."

So polite. I exchanged a glance with Mother Eulora, who appeared both amused and approving.

But as soon as Cecelia spied Mungo, the mature young woman was gone. "Oooh! Puppy! Can I pet her? Please, please?"

"He's a boy, and his name is Mungo," I said.

My familiar, ever the ham, stood on his hind legs and wagged his tail so hard, I thought he'd fall out of the tote. Quickly, I grabbed him and lifted him down to the porch. He beelined over to his new fan, who sat on the top step and patted her leg. I winced as he bounded into her lap, wondering how much of his charcoal-colored fur would end up on her white shorts, but she didn't seem to care.

"Oh, you're such a cutie! Who's a good boy? Mungo's a good boy!"

I grinned and moved over to where Eulora was looking down at both of them with an indulgent smile.

"I hope you don't mind that I brought him along," I said, setting the bag of pastries on the table between us.

"Of course not," she said. "He *is* a cutie."

Mungo lolled his tongue at her over Cecelia's shoulder, and Eulora laughed.

I shook my head at his over-the-top antics. "I hope I'm not inconveniencing you, dropping by like this. I know Emily Post would disapprove, but I don't know your phone number, and I wanted to talk to you about something."

She moved her hand as if flicking away a bug. "Bah to Miss Post and her ilk. You come on by here anytime you want." Her eyes were knowing. "After all, we have a lot to talk about."

Cecelia moved Mungo off her lap and stood. Regret oozed from every pore. "Grammy, I gotta go."

Eulora inclined her head. "I know, honey. Your daddy's expecting you."

"Maybe you could call him? Tell him you need me to stay?" She looked down at Mungo as she said it.

"I'm sorry, child. I have some business with Katie here. Come back tomorrow at the same time, okay?"

The girl's shoulders slumped, but she nodded. "Tomorrow." Cecelia looked a little worried. "Tanna?"

"I'll let her know she needs to run an errand. It's okay, honey. You'll be in school soon. We've got to take advantage of the summer."

"Okay, Grammy." Cecelia went over and kissed her grandmother's crepe-papery cheek, then nodded to me. "Nice to meet you." And then to Mungo. "And you, too!"

Yip!

"Oh!" she giggled, then groaned, "He's too cute to leave."

"Come by the Honeybee bakery down on Broughton. Sometimes Mungo hangs out in the reading area." I pointed at the paper bag. "In the meantime, how about a cookie or a muffin?"

Cecelia peered inside and carefully selected a chocolate-chunk cookie. She thanked me, said good-bye to her great-grandmother, and skipped down the steps to her bike. Seconds later, she was sailing away down the sidewalk.

"Come and sit," Eulora said, fanning herself with a fold-out fan.

I did as she said, sinking into the rocking chair while Mungo explored the not so far corners of the small porch.

"Thank you for the pastries. I should have had Cecelia get you some lemonade before she left."

"Oh, I'm fine," I said, then saw the look in her eye. "And I'm not worried that you're going to do me in with some voodoo drink

273

spell, either."

"Ha. Well, that's good."

"I take it Tanna isn't here," I said, hoping I was right.

Eulora shook her head. "She finds errands to run when Cecelia comes to see me. They don't get along."

"How could anyone not get along with that girl? She's adorable."

She didn't smile. "Cecelia is my apprentice. So is Tanna, of course, but Cecelia is family. Tanna is not. It sometimes creates . . . conflict."

I thought of Lucy and Iris and that tiny green arrow I'd felt when I'd seen them together. I'd brushed it away, but I was Lucy's family. I knew I didn't have to worry.

"She's jealous," I said flatly.

"She's . . . overprotective of me, and, yes, perhaps a bit jealous. I teach them the same, or at least the same according to their own strengths and abilities."

"But your great-granddaughter is only what? Twelve?"

"Thirteen just last month. Poor Tanna. She has no family left, and her husband passed several years ago."

But she's the grown-up, I wanted to say. For once I kept my mouth shut.

"Shall we go inside?" Eulora said, changing the subject. "It's cooler today, but I'm still a bit overheated."

I sprang to my feet. "Of course!"

"Bring the little dog, too." She rose, examining him as she did so. "He's more than your little dog, though, isn't he?"

Nodding, I asked, "How did you know?"

"Because you are a lightwitch. You are bound to have a strong familiar, and small though he might be, that one is strong indeed."

CHAPTER 17

Holding her elbow, I helped her inside. She seemed frailer than the day before, and I wondered how much our visit had taxed her health. Maybe Tanna wasn't overprotective after all. I ran back outside and retrieved the empty glass and pastries from the porch and brought them into the kitchen, then began looking through the cupboards for a plate.

"Next to the refrigerator," Eulora called from her perch on the living-room sofa.

"Got it," I said. Moments later, I brought in a plate piled with the Honeybee baked goods and the pitcher of lemonade I'd found in the refrigerator. "I changed my mind about something to drink. I hope you don't mind."

"Heavens, no," she said, a smile crinkling the skin around her eyes even more. She reached for a fig muffin. "I see you're wearing the bracelet. Good. Have you had a chance to look for the gris gris since yesterday?"

I sat in the same chair I'd chosen the day before. "Yes, but not with the best of luck. We — my coven and I — tried a location spell last night. More than one, actually. I found a likely possibility."

She leaned forward with an eager expression. "And?"

"It was where Franklin rented a room. But he hadn't paid his rent, and his room has been cleared out and rented. The landlady wouldn't let us look at what he'd left behind. She's not feeling very trustful."

She tipped her head to one side. "Did something happen to make her feel that way?"

"There was a break-in last night. Nothing seems to have gone missing," I said. "But the timing seems a bit, er, coincidental. She agreed to give Franklin's possessions to Detective Quinn, however. I have a call in to him."

Eulora's took a bite of muffin, looking thoughtful. "I agree that break-in is suspicious, especially since only last night you discovered the location of the gris gris with your spell. Could anyone have observed you?"

My fingers crept to my lips. "You think

someone was watching us cast? The blinds in the Honeybee were all closed."

Her eyes flashed purple. "There are many ways to watch someone. Not all are literal."

The enormity of the enemy I was up against settled in my stomach. "Mother Eulora, I don't know what to do."

She shook her finger at me. "Of course you do. You might not realize you know yet, but you do."

I stared at her. *What the heck?*

"Eulora," I said slowly. "Franklin said I was a lightwitch, but other than telling me I was unable to engage in black magic, he didn't tell me what being a lightwitch is supposed to be all about."

Her eyes went wide. Shaking her head, she looked toward the ceiling. "Franklin, what were you thinking?"

I stood. "What?"

Eulora pushed herself to her feet. "Come with me. I want to show you something."

Obediently, I followed her down a back hallway with Mungo trundling along at my left heel. But I was fuming. Had Franklin lied to me?

We passed a neat, austere bedroom. "Tanna's," she said. "She moved in a few months ago. To take care of me." She breathed a small sigh.

We moved farther down the hall to what must have been Eulora's own bedroom. Stuffed hedgehogs were piled on the neatly made bed. More overflowed the top of the dresser, the deep windowsill, and a small bookshelf. When she opened the walk-in closet to reveal a recognizable altar, it threw the collection of fuzzy, sweet toys into sharp relief.

A small table, waist-high and covered with a white cloth, snugged against the wall. It was covered with photographs ranging from old-fashioned sepia daguerreo-types to modern snapshots. A vase of silk lilies, the same dark aubergine of Mother Eulora's eyes, dominated a back corner. A crystal bowl held water, and a white candle sat in a bowl filled with M&M's. Another bowl held what looked to be plain old soil — only I remembered the vials of graveyard dirt in Marie LaFevre's shop and doubted it was plain at all.

The item that grabbed my attention and wouldn't let go was the two-foot length of dried snakeskin curled in the middle of the altar. The red, black, and yellow stripes were faded but still managed to look deadly.

I pointed to it. "Detective Quinn said they found snakeskin in the warehouse where they found Franklin. Feathers, too."

She slowly nodded. "Voodoo of some kind is no doubt involved in his death, then."

I couldn't help but shiver, recalling the slither of snakes in the depths of Mimsey's shew stone.

Mother Eulora saw my reaction and said, "In our legends, Damballa is the serpent god who created the world. His coils form the stars, his skin the oceans. He is married to the rainbow, Ayida Wedo. This brings me comfort, but not because it protects me or can keep me from age or illness. It is my heritage, and these things have meaning to me." She took my hand. "I do not call myself a mambo nor a priestess, but a spiritualist. That is a choice."

Turning to look up at me with her sweet face and deeply knowing eyes, she said, "Franklin was wrong to tell you lightwitches can't cast black magic."

I felt the blood drain from my face. "But . . ."

She patted the bed. "Sit."

I sat on the chenille coverlet. Eulora shut the closet door and sank into the chair by the window with a grateful sigh. Our knees were almost touching. Over her shoulder, I could see a tidy rose garden flourishing in the backyard.

She reached for a stuffed hedgehog on the

windowsill and placed it on her lap. "Light-witches are more powerful than your every-day witch, or sorcerer, druid, mage, houdon — anyone who comes to magic to learn and develop the inherent power we all possess. You were *born* with power, deep power. One or the other of your parents was gifted through the generations."

"Both," I said. "Hedgewitchery and Native American shamanism."

She clapped her hands, delight playing across her features. Once again she reminded me of Mimsey.

"Of course! That explains it. You are, shall we say, supercharged from birth. All magic can be learned, augmented, improved over a lifetime. But you are a magical savant, if you will."

I looked down at my hands, clasped in my lap. "Sometimes I glow."

"You . . . ?" She gave a full-throated laugh. "Oh, yes. I remember Franklin telling me. It was what alerted him to the depth of your power in the first place. But, honey, don't worry. That's only when you're under duress, I'm sure." She absently stroked the stuffed animal in her lap.

I looked up to find her looking at me with concern that belied her words. "Then why are you looking at me that way?" I asked.

"Franklin lied to you, at least in a way. He had his own agenda, you see. To fight the dark. Once he discovered how powerful you really are, he tried to force you to do only good by telling you that you had no choice."

"I have no interest in practicing dark magic," I said.

She held up her hand. "I'm happy to hear that, of course. But you need to understand that the gift of the lightwitch demands choice. Informed choice. Balance and intention are key to power. Even angels can't be forced to serve the light."

A grimace crossed my face. "Well, I'm no angel."

A small smile touched Mother Eulora's lips.

I sighed. "But I haven't been like this my whole life. The glowing and all."

"You've had magic in you your whole life, though. You know that, surely."

Slowly, I nodded. "It took me a while to realize that after my aunt told me about my witchy heritage a year and a half ago. But then I remembered all sorts of evidence of my latent abilities." I folded my arms over my chest, and my voice rose. "Out of fear, my mother kept that knowledge from me, and now I find out Franklin lied to me, too. I'm getting pretty darn sick of other people trying to control me!"

Mother Eulora's eyes shone. "Good. Don't allow that to happen anymore."

I blinked.

"It's your choice," she said.

A door slammed somewhere on the other side of the house. Eulora rose to her feet, and I did the same. "Tanna has returned. I assume you want to keep this conversation private?"

"Yes," I said. "But please, before I leave, can you tell me just a little more? What does it *mean* to be a lightwitch? Is there such a thing as a darkwitch?"

She tipped her head to the side. "I suppose there might be, since everything has its opposite, but I've yet to meet one. Lightwitches bring balance to the universe, you see. It's very simple. Sometimes it's a small thing — balancing the sadness, the anger or loss in someone's life with a positive herbal remedy like you do in your bakery, or even a smile or word of encouragement. It can also mean going head-to-head with greater evil, if that is the choice you make. Large or small, it's all part of the same calling. Anyone can do the small stuff — and should. But we often don't take those opportunities to bring a bit of beauty or kindness or laughter into the world, do we? It all adds to the positive, though, and acts against the jealousy, violence, greed, and hate." She paused, her gaze penetrating my mere physical body and seeming to look deep into my mind.

Maybe even my heart.

"You are able to engage with larger evil than most of us," Eulora went on. "However, it's not a gift you're obligated to use. You must understand that."

I nodded.

"However, if you don't, it is a great waste."

We heard a rustling from somewhere down the hall. Closer now.

Putting my hand on Mother Eulora's arm, I rushed my words. "Thank you. Perhaps I did know this all along, but I feel a new clarity about being a lightwitch. I can't tell you how much that means to me."

She patted my hand again. "Of course —" Her eyes widened and her head whipped toward the hallway.

At the same time, Mungo went crazy, barking and bouncing, high and loud and fast. He ran to the doorway and his barking grew even more frantic.

"What the . . . ? "The mother-of-pearl bracelet seemed to tighten against the pulse point on my wrist as I ran to join him.

What I saw didn't register at first.

Fog seemed to be creeping along the ground, billowing along the wall-to-wall carpet from the direction of the living room, crawling toward us as if impelled by its own life force. I watched it in a trance, Mungo's barking a strange background noise.

Eulora shook me. "Katie! We have to get out of here!"

I blinked, inhaled a whooping breath, and smelled the foulness of the air. The rustling sound grew louder, turning to a crackling, and, finally, though it only took a few nanoseconds, my brain put it all together.

Fire.

A quick glance confirmed the window was too small to crawl out of. No way could the older woman have hoisted herself up to that level, anyway.

"Come on." I grabbed her hand and pulled her out of the room. Mungo had fallen silent now that he'd sounded the alarm, and followed me like a wraith. I thought about picking him up, but instinctively decided he'd be better off near the floor. The hallway was full of smoke now, as it rose toward the ceiling, acrid and nasty smelling. The crackling grew louder. I veered into Tanna's bedroom and pulled back the curtains.

Yes!

This window was much larger and lower to the ground. We could all get out! I reached for the latch and unlocked it.

Mungo started barking again as sudden flames whooshed upward from the floor molding. *What? Where did that come from?* But it drove me back from the window.

This isn't a normal fire. This is something different. This is something very, very wrong.

I grabbed the pillows off the bed, stripped off the cases, and ran into the bathroom across the hall. Quickly, I doused them both and wrapped one around my face and the other one around Eulora's, muffling everything below her sharp, assessing eyes. At least we could breathe.

But Mungo started coughing at my feet, and new terror winged through me at the thought of smoke getting into his little lungs. I swooped him up in my arms and nestled him against my shoulder so he could breathe through the wet fabric as well.

Eulora and I stumbled down the hallway, hand in hand, toward the living room. I didn't know how long the fire had been burning, perhaps several minutes before we noticed it, but it was accelerating at a dizzying pace. The smoke was making me woozy, too, and my throat ached from breathing the hot, harsh air even through the wet pillowcase.

"Katie!" Eulora called through the roar of the flames. She pointed.

Flames licked the walls, filling the arched doorway to the kitchen and roaring to a crescendo all around us. Looking back, I saw it had spread to the bedrooms we'd just been in. Then I saw something that made my pounding heart almost stop: Dark streaks reached through the flames, flickering with a life of their own. Antifire in the midst of fire, something I sensed was so cold, it only made the feverish heat hotter. With an eerie intelligence, it reached destructive fingers toward us.

Seeking. *Hunting.*

It nudged flames toward fabric and books and the more combustible items in the room. The wooden apples burned brightly within their ceramic bowl, a sinister centerpiece in the middle of the glass coffee table. Wisps of magazine ash swooped through the room, buffeted by hot currents of air. A whiff of burnt sugar reached my nose from the wreckage of the Honeybee pastries cremated right on the plate.

The gauzy curtains went up in a flash, and a wave of heat tumbled over us. I bent down, hunching over Mungo as I moved away, then straightened to find the entire room engulfed in fire. Loud popping came from the direction of Eulora's collection of ceramic hedgehogs, and a piece of super-heated shrapnel struck my left shoulder. I cried out, and Mungo yelped. The caustic smell of burning upholstery filled my nostrils as the blazing sofa slumped in upon its springs, the polyester stuffing melting and giving off a putrid, yellow cloud.

I held Mungo to my chest with one hand and squeezed Eulora's hand with the other. "Help me fight it!" I cried, focusing all my panicked energy into clearing a path to the doorway. I felt her considerable power rush to meet my own, and there was the lupine energy I knew was Mungo's essential wolfish nature that merged seamlessly with mine. I felt my skin grow oddly cool and saw white light like static pulse beneath my skin.

Closing my eyes, I gathered all our energies together and *pushed.*

I felt the dark flames retreat, try to surge back as if fighting me, but one more push and the fire died between us and the door. We rushed forward, and I reached for the doorknob.

Eulora slapped my hand away. "Hot," she rasped.

I could barely hear her, but nodded. *Stu-*

pid. Unwinding the pillowcase from my face, I wrapped it around my hand and used it to grasp the metal handle.

It wouldn't turn.

A wall of flame like the one in Tanna's bedroom flared from the bottom of the door, driving us backward.

"Help!" I screamed in desperation.

Eulora grabbed my hand again, and I felt our energies melding once more.

"Baby dog, I have to put you down for a sec," I murmured to Mungo. Fighting every instinct to keep him as close to me as possible, I set him at my feet. He leaned against my leg, still helping Eulora and me as we directed our attention toward the flames now obscuring the exit in front of us.

The fire fought back. I gritted my teeth, summoning everything I had, ready for one last effort. But then Eulora's grasp loosened in mine, and her other hand moved toward her chest. She leaned against me. Mungo whined at my feet.

"No!" I screamed, my rage at whatever force was at work overcoming my fear. The word cut through the incinerating roar, and the flames seemed to pause.

A sudden, cool calm descended through my frantic thoughts. *There is evil in the fire, but fire itself is not evil. It is an element, and I am a witch. I work* with *the elements, not against them.*

Putting one arm around Eulora's shoulders to help her stand, I closed my eyes against the blaze and smoke, concentrating. "I call upon Michael, archangel of the south, of fire, of protection and courage," I whispered. "With gratitude and reverence I call upon Fire." My voice was louder this time. "To help and not hinder, to warm but not burn." I thought of all the magical associations of fire the ladies of the spellbook club had taught me, concentrating on the good and beneficial.

Summer, sun, laughter and joy, playfulness, motherhood, the third chakra . . .

I sensed a shift of energy in the room, as if the clean fire was listening, shrugging off the bitter power controlling it. Gathering itself. Offering itself to my will.

"Thank you," I said, my fear and anger draining away in a wave of gratitude.

Holding the essence of fire in my mind, I wordlessly asked it to move away from the door. When I opened my eyes, the path had cleared. The charred wood of the door no longer burned. A sound behind us made me turn my head, and I saw that wasn't all. The fire had turned away from the combustibles in the room, had turned upon itself, eating the icy darkness within.

With a crash, the door burst open, and Declan filled the frame.

"Och, yer all right, then," he bellowed.

Or, rather, Connell did.

Yip!

CHAPTER 18

Mungo ran out to the front yard and began barking in earnest to anyone who would listen. Connell blinked at me once, smiled ruefully, and was gone. The smile dropped, and Declan's worried gaze took over. "Katie!" He pushed into the room. Heat flared against my back, the fire returning, real and untainted now but still hungry.

"Are you okay?" Declan shouted and reached for my arm.

"I'm fine." My voice rose as I shifted to look at Mother Eulora. "But she's not. I think there's something wrong with her heart, and I know she inhaled some smoke."

Declan took one look at my companion and scooped her up in his arms with a grunt. We ran outside as the roof above the porch caught.

A ladder truck and ambulance roared to the curb. Joe Nix jumped out and began pulling a gurney out of the back of the van as Declan lowered Eulora gently to the ground. I grabbed one of her wrists and chafed it, as I'd seen her apprentice do.

"She's on medication, but I don't know what," I said to Declan, as he felt for her pulse and checked her breathing.

"Tanna," she muttered. Her eyes flew open, pinning me where I leaned over her prone form. "She came home. She was inside."

"Shh," I soothed. "We didn't see her. She must have gotten out."

"Tanna," Eulora said again, her eyes drifting shut. And then the paramedics were there with the gurney and bags of equipment, crowding me away.

Declan, still kneeling beside her, raised his head and raked me with his gaze. I could see him mentally running through a checklist as he assessed my physical well-being. I forced a smile and backed away. I wanted him to concentrate on Mother Eulora, not worry about me. I was fine.

Well, as fine you could be after escaping a magical fire.

I called Mungo over and checked him for injuries. Other than a few singed hairs on top of his ears, he appeared none the worse for wear. Together, we melted to the edge of the activity, watching numbly.

Where was Tanna? I'd assured Eulora she must have escaped the fire, but I also knew she'd be by Eulora's side if she were able. Had that even been her we'd heard coming in the door? Wouldn't an arsonist have been a little quieter?

We couldn't even see into the kitchen. Tanna could have been trapped there. My stomach tightened at the thought.

The fire crew had hooked up to the hydrant and was directing jets of water at the blazing home. The rear of the house had already fallen into a pile of charcoal defeat, now wetly burping smoke from the crevices. It would be a complete loss, hedgehogs, altar, and all.

Glancing at my watch, I felt a sense of disorientation. I'd been gone from the Honeybee less than an hour.

"Katie?"

I turned, and Declan swept me into his arms.

"Ouch!"

Instantly, he was checking me over. "This is a bad cut on your shoulder," he said. "You'll need stitches."

Craning my head, I tried to see. "It doesn't hurt that much." The wound was deep, though, now that I really examined it. At least an inch, and four inches long. The sharp ceramic from the exploding tchotchke had acted like a bullet.

He grimaced. "It will. Come on. We'll get it numbed before the adrenaline wears off."

I began to protest, but a wave of weariness almost brought me to my knees. Weakly, I nodded and allowed him to take me toward the ambulance.

"Mother Eulora?" I asked.

"Probably a heart attack, but she's stable."

The ambulance started up and pulled away. "How will I get to the hospital?" I asked in bleary voice.

Declan laughed. "In my truck, silly." Then, more gently: "Don't worry, Katie. I'll take care of you."

I nodded again, relieved to let my lethargy take over. He *would* take care of me.

There was a prick of pain on my upper arm, and Joe Nix was smiling at me over a hypodermic needle. "You've had one hell of a week, Lightfoot."

"Uh-huh," I said.

Declan led me toward his king-cab pickup. He lifted me in, placed Mungo on my lap, and closed the door. The voices on the dashboard scanner nattered away, oddly soothing. But as he pulled away and turned in the direction of Candler Hospital, I finally put my finger on something. "Why are you in your truck when you're on shift?" I asked. "Were you doing something separately from the rest of the crew?"

His silence went on for long enough that it pulled me out of my stupor. "Declan?"

"I didn't come in response to the 911 call. That came in after I was already on my way. And the others couldn't come just because I told them you were in trouble." He licked his lips. "I'm pretty sure they think I'm crazy."

"But you were right — Wait. How did you know I was in trouble?"

He shot me a look.

I remembered his expression when he'd broken open Eulora's door, the shouted words. "Connell?"

"Connell."

"I saw him there in the doorway when you came in. Did he, uh, make life difficult for you with the other firefighters?"

He gave a small shudder. "No. At least he didn't do that. But he came to me, told me your life was in danger, that you were being attacked. He guided me to where you were."

I sat back against the seat. "Well, I have to thank him for that."

Declan half smiled and turned into the emergency bay behind an ambulance. "I've already thanked him." He put the truck in park and faced me. "He's taken quite a shine to you. I'm glad he's not only looking out for me, but for you, too. But, Katie?"

"Yeah?"

"What was he talking about when he said you were being attacked?"

"That fire . . ." I faltered, remembering. "It wasn't natural. It was fast, hot, and —" I paused.

"What?" he asked, using the smooth, calming tone he'd developed on the job. But I could see the dread in his eyes.

"Smart," I finished.

He paled. "You mean it was *sentient*?"

I shrugged carefully, no longer feeling bleary. My shoulder was starting to really ache. "I don't know. Maybe it was my imagination. But I'd sure like to know whether your investigators find any evidence of arson."

He looked away, processing what I'd said. "A fire that fast had to have an accelerant."

"I figured. And, Deck? There's a possibility Eulora's apprentice, Tanna, was in the house, too. We heard someone come in before we realized what was going on. It could have been her."

"Or it could have been the arsonist," he said, echoing my thoughts. He opened his door. "I'm calling Peter Quinn while they stitch you up."

The scent of disinfectant almost overrode the smell of smoke that seemed to emanate from my every pore. I wondered if I'd ever get it out of my hair as the nurse, a middle-aged man whose name tag read MIGUEL, made short work of patching up my shoulder. He bandaged it elaborately with gauze and tape, and repeatedly warned against getting it wet for the next few days. Declan had parked his truck and checked on Mungo, and now stood quietly in the corner.

The overhead light gleamed off Miguel's shaved head as he leaned over and inspected his work before straightening. "Here. Take two of these." He handed me a blister pack with six tablets. "I'll get you some water."

"What are they?" I asked.

"Hydrocodone. The doctor'll write you a prescription for more."

"Will they make me feel funny?" I asked.

"Probably." He grinned.

I nodded. "Okay. But I'm going to wait and see how bad the pain is without them."

"Your choice, but you generally want to stay ahead of the pain."

"Katie —" Declan began.

I cut in before he could chastise me. "I

want to check on Eulora." I slid to the edge
of the examining table and put my feet on
the floor. He grabbed my good arm as I
wobbled, but then I straightened and took a
couple of steps.

"You go sit in the waiting room," he said.
"I'll find out what happened to her."

I nodded, and he strode away on long legs.

"You're looking for that other lady who
was in the fire? They admitted her," Miguel
said, tidying the area in preparation for the
next customer.

"Is she okay?" I asked.

"For now," he said, meeting my eyes.
"They took her to the cardiac unit. They'll
monitor her very closely — I promise."

I allowed myself to feel a frisson of relief.
"Where's the cardiac unit?"

Miguel shook his head. "You should do
what your boyfriend says. Go sit down, take
it easy. He'll be back soon enough."

My lips thinned. "I want to see her. What
floor?"

He lifted one shoulder, let it drop, and
gave me the directions I'd asked for.

"Thanks," I said.

"The elevator's that way." He pointed.
"And you might want to stop by the restroom. You have a bit of ash on your face."

I left the curtained area, shoulder throbbing, impelled by worry and guilt. If I hadn't dragged Eulora into whatever mess Dawn had pulled me into, she wouldn't be in the hospital, possibly fighting for her life.

The "bit of ash" turned out to be a smear across one whole cheek and part of my forehead. Why hadn't anyone told me until now? Standing over the sink, I scrubbed until my face was pink and clean. Then, stepping off the elevator, I followed the signs to the cardiac unit. The hallway opened into a forty-foot-square waiting room. I heard the voices before I stepped into it, so I wasn't surprised to see a dozen people standing or sitting, chatting in low tones. I recognized a few of them from the photos on Eulora's altar.

Family.

Then I noticed Cecelia. She saw me and waved.

I waved back and turned to the nurses' station positioned near the door to the stairwell.

"Excuse me," I said to the efficient-looking woman seated there. "Can you tell me what Eulora Scanlon's condition is?"

She quirked an eyebrow. "Are you related?"

"Afraid not. But the fire she was rescued from? I was caught in it, too."

The RN looked at my bandaged shoulder and my wild mess of smoky hair, then back at my face with sympathy. "She's stable."

My lips thinned. "That much I know. Can you . . ." A movement in the window to the stairwell caught my eye, and I felt my jaw slacken. "Tanna?"

The woman disappeared from behind the reinforced glass.

"I'll be right back," I said to the puzzled nurse and hurried to the door. Pushing it open, I heard receding footsteps from the next floor down and took off down the stairs. "Tanna," I called. "Wait."

She didn't wait. Using the railing to pull and steady myself, I clattered down the steps as fast as I could. My left shoulder throbbed. After two floors, my head was keeping time with it. I stopped, panting as if I'd never run a day in my life. No way was I going to catch up with Tanna if she didn't want me to.

But why on earth was she running away?

Could *Tanna* have set the fire? Was her protective attitude toward Eulora a ruse? For what? And was Eulora still in danger?

Slowly, I clumped back up the stairs. The nurse had left the desk and was talking to a gaunt, long-necked man in the waiting room. As I watched, Cecelia approached them, listening hard as he put his arm around her shoulder. The RN returned to her post, eyeing me with a mixture of curiosity and distaste. Apparently, taking off and shouting down a stairwell did not win me any prizes.

Eulora's great-granddaughter approached with the man the nurse had been talking to. I could see where Mungo had shed black fur on her white shorts only a few hours before.

"Hi," she said with a sad smile. "You were with Grammy when the fire happened?"

I nodded.

"You're okay?"

"I'm okay."

"What about Mungo?" she asked in a worried tone.

"Don't worry. He's not hurt. He's outside, waiting for me in my friend's truck."

Her face cleared. "Good! Katie, this is my granddad."

I stuck out my hand. "Hi. You're Eulora's son?" His grip was dry and warm, his expression troubled.

"Aaron Scanlon," he confirmed. "My mother tells me you saved her."

"We saved each other," I said quietly. "And the firefighters came to our rescue. We would have been trapped in the house without them."

Without him. Declan saved our lives. With Connell's help, but still. A tremor ran through my core as I finally realized how close I'd come to dying.

I shook myself. "How is Eulora?"

"Stable," he said. I was really starting to dislike that word. "She's in some pain, and will need rest. The doctor is talking about a pacemaker. Of course, he's talked about that for a while. She's asleep right now. How did it start?"

"The fire?" Had Eulora told him about the magical nature of the fire? Or how we'd combined powers to battle it? But I didn't see suspicion in his gaze or get any strong vibes from him other than curiosity and concern.

I closed my eyes and shook my head. "I have no idea. It seemed to come out of nowhere."

Cecelia looked on, lower lip firmly clamped between her teeth. Her father was silent for a moment, then said, "Just now — you saw someone on the stairs?"

"I thought it was your mother's . . . assistant." I assumed he knew his mother was a voodoo spiritualist if she was training Cecelia, but I didn't want to step on any toes.

His jaw set, and he looked away. "Tanna."

"Had she been to visit Eulora?" I asked. "We didn't see her after the fire, and your mother was so worried that she hadn't made it out of the house."

"She hasn't visited. I'll tell my mother you saw her, though. That should put her mind to rest."

Something was off. Aaron still wouldn't meet my eye. Cecelia looked unhappy.

"Eulora told me Tanna leaves whenever you come over," I said to her. That got her father's attention.

"She is very protective of my mother," he said. "She takes good care of her — at least that's what Mom says. But she's also a bit . . . possessive. Doesn't pass on phone messages, tries to keep Mom to herself." He considered me. "Of course, if you're friends with my mother, you already know how Tanna is."

"Watch for her," I blurted.

His eyebrows rose. "I see. Yes, believe me — we all will. Now, if you'll excuse me."

"Of course. Tell Eulora I was here?"

"I will," Cecelia said. Her grandfather smiled down at her and put his arm around her shoulders again as they joined the rest of the family.

I headed back to the elevator. My shoulder hurt with every inhalation, but I still passed the drinking fountain without taking any pain pills. There was one more stop I wanted to make, and I wanted the clearest head I could manage. The nurse was happy enough to give me directions.

CHAPTER 19

The intensive-care waiting room was empty save for a woman who stood looking out the window. Her hands were clasped behind her back, her shoulders bowed. She looked up as I approached, blinking at me with quiet fatigue. Her white blond hair was layered just over her ears, and her short, blunt bangs framed light blue eyes very similar to the ones that had haunted my dreams for the past two nights.

"Mrs. Taite?" I asked.

She looked surprised. "Yes." Her voice was high and soft. "Do I know you?"

I shook my head, trying to ignore the low ache from my arm that reached all the way up my neck now. "My name is Katie Lightfoot. I'm one of the owners of the Honeybee Bakery."

Dawn's mother looked blank.

"Your daughter collapsed there," I said gently.

Her expression cleared. "Oh. Right." Then she frowned. "So, you're her friend?"

"I'm afraid I only met her briefly before she fell ill."

"It's very nice of you to visit her," she said. Her voice rasped at the edges, but her eyes were dry. She turned to the window again, watching the breeze blow the United States and the Georgia state flag on the pole outside the hospital toward the east.

"Is she any better?" I asked.

"No," she said simply. "I don't understand what happened to her. We'd fallen out of touch lately. She left school, you see. She was studying sociology. Only had one semester to go." She paused.

I remained silent. Mrs. Taite wasn't talking to me in particular. She just needed to talk to someone, and I was there.

A few beats later, she continued. "She told me she wanted to work with her uncle. Franklin. My husband's brother."

My ears perked up.

"He was a bit of a black sheep, but Dawn likes black sheep. That's probably why sociology interested her. She was interested in *outsiders,* as she put it. Puts it, I mean." She stole a glance at me.

I offered an encouraging smile. She turned back to the window and rubbed her hand over her face.

"Dawn's father died in an accident when she was a teenager. We were never close with Franklin after that, and I was surprised when Dawn told me he'd come to see her on campus. He'd apparently left the police department — he was a detective, you see. But he threw that away the same way Dawn threw away her education. He went off to be some kind of private eye, and asked my daughter to quit school and work for him. What kind of man would do that to his own family? Of course, Dawn insisted Franklin was more than a private eye, but when I asked for more details, she refused to tell me." Her head tipped to the side. "We fought. Mothers and daughters always fight, of course, and we were no exception, but this fight was different." She backed away from the window and went to sit in one of the cool-colored chairs lined up against the wall. "She hasn't spoken to me for months. Now her uncle is dead and something happened to her, and I don't know what." Tears in her voice now. "I don't know how to help her."

I walked over and sat beside her. "I'm sorry."

A long silence, then: "Thank you."

"Do you think I could see her?" I asked.

She rose. "I'll ask the staff."

Less than two minutes later, I was gazing down at Dawn, while Mrs. Taite took a break to get something to eat. Her thin frame was hardly discernible under the sheet and thin blanket. Machines sighed and bleeped around the bed, and an IV drip was taped to her arm. A strand of her scraggly dishwater-blond hair had fallen over one eye. Gently, I brushed it back with my fingertip.

"I found the voodoo queen," I said in a quiet voice, so the nurse across the room wouldn't hear me. "She's in this same hospital. Her name is Eulora, and your uncle knew her well." Her heart beat in waves across the monitor. "I'll find the gris gris. I'll figure out some way to help you."

With one last look, I turned and left.

I rounded the corner into the emergency room. Declan stood talking with an orderly, his expression urgent. Lucy and Ben sat side by side, and Mimsey had made the trip, as well. And wouldn't you know it? Steve Dawes was right there in the mix, off to the side and well away from Declan. My aunt's tone and gestures were animated as she described something to Mimsey. She raised her hands in the air, then saw me and stopped midsentence. An instant later, my aunt was on her feet and running to me.

"Katie! Sweetie, what *happened*? Are you okay? Oh, my heavens, you're really hurt. Look at that shoulder. What did the doctors say? I wanted —"

"Lucy! I'm fine." I struggled not to grit my teeth against the pain and slowly lowered myself onto a chair.

Steve watched me in silence. I could feel him gauging whether I was telling the truth.

Declan had turned at her words, and now hurried over. "Where have you been? I've been looking all over for you. I was about to have the hospital put out a BOLO for you."

"I went to see Eulora." I felt tears threaten, and hung my head. "I feel so awful about what happened. If I hadn't barged into her life and started asking questions, she wouldn't be here — she'd be nice and safe at home. And now she doesn't even have a home. It's completely gone. I put her in terrible danger."

"She was already in danger," Mimsey said. "Lucille here was just telling me about Mother Eulora, and the truth was that she was involved with Franklin Taite. He's dead now. Do you think you're responsible for that, too, Katie?"

Slowly, I shook my head.

"Well, then, how could you think you're in any way responsible for the fire at Mother Eulora's?"

Because I'm a catalyst.

But that just sounded egotistical. So I said, "Because I've been asking too many questions, and that made someone angry. Because I know Franklin was murdered, and I'm going to find out who did it — and why." The rush of words made me feel better. I'd been called to find the truth, and, by the goddess, I was going to do it.

Never mind that I had no idea what to do next.

Declan put his hand under my chin and tipped it up, looking into my eyes with a professional air. "I found out where Eulora was and went to find you. You'd already left the cardiac unit. Did you get lost?"

"No. I visited Dawn Taite," I said.

Silence greeted that announcement. Finally, he said, "Yeah. I guess you'd want to check in on her as long as you're here."

"She's in intensive care still, but they let me in. Her mother asked them to. I could tell she's been here with Dawn more or less nonstop since she got into town." I sighed. "But she has no idea what might have happened to her daughter — or to Franklin."

A sharp pain emanated from the increasingly vivid ache in my arm. I pulled the pain pills out of my pocket and removed two from the blister pack. "Could you grab me some water?"

Ben jumped to his feet before Declan could respond. "Back in a jiff," he said, and hurried to the cooler.

"Who's minding the Honeybee?" I asked.

Lucy said, "Iris is, honey. She'll be fine. Annette next door said she'd come over and help out if there's a big rush. And she has our cell numbers."

Ben returned and handed me a paper cup of water. I washed down the pills and sat back in my chair. "Golly. You guys didn't all need to come."

I caught Steve's eye. The corners of his lips turned up a fraction, and he finally spoke. "I wanted to see for myself that you're okay."

Declan glowered. "I have that covered, Dawes."

Oh, for heaven's sake.

"Jaida and Bianca will be here soon unless I call them back," Mimsey said. "And I left a message for Cookie with Oscar." She tsked. "We're family, Katie. We stick with our own."

"Would you mind calling them?" I asked. "I'm ready to head home, and I don't want

312

them to make the trip for nothing." I stood.

Mimsey nodded and fished out her phone. "Of course, darlin'. You need a nap more than anything else."

The door whooshed open, and Samantha Hatfield swept into the emergency room like Sandra Dee onto a movie set. She wore a crisp cotton circle skirt in eye-searing vermillion, a white short-sleeved blouse, and white canvas sneakers. Her shiny, flaxen hair was held back from her face with a wide headband the same color as the skirt. She took in the waiting room and us with it before fixing her attention on me. Her eyes got big, and she hurried over.

"Katie! Goodness' sake, are you all right, girl? I just couldn't believe it when Steve called and told me what happened."

Steve rose and walked over to put his arm around her shoulders. I dared a glance at Declan. Hostility rolled off him in waves, though I was surprised to see that his eyes were narrowed at Samantha rather than Steve.

"I'm fine," I said again, hoping the dry tone of my voice would be attributed to smoke inhalation. "How did you find out about the fire?" I asked Steve.

He shrugged. "You know. The usual."

Samantha's lips thinned, but then she

quickly laughed. "The usual! I *declare*!" Ms. I Suddenly Seem to Think My Name Is Scarlett eyed my bandage. "You're not entirely fine, I see." Was that satisfaction in her words? Steve didn't seem to hear it, but I saw Mimsey's sharp gaze as she watched Samantha.

The hydrocodone was beginning to kick in. I struggled to rally. "Samantha, this is Mimsey Carmichael, and this is my boyfriend, Declan McCarthy."

"Mimsey! What an *adorable* name!" Her accent had deepened. "I'm so very pleased to meet you!"

"Enchanted," Mimsey said with a gracious smile and shook her hand. But I knew that look. Steve's girlfriend wasn't pulling the wool over that witch's eyes.

"And, Declan. My, you are a handsome one." Her hand popped out again.

He took it with a dazed look. "Nice to meet you," he said.

Her other hand rose so that she was holding his hand in both of hers. Steve looked on with an expression of mild indulgence. Was he faking it? Because maybe the meds were making me cranky, but I wanted to slap her. I looked back at Declan, who stood transfixed, staring down at her double grip.

Then I saw it, too. A diamond so big, it

actually looked heavy on the third finger of her left hand. At least two carats of faceted stone.

How impractical. You'd never be able to knead bread . . .

And then: *What the heck?* And finally: *Oh, dear. Something is terribly wrong here.*

"It looks like congratulations are in order," I managed in a strangled voice.

Goddess help me, she smirked. "Thank you so much, Katie! Yes, we're very happy." She finally dropped my boyfriend's hands and wrapped her arms around Steve's waist.

Steve's eyes met mine. They held a smidge of embarrassment, a tad of apology, and a good dose of defiance, but all were dusted with his usual self-assurance. And when he looked down at his fiancée and grazed the crown of her head with his lips, his gaze held only adoration. "Very happy, indeed."

Engaged? After what — a month at the most? No. It wasn't like Steve. None of his behavior around Samantha seemed normal. Something else was going on. And it wasn't the book on how to get what you wanted that she'd found at the Honeybee. No self-help book was that effective, especially when a druid was involved.

She got a love potion from Mambo Jeni and is using it on my friend. I wonder if Heinrich

*knows about this engagement yet. Though,
by the sound of it, she might be using the love
potion — or some variation — on him, as well.*

I swallowed against the thickness in my
throat and looked away. Normally I would
have been outraged, but I was too tired and
my shoulder hurt too much to deal with all
this right now. Then I remembered something I'd been thinking about in the elevator on the way back down from intensive
care.

"Steve, can I talk to you a sec?"

He tore his attention away from Samantha. "Sure."

I pointed. "Over there?"

He looked surprised. *Too bad.* I wasn't
going to broach the subject in front of just
anyone, and certainly not in front of her.

Samantha frowned. "Honeybuns, I think
you two can talk about whatever you need
to right here," she said.

"It's okay," Steve said to her. "I'll be right
back."

She glared at me. "No. We don't have any
secrets. Just like Katie and Declan don't.
Right?" She turned to Declan with a wide
smile. "Right?"

"It's not about a secret," I said.

"Could it wait, Katie?" Steve cut in.
"Because if it's not urgent, you need to go

home and get some rest. You look awful."

Samantha smiled at that.

"Why, thank you," I said, weighing my options. "Yes, it can wait." I returned Samantha's smile as I added, "I'll call you, Steve."

Her pretty little nostrils flared. "Come on." She pulled Steve toward the door.

"You take care of her, Declan," he called over his shoulder.

The room wavered in front of me, and I grabbed the back of a chair as they exited. Lucy gasped, and Ben started toward me, but Declan already had his arm around my waist and was helping me to sit down.

Lucy perched on the other side of me. "Katie, honey, we have to get you home."

"I'll pull the car up," my uncle said, and started for the door.

"Wait, Ben," Declan said. "I'm going to call into work and get someone to cover the rest of my shift."

I shook my cotton-filled head. "You don't need to do that. Ben needs to get back to the bakery. If you can take him in the truck, then Lucy can take me and Mungo home — right, Luce?"

"Of course, honey."

I looked up at Deck. "I'm going to go straight to bed. No need for you to miss work so you can watch me sleep."

He frowned, unconvinced and unhappy.

"Really," I said. "I'm a bit dizzy right now from the pills, but that's all. And you know what?" I gingerly moved my elbow to make sure. "I already feel a lot better. That hydro-whatsit is kind of awesome."

"Well, okay." His tone was grudging. "But you call me if you need me, Lucy, and I'll be there in a flash."

She patted his arm. "I promise."

I'd retrieved Mungo, said good-bye to Mimsey and Ben, and kissed Declan hard on the lips after assuring him yet again that he could go back to work. I was waiting in the late-afternoon sunlight for Lucy to unlock their vintage, baby blue Thunderbird when a black Chevy Tahoe screeched into a spot two cars over. Detective Quinn clambered out and strode toward me.

Suppressing a tired sigh, I said, "Fancy meeting you here."

"Lightfoot, what have you gotten yourself into this time?"

"A fire." I didn't have the energy for witty repartee. "What are you doing here?"

He stopped in front of me and pressed his lips together. "You left me a message, remember?"

"Oh, right." I shook my fuzzy head.

"And then McCarthy left me a message about the fire, that you were here, and that he suspected arson."

"But you don't investigate fires . . ."

"I investigate homicides and attempted homicides. If it was arson, then it's possible someone tried to kill you — Oh, sorry, Ms. Eagel."

Lucy had come around to stand at the back of the car, her lips parted as she listened.

"Er, and it sounds like there may have been another person in the house," Quinn went on in a gentler tone. "Someone who didn't make it out."

"Tanna," I said. "Mother Eulora's, uh, caregiver. Sort of. I don't know her last name. Eulora and I thought we heard her come in, but Declan wondered if it couldn't have been someone setting the fire. I think he might be right."

"Eulora Scanlon is the homeowner, right?"

I nodded.

"Well, the actual fire investigation is out of my hands. But I'll be involved if I need to be."

"Thank you," Lucy said with feeling.

"I don't think you need to worry that Tanna was caught in the fire," I said. "I'm

319

pretty sure I saw her in there." I gestured toward the building looming behind him.

His gaze sharpened. "Where?"

"In the stairwell, outside the cardiac unit, where Eulora is being treated. Apparently, she doesn't get along with the family. She ran away when I tried to talk to her, though."

Lucy's eyes grew wide.

Quinn whipped out the tiny notebook he always carried and scribbled a quick line before looking back up at me. "But you called me before the fire, didn't you?" he asked.

"Oh! Yes. I wanted to tell you about Franklin's landlady. She thought he ran out on his rent and re-rented his room, but she packed up his things. She wouldn't give them to me, but she said she'd give them to you if you stop by. Her name is Cozie Temmons. Her rooming house is by Forsyth Park."

He stared at me.

"What?"

"For the past two days, I've been trying to find out where Franklin was staying, with no luck. How did you find out?"

"Um." I glanced at Lucy.

She smiled her encouragement. "Tell him about Mother Eulora."

"The other fire victim? What in Sam Hill does she have to do with Frank Taite?" he demanded.

"Hey! Show some respect." The pain meds were making me both cranky and cocky. "She had a heart attack in the middle of that fire. She's lucky to be alive."

He looked down at the asphalt, then back up at me. "Okay. So who was she to Frank?"

Poppa Jack had said Eulora was well-known in town, and she didn't act secretive about her skills. I didn't think she'd mind if I told Quinn. Besides, I was too tired to make up a lie. "She was his voodoo spiritualist."

Quinn snorted before he could help himself.

"Listen. Franklin died from a snakebite, right? And you found feathers, snakeskin, and that other stuff near his body."

"Yeah . . ." His interest was piqued now.

I grabbed the car handle and hugged Mungo tighter. "And you know that Franklin had an interest in the occult. Well, Mother Eulora calls herself a spiritualist, but she was referred to me as a voodoo queen. It turns out she'd helped Franklin on some of his cases involving the paranormal." I chose my words carefully. "She told me voodoo was likely involved in

Franklin's death, and she told me where he'd been staying in Savannah when she last saw him — which was about three months ago. That's how I knew where to look."

"Why didn't you tell me?" he asked. He didn't seem angry, just curious.

"First off, I didn't know if I'd find where he'd stayed. Plus, when I heard *voodoo,* I knew you'd be less than receptive."

He folded his arms and leaned against the Tahoe. "Katie, I know you think I'm a curmudgeon, but I'm just a practical guy. I don't buy all that woo-woo stuff, only my own gut hunches. But I do know voodoo is alive and well here in Savannah, so I'm not discounting anything you've told me. I do wish you'd told me sooner, because if Franklin died as part of some kind of ritual, that changes everything. Is there anything else you haven't told me?"

I visually checked with Lucy again. Between the pills and still feeling a little shocky I didn't entirely trust my own judgment. Should I tell him about the other voodoo queens? About Poppa Jack? Without a good reason, that felt like a betrayal — to them, and certainly to Cookie.

"Maybe he can help," she said.

Quinn rolled his eyes. "Oh, God," he groaned. "There *is* something else."

Well, there was one thing I could tell him. "A gris gris, a voodoo talisman, is missing," I said. "Dawn Taite said something about it before she collapsed at the Honeybee." I considered telling him Franklin had told his niece to find me if she got into trouble, but stopped myself in time. I could only imagine what Quinn would think if I claimed to be a super-duper, black-magic-fighting light-witch. "It sounded important," I said. "And I wondered if it might have something to do with what happened to Franklin. So I was trying to find it," I finished, sounding lame even to my own ears. "So, will you pick up his boxes from Cozie Temmons?"

"Try and stop me." His tone was grim.

"Is there any chance you'll let me know what's in them?" I asked. "In particular, a metal amulet with white fringes."

Lucy grinned. "Of course he will. Won't you, Peter?"

"We'll see," he said. "But you have to promise to stop keeping things to yourself that might help me."

I pointed at him. "As long as you're willing to hear what I say — not yell at me like you did when I told you about Franklin contacting me through a psychic — then I promise."

He shook his head. "Deal. But that psychic

stuff was off the mark. Franklin wasn't even dead back then."

At my noise of protest, he held up his hand. "Anyway, I also want to ask you about how that fire —"

I staggered. He took a big step, catching me by my good elbow.

"Peter Quinn!" Lucy stepped forward. "This poor girl has been through a lot today. She's exhausted, not to mention wounded. You have to let her go home and go to bed."

"I'm sorry, Katie. You do look awful."

I wished people would stop saying that.

He opened the car door and helped me inside. Lucy hurried around to the other side and got in, keys at the ready. As she started the engine, I caught Quinn's arm. "The fire? I don't know how it started. We were in the back of the house, and it could have burned for a while before we realized. But I can tell you it wasn't a normal fire."

"Okay, Katie. Thanks." He shut my door, and I thought he was humoring me until I saw the deep concern shining from his eyes. Then it was replaced by his usual professional poker face.

Even though she could barely see over the steering wheel, Lucy skillfully backed the big car out and turned toward my place in

Midtown. Mungo curled into a tight ball on my lap, and I rested my hand on his back as I allowed the seat to envelop me in comfort.

"I can't believe they got engaged so quickly," I heard myself say.

"Steve and Samantha, you mean." Lucy shrugged and nodded. "It is a bit sudden, but there's no accounting for true love."

"If that's true love, I guess you're right," I said. But that's not what this was. Or was it? Was Samantha really using a love potion, or was I just a bit jealous?

"Ben and I had a very short courtship." A soft smile smoothed the worry lines from her forehead.

"Only a couple of months, right?"

"Less than that. But we knew right away. You know."

Actually, I didn't. Declan and I were taking things slow, and that was largely my doing. I was admittedly a tad gun-shy since Andrew had broken up with me right before our wedding back in Akron, though it had been well over a year ago. I couldn't help it if I liked my life the way it was. Still, Declan had dropped enough hints about living together, marriage, even children that I knew he wanted more.

Darn it, just because we weren't jumping into matrimony didn't mean we weren't in love, though. And that ring Steve had bought Sam was ridiculous.

"And then there's Cookie and Oscar," Lucy broke in to my thoughts. "They got married very quickly. Within weeks of meeting each other."

"That's not the highest recommendation," I said.

She turned her head. "What do you mean?"

"Nothing," I said.

"Katie? Are they having problems?"

"I'm sure it's the same getting-used-to-each-other things all newlyweds experience," I said. *Another good reason to take it slow.*

We rode in silence for a few minutes. I was beginning to doze when Lucy asked, "What were you going to ask Steve in there?"

"What?" I startled awake. "Oh. I was hoping he might be willing to help Mother Eulora."

She turned onto my street. "Help her how?"

"Well . . . we've healed together before. I thought maybe we could help her."

My aunt pursed her lips. "I doubt Samantha would have liked that. Or Declan."

"Oh, for heaven's sake, Lucy. I'm talking

about healing magic, not sex. I feel so guilty about what happened," I said. "If I could make Eulora feel better, maybe help her heart condition . . . well, I couldn't do much right now, anyway, not feeling like this. So I let it go. Still, maybe I can talk to Steve about it when I have my strength back." I looked out the window. An athletic-looking woman pushed a toddler in a stroller with one hand, her golden retriever's leash trailing from the other. "I also thought about trying to pierce Dawn's coma somehow, but Mother Eulora said we need to know if the talisman was involved, and, if so, who used it before we could break the curse. Besides, I don't know how we could manage any spell work in front of the intensive-care staff."

She made a wry face. "You have a good heart, Katie. But you need to stop feeling guilty. Mimsey was right. None of this is your fault. You didn't start that fire."

"Well, I'll tell you one thing," I said. "I'm sure as heck going to find out who did."

CHAPTER 20

It seemed like a lifetime since I'd seen my own front door, but it was just before five o'clock when Lucy pulled to the curb in front of the carriage house. Iris and Ben would be sweeping up and cleaning out the espresso maker before locking up the Honeybee for the evening. I hoped Iris had remembered to mix the sourdough to rise overnight. And who knew what kind of prep work we'd need to catch up on the next morning?

Mungo jumped from my lap, doing his business without ceremony and heading straight to the porch to lie down and wait for us. I wasn't the only one about to drop.

Inside, Lucy shooed me toward the bedroom. "You go lie down right this instant, honey. Take Mungo with you. I'll be in soon with a nice, cool drink."

"Shower first," I muttered. "I can't stand smelling like this."

A quick nod. "Of course. Scoot on in there and clean up. Tea?"

I bobbed my head and made my woozy way to the bathroom. "Sorry, little guy. I don't think I can manage a bath for you right now. I know you want the stink of the fire out of your fur. Give me a few hours?"

Yip!

With the plastic bag Lucy brought me wrapped around my bandage, I washed my hair three times, slathered on rosemary conditioner, and scrubbed my whole body with a loofah imbued with lavender and tea tree soap. Carefully, I toweled off and climbed into yoga shorts and a tank. Back in the bedroom, Lucy had pulled the covers back, plumped my pillow, and placed a glass of lemon-infused herbal tea on the side table. One sip revealed the flavors of sage and oregano, as well as sweet marshmallow root and slippery elm, all heavily laced with honey. I suspected she'd steeped a bit of Saint-John's-wort in the mixture, as well as adding a heartfelt incantation to the brew. I said a word of gratitude, added my own healing intentions, and downed the whole thing while sitting on the edge of the bed.

Then I removed the picture of the fringed gris gris Mother Eulora had given me from the drawer in the bedside table and leaned it against the lamp. I stared at it for what seemed like a long time. A grunting snore from where Mungo sprawled on his back reminded me that I needed rest.

Rolling carefully onto my back, I propped my elbow on a pillow and pulled the sheet over me. Seconds later, I was probably snoring as loud as my familiar.

The fragrances of garlic and basil, seafood, and fresh bread slowly pulled me from a vague dream in which I was chasing Tanna and she kept turning into a puff of sulfurous smoke. Shaking off drowsiness, I swung my feet out of bed and pushed myself to a sitting position. An odd, sour scent surfaced below the yummy food smells. Then, suddenly, it was gone. The rattle of cookware drifted down the short hallway, and voices murmured in the living room. Mungo was uncharacteristically absent. The solid wood floor felt cool on the soles of my feet as I crossed the bedroom to retrieve my robe. Wrapping it around myself, I stumbled into my living room.

Ben looked up from where he sat on one of the wingback chairs, hunched over the Civil War trunk. Detective Quinn sat on the sofa, and together they had managed to spread an assortment of papers over every flat surface within reach. Four boxes were piled over by the bookcase.

"Hey, darlin'. How are you feeling?" Ben asked.

Lucy poked her head around the corner of the kitchen. "You up already? I thought you might be out until morning. I called your parents to let them know what happened and that you're okay."

I yawned wide, quickly covering my mouth. "You're a gem, Lucy. Actually, I feel a lot better. See? I can even move my arm a bit more."

"Well, don't," she admonished. "You don't want to break those stitches open."

Mungo bounded out of the kitchen. I bent over to pet him. "Why, look at you! You got your bath after all." He even had a little bandanna around his neck.

Yip!

"I came over as soon as we closed down the Honeybee, and first thing gave him a good scrub in the backyard," Ben said. "He didn't seem to mind a bit."

"I don't imagine he did. Thanks, Ben."

"No problem. It was the least that I could do."

I straightened. "Quinn," I said by way of greeting. He'd watched our exchange in silence.

He shook his head and grinned. "Boy, it really takes a wallop to keep you down, Lightfoot. Your aunt said you only went to sleep a couple of hours ago."

I glanced out the window. It was still light. But with my sleep disorder, two hours was like a full night's rest. All I said was, "Sometimes a nap is all you need." I indicated the mess. "What's all this? And, Lucy, what on earth do you have on the stove? It smells like heaven in a pot."

She grinned. "Close enough, honey. Fresh pesto with basil from your garden, grilled shrimp, and garlic bread courtesy of the Honeybee Bakery. It'll be done in a few minutes. You're more than welcome to stay, Peter."

"Thanks, Ms. Eagel. I might just have to take you up on that. Katie, you see before you the remains of Frank Taite's worldly possessions — at least the ones he left at Ms. Timmons' boarding house. She gave them to me without any problem. And it turns out, there are some interesting things here." He leaned forward and looked me up and down with such thoroughness I pulled my robe tighter. "You do look a lot better than the last time I saw you."

Have we found the gris gris? The thought sent a bolt of hope through me. Eagerly, I perched on the edge of the second wing-back chair. "Interesting, like how?" Now that I was closer to the boxes, I felt an energy that felt sharply sour. Could that have been the vinegary tang I thought I smelled from the bedroom? One of the boxes by the bookcase seemed to exude a smoky yellow aura. Could it be the talisman? I felt my bare toes tapping on the floor in anticipation, and had to stop myself from barreling over and tearing off the lid. Detective Quinn would think I was nuts.

Ben leaned back and pressed his lips together. "Peter's been here for an hour, and we've gone through absolutely everything. Twice. Two boxes of clothes and toiletries, a laptop computer that's password protected, and a few personal items."

"The talisman?" I couldn't keep the eagerness out of my voice. "Did you find it?"

Both men shook their heads.

"Are you sure? It looks kind of like a necklace, metal and fringed. Here, let me get you a picture." I bolted up and trotted to the bedroom to get the photo off the nightstand. Returning, I held it out to them.

Quinn took it with a frown. "Where did you get this?"

"From Mother Eulora. This is the talisman she gave Franklin — the one I told you about."

"Sorry, hon," Ben said. "Nothing like that in any of this stuff."

My eagerness faded, the frustration I'd come to associate with almost everything about the situation returning full force. "Dang it!"

So, what's over there in that box?

"But take a look at what Peter found," my uncle said. The anticipation on his face gave me pause.

I scooted closer. Lucy stood in the kitchen doorway, watching the stove and listening to us with a wooden spoon poised in her hand.

Quinn said, "Who knows what we might find on that computer, but Frank kept hardcopy records of his cases, both on and off the force. This is the one I think you might want to see." He held a manila file out to me.

I took it, still aware of the force surrounding the closed box across the room. "Luce, are you using vinegar in anything you're cooking in there?" I asked, opening the file.

"No." She sounded puzzled.

I looked up. "Anyone else smell that?"

"Well, I sure smell lots of good things, thanks to your aunt's hard work," Ben said.

Quinn cocked his head and sniffed.

One thing at a time.

Quickly, I perused the contents of the file, skimming through the pages and then going back to check on a few things.

"So, human sacrifice was involved in this case." I sat back in the chair. "Pretty freaky, but not exactly shocking, given what his lieutenant in New Orleans told you about his last case before he left the force. This is the same one, right? I mean, this isn't the official police report, just his personal notes, but the dates seem right."

Quinn nodded.

I went on. "Plus, Franklin mentioned human sacrifice to Mother Eulora when he came to see her in April." I bent my head over the file. "Still, he stopped the sacrifice before anyone was harmed. Wait a minute." I flipped through the pages again. "Who was the mastermind behind the whole thing?"

"We think Frank took part of that file with him." Quinn tipped his head toward the folder I held. "I've got a call into the NOPD to find out what the official story is. And I'm hoping that information will be on his computer. Because there's . . . well, keep reading."

Lucy disappeared into the kitchen for a moment, then came back out to join us, the spoon still held absently in her hand. She sat lightly on Ben's knee, and he steadied her with his arm. Watching me with a grim expression, he stroked his beard with his other hand. Mungo had snuggled down on the throw rug next to my foot.

I returned my attention to the papers in my hand. "A coma? Whoever it was induced a coma and then was going to kill the victim with — Oh, my God." I looked up. "A snakebite? Quinn! It says they got away! It says here they escaped without making their sacrifice, but they were never caught. It says — let's see here — it says they kept their victim for only a couple of days before trying to complete the sacrificial ritual." I met the detective's eyes, scrambling for the right words to convince him of what I was thinking. "Do you think it was more than one person?"

Slowly, he nodded. "A complicated plan like that, it would make sense for there to be more than one perpetrator."

I reached down and scritched Mungo behind the ears. "Franklin disappeared without a trace from Cozie Temmons' rooming house in April. He visited his friend, Mother Eulora, around the same time, but then never came back to see her. I think he would have if he could have. I think he would have contacted me, too."

"Why?" Quinn asked.

I shook my head. "I just do. But he didn't die until just a few days ago. So, where was he that whole time? Is there any indication of another case he was working on during that time? No, wait. There wouldn't be because he *disappeared without taking any of this stuff with him.*" I licked my lips. "Here's the thing: Those people he stopped from sacrificing their victim were never caught. And their plan had been spoiled by Detective Franklin Taite." I hugged myself, almost glad for the twinge in my shoulder to remind me that this wasn't a dream. "They got to him, Quinn. I think he was in a coma for months, and then they managed to go through with their snake-bite sacrifice. And now Dawn's in a coma, too."

His poker face didn't waver. Out of the corner of my eye, I saw Ben hold Lucy a little tighter. "That's crazy," Ben said.

"That doesn't mean it isn't true," I insisted. "Quinn, how hard would it be to check hospitals here in Savannah and the surrounding towns for long-term coma patients?"

The silence that followed seemed to stretch into minutes but was probably only seconds. Finally, he spoke. "Not too hard."

I grinned. "You'll do it?"

"No."

My smile dropped.

"I'll have a lackey do it."

Ben laughed. "You know Katie's right more often than not."

Quinn allowed the ghost of a smile to cross his face. "If I didn't, I wouldn't agree to this nonsense." He reached into the pile of folders on the table. "There's something else. About his niece."

I leaned over and grabbed the file before he could properly offer it to me. Another quick scan, shorter this time because there was only one page. "Dawn was in North Carolina for the past two months?"

Quinn nodded. "Frank had her infiltrate a cult headed by some nutso prophet."

"A cult!" Lucy said. "How could he?"

"I've heard of this bunch. They're pretty harmless — mostly woo-woo pagan stuff. Not exactly another David Koresh. It looks like Frank sent his niece to bring a girl back to her parents."

Lucy still frowned.

"I'll check into it," Quinn continued. "Obviously, she finished what he sent her to do and came back to Savannah. I doubt that it has anything to do with Franklin's death or her current condition. You never know, though." He began gathering the folders into a neat pile. "Any chance that dinner invitation is still open?"

My aunt bolted to her feet. "Oh, heavens. I turned it all off, but it's ready. Come in and help yourself." She darted back into the kitchen.

Ben and Quinn got up as the dish-rattling sounds began again.

"Quinn," I said quietly.

He paused. Ben noticed, but went ahead to join his wife.

"Are you worried that someone might go after Dawn? At the hospital, I mean. For another, er . . ." I trailed off, unwilling to say the words.

The detective wasn't so squeamish. "Human sacrifice?"

I nodded.

He looked thoughtful. "Honestly, no. And I can't justify putting a guard on her. She's in the ICU still, though that might change. But let me see what I find out about coma cases in area hospitals."

My brows pinched together, and I bit my lip.

"In the meantime, I'll alert hospital security to be on the lookout for anything strange."

"Okay," I said. At least he was doing the

best he could.

Quinn joined my aunt and uncle in the kitchen, and I got up and went to the box that had caught my attention. Mungo followed, his tiny toenails making wee clicking sounds on the wood floor. Sinking to my knees in front of the bookcase, I carefully nudged the top off the box. Sure enough, the sour aura became stronger. Not only that, but Mother Eulora's bracelet grew significantly warmer. Could Ben and Quinn have overlooked the gris gris?

With thumb and forefinger, I moved a few things around. A picture of two boys — Franklin and his brother, I guessed. A couple of bow ties, which was odd, yet I could totally see Franklin Taite wearing one. Three mystery novels were stacked in the corner. I wondered if he'd had a chance to finish them. There was a ceramic figure of a hedgehog that made me think of Mother Eulora. Perhaps he'd been planning to give it to her. There was no talisman or anything that looked like it could conceal the talisman. But I had found the source of the strange energy.

It was a poppet. Only not a poppet like the spellbook club had used before, but a doll like the ones I'd seen in Marie La-Fevre's shop. A voodoo doll, seven inches long and sloppily sewn like those, only this one was made of black velvet and had red-stitched X's for eyes. Another vermillion X represented the mouth, and a fourth one marked the middle of the poppet's chest. That X was bigger than the rest. I glanced away, and it seemed to throb like a heart beating in my peripheral vision, but when I looked back, it was plain embroidery floss on plush fabric. Still, I felt my hands shaking.

Then I saw that the doll had no stuffing. It was a completely empty husk.

I couldn't make myself touch it, but I'd tell Quinn about it over dinner. Because, oddly enough, this was the only thing in Franklin's effects that really indicated voodoo had been involved with either of the cases Quinn had showed me.

Other than the planned sacrifice by snakebite, of course. That smacked of voodoo through and through.

Quinn ate and ran, taking all of Franklin's possessions. I'd insisted on going through them myself, just to make sure they hadn't missed the gris gris in one of his pockets or tucked into a sock. Thankfully, neither my uncle nor the detective took offense. Still, I didn't find anything. Quinn promised to give the voodoo doll to the crime lab for testing.

"Will you let us know what you find on his computer?" I asked.

He looked at the ceiling for a moment, ignoring Ben's grin. "Depends on what we find, Katie. It's looking more and more like Frank's death was a homicide —"

"Which you wouldn't have known without my interference and meddling," I pointed out, using words I'd heard him use before when referring to the help I'd given him.

"Yeah, well. I'll let you know what I can."

I gave him a look.

"Good Lord, girl. I brought Frank's stuff over here before even taking it to the department. Give me a break."

"You're right." I hung my head.

"Well," he mumbled. "That's better."

Lucy took my arm. "Come on, honey. Let's get you back to bed."

My cell tone went off as Quinn went out to his car. I heard the sound of the Tahoe's engine fade as I read Declan's text.

Just checking in to make sure you're okay. Have called twice and Lucy must be starting to think I'm crazy. I am, of course. Crazy about you. Call me when you get this any hour.

"Aw," I said.

Lucy grinned. "Declan?"

"Yup."

"Katie!" Margie stood in the still-open doorway. Alarm thrummed through her voice. "Miss Lucy, Ben, what on earth is going on? Why were the cops over here? And what happened to your poor arm, Katie?"

Baby Bart rested in the crook of her elbow, his arms around her neck and his head leaning against her shoulder. He blinked sleepy blue eyes at me.

"Wasn't our doing," Ben said with a smile. "She gets into trouble without any of our help."

The JJs appeared on either side of her, clad in pajamas and both wearing bunny slippers. Jonathan's were brown, and Julia's a dingy pink.

I smacked my forehead. "We were supposed to have a girl's night tonight. Oh, Margie, I'm so sorry. I completely forgot!"

"Never mind that. Are you in trouble?"

I laughed. It felt good, and I realized it had been a while. "Not the kind you mean."

She pressed her lips together.

"Really," I assured her. "I was in a fire, and Declan and his crew showed up. I got a pretty deep cut in my shoulder, but they patched it up nicely at the emergency room.

343

Oh, and that policeman who was here had some questions about the fire. You've met Detective Quinn before, haven't you?"

She nodded, still thin-lipped. "He seems to be here pretty often."

"He's a family friend," Lucy said, and I watched the suspicious look drop from my neighbor's face. What — did she think I was having an affair with Peter Quinn? A bit old for me, Declan or no Declan. Astroy and Rowanna Bronhilde, the author of the spellbook I'd suggested for the coven's review during our last meeting, suddenly came to mind.

I shook my head to clear it. "Margie, I don't think I can hang out tonight after all. I'm sorry."

"Oh, bless your little heart, Katie Lightfoot. I wouldn't dream of dragging you over to listen to me natter on and drink pink wine after you've been wounded in a *fire.* Good heavens, girl. You better take yourself some aspirin and get right on back to bed."

Lucy looked amused. "I'll make sure she does just that."

Margie gave a definitive nod and turned to go. She whirled back. "Hang on. I heard about a fire this afternoon. You're weren't at Mother Eulora's, were you?"

I felt my mouth go slack. Struggling to

344

recover, I managed, "You know Eulora?"

She flipped a hand. "Oh, heavens, yes. Honey, I'm a born-and-bred Savannahian. I bet I've run across everyone in this town at one time or another. Especially folks that have been here as long as she has. Beside, my mother-in-law consults with Mother Eulora pretty regularly ever since Redding's daddy passed on."

"Will wonders never cease?" I heard Lucy mutter under her breath.

Margie shook her head. "I must say, I'm surprised as anything that you go in for that woo-woo stuff. I always thought you were one of the most practical people I know."

Behind me, Ben muffled a laugh.

I grinned. "What about you? You believe in spirits and haints and spells and the like?"

She flushed but looked defiant. "Maybe a bit. Hard telling what might be around — just because we can't see it doesn't mean it isn't there. Besides, we live in the most haunted city in the entire United States, you know."

"I believe it," I said. "And, yes, I was, uh, consulting with Mother Eulora when the fire broke out." All my humor drained away. "It was horrible. Her whole house it gone, Margie, and Eulora's in the hospital. Her family is there, but she could use the prayers of anyone who knows her."

Margie's expression softened. "I'll tell my mother-in-law. I'm sure she knows some of Mother's other clients. We'll spread the word and get some good vibes going her way."

"Thank you. You're a gem."

"Nah. Saint Margie, remember? Come on, kids. Let's get you to bed. And, Katie?"

"Mmm?"

"I know Declan's on shift, so if there's anything you need — anything at all — you just let me know. Okay? I'll be around, and I can run right over."

"Thank you," I said with feeling. "You're the best neighbor ever."

She looked pleased but waved it away. "Pshaw. Anyone else would do the same. You take care."

"I will."

Ben shut the door behind the Coopersmiths. "I think we might have to be going, too. Unless you want us to stay the night? You still have that futon in the loft, don't you?"

"No need, Ben. I appreciate it, though. I'm going to have another glass of Lucy's amazing healing tea, check in with Declan, and settle in for some more shut-eye."

My aunt and uncle exchanged a long look

before he dipped his chin in agreement. "Okay."

"The rest of the tea is on the counter," Lucy said, reaching for where her purse hung from the back of one of the wingbacks. "And there are plenty of leftovers for both of you. Mungo's pasta doesn't have garlic, and is in the blue container in the fridge."

"Thanks, Lucy. I'll see you in the morning," I said.

My aunt spun around. "What? Oh, no, Katie. You most certainly will not. I've already called Iris, and she can come in early. We'll handle the baking tomorrow. You stay home and rest."

"I'm not sick," I began to protest, but she cut me off.

"I won't hear another word about it," she said. "Come on, Ben."

And that, apparently, was that.

CHAPTER 21

Jaida called, then Bianca, each of them checking on my welfare and giving me lots of love and sweet get-well-soons. I drank them up like ambrosia, happy for their good wishes and the company of their voices. While I spoke with them, I sipped the rest of Lucy's tea. I swore I could feel it knitting my wound and returning my energy to something like normal.

After speaking with them, I called Declan. His relief was palpable when I told him I was feeling much better and to stop worrying. We hadn't made it very far into the conversation when the crew was called out to a carbon-monoxide alarm, and he had to hang up. I promised I'd call again in the morning, as I was longing to talk to him more but grateful he didn't have to respond to another fire on this shift. At least not yet. He had another day to go, but by now I knew the majority of the calls Five House

— and all the others — responded to didn't involve any kind of blaze at all.

Thank heavens, I thought, honestly feeling shakier about the fire that afternoon than I had since escaping it. A hefty dose of adrenaline and the necessity to stay in the moment had shoved the enormity of almost dying to the back of my mind. Now, rested and alone except for my familiar, it came roaring back with an intensity that frightened me nearly as much as the fire itself had.

So, when I heard the knock on the front door, I jumped off the couch. Margie must have come back to check on me, and I hadn't taken another dose of pain meds yet, so maybe some pink wine was in order after all.

However, when I checked through the peephole, it wasn't Margie standing on my tiny porch, the amber light from over the door turning the fuchsia streaks in her hair to dark orange. It was Cookie, her cheeks streaked with mascara.

I threw open the door. "Oh, honey! What's the matter?" I ushered her into my dimly lit living room. She appeared almost frail in oversized cutoff jeans, a shapeless T-shirt draping off one shoulder, and plastic thongs.

She threw her arms around me, almost

knocking me over. I winced as she brushed the dressing on my shoulder, but returned her hug. I'd never seen her so upset. She let out a couple of sobs, then took a deep breath and seemed to gather herself. Pushing away from me, she held me at arm's length and regarded me with a searching, if somewhat soggy, gaze. "I'm so sorry, Katie. I failed you."

"What on earth are you talking about?" I shut the door, pulled her to the couch, and made her sit down.

"I wasn't at the hospital when you had to go to the emergency room after that horrible fire."

"Oh!" I laughed. "Please don't worry about that. I asked Mimsey to call Jaida and Bianca off, too. I just spoke with them on the phone a few minutes ago."

She sniffled. "Mimsey called me back, too, after you left the hospital. But you must know I would have come if I'd known you were there in the first place. Really, I would have. Oscar answered my cell phone but didn't give me Mimsey's message. It wasn't until the second time she called that I knew what had happened to you and Mother Eulora."

I held up my hand. "Wait a minute. He answered your cell and then didn't give you the message?"

She nodded, looking miserable.

"Cookie, your husband has some serious boundary issues. That's not right."

"I know!" She gulped. "We've been fighting about it. About a lot of things, actually, but mostly about how crazy he gets about me helping you find the gris gris."

"What's his problem?" I said. "Is it me?"

She shook her head, lower lip quivering. "It's the voodoo. He says he's protecting me, that he knows how it upsets me."

"It does upset you. I know that. I'm sorry I had to drag you into all this."

Her sharp chin lifted, and her lip stilled. "Oh, Katie. I love Oscar like I've never loved anyone. And I know he loves me. It hurts his male pride that I don't believe I need his protection. And I'm here of my own free will, not because anyone — including you — made me."

I couldn't help smiling. "And I'm glad you are."

"Good. Then let's get started," she said and reached into her hobo bag.

"Started?" I asked, confused.

She paused, her hand still in the leather bag. "Jaida told me about the other night. How you located the gris gris with the dowsing rod and then you two went to see

Franklin's landlady. But you didn't find the gris gris. Yes?"

"Yes. I mean, no, we didn't. And Detective Quinn left just a while ago after bringing over Franklin's possessions. The landlady gave them to him."

Cookie looked speculative. "And the gris gris wasn't in them." It wasn't a question. She looked toward the shutters and nodded to herself. "Yes. Let's get started. Katie, make sure the windows are tightly closed and the shutters latched. The lights are fine, down low like this. Mungo, you may help."

"What do you have in mind?" I asked, jumping to my feet.

"I'm going to try to remove the hex that's hiding the gris gris from you."

. . . The object yer seekin' is hidden between layers of magic.

I grinned and hurried to check the windows. "Let me put on some real clothes first."

"No need," she said, pulling out a velvet pouch. "Robes are appropriate attire in most traditions. Are you skyclad beneath?"

"Naked? Uh, no."

"Oh, well." She shrugged. "Come sit down. Wait — Do you have a black altar cloth? I didn't think to bring one."

"Will a silk scarf work?"

"Perfectly."

I got the scarf from the wall peg by the back door and spread it on the old trunk. Cookie slid to the floor, kneeled in front of the coffee table, and began placing items on the flat surface: the velvet pouch, a length of shiny red thread, three cloves of garlic, a black candle and lighter, and, to my surprise, a small ball-peen hammer. She lit the candle, returned the lighter to her bag, and then drew out a box about three inches by five inches. It was formed of stained glass, jagged geometric shards in all the colors of the chakras arranged in no particular order, but startlingly beautiful in its primitive way. She placed it by the candle, stroking the side of it with affectionate fingertips.

"It's lovely," I said.

"It was my father's," she said. Giving a small shake of her head, she reached for the velvet bag.

"What's inside the pouch?" I asked. My voice was practically a whisper.

"Vervain, curry, dill, and ginger." Her tone was practical.

"Sounds like you're a bit of a *grune hexe* yourself," I ventured.

A wisp of a smile crossed her face. "I double-checked with Poppa Jack for some of the details. But hex breaking is hex breaking, whatever the school of magic. It's all about —"

"Intention," we intoned together.

"Okay. What can I do?" I asked.

"We need the picture of the actual talisman!" she said.

I got up and went to the bookshelf where I'd put the photo after showing it to Quinn and Uncle Ben. Sitting down opposite Cookie, I handed it to her.

She studied it for several seconds before opening the delicate box and placing it inside. She carefully nestled the velvet bag of herbs on top and closed the box. Then she picked up the length of red thread and began tying knots in it at roughly two-inch intervals. "The box symbolizes one layer of magic, this cord another." She finished with the knots, wrapped the thread around the stained-glass container, and tied it with another knot on top.

Then she sat back and regarded me. "Sit back and cover your face."

"Don't you want my help?"

"Trust me."

"Well, okay." I scooted back on the floor until I was sitting between the two wingback chairs. Cookie nodded her approval. "Your face. And, Mungo, go sit behind Katie."

Baffled, I did as I was told. So did my familiar. Still, I peeked out through my laced fingers.

Cookie grabbed the small hammer tightly in her fist. Her lips moved without sound for a few seconds. She nodded once, took a deep breath, and raised the hammer.

"What was done is now undone!" she shouted and brought it down hard on the dancing colors of the glass box.

The sound of it shattering was obscenely loud, louder than a baseball going through a plate-glass window, and it reverberated like an ancient gong. I saw the shards fly away from the hammer blow as if in slow motion, the sharp colors floating like so many butterflies in the artificial gloaming of the fringed floor lamp.

A sudden flash filled the room with impossible brightness, a cosmic flashbulb overexposing the world, temporarily blinding me despite my hands over my eyes. I felt my own power surge in response, light meeting light . . .

Only the mulicolored flash was already gone, and Cookie was lying on her back by the couch, legs akimbo, eyes closed.

"Cookie!" I scrambled across the floor toward her, scattering broken glass.

Mungo skipped nimbly between the sharp

shards and reached her first. He immediately started licking her face and pushing at her with his nose. By the time I navigated around the furniture to her side, her eyelids fluttered open.

"Cookie." I shook her. "Are you okay? What happened?"

She began to sit up, and I pulled on her arm to help. Her eyes were wide, and her breath came in little pants. She blinked and rubbed her face. "Why is my skin wet?"

"Mungo slobber," I said. "Sorry."

He nosed her leg. She looked down at him as if she didn't recognize him. Then suddenly she snorted out a giggle.

I stared at her. "Cookie?"

She giggled again, covering her mouth with her hand to stop herself. Her green eyes danced behind her long lashes.

She's hysterical.

"I'm going to get you a paper bag to breathe into," I said, standing and shaking glass out of my robe. "You're about to hyperventilate."

Her hand dropped, and she pushed herself to her feet. "No, I won't." She grabbed my arm. "I think it worked. I felt something . . . *pop.* You know?"

I shook my head. "All I saw was a flash of colors, and then you were *unconscious.*" I'd certainly felt the burst of some kind of force, but it had happened so quickly, I didn't know what to make of it.

She waved her hand as if the backlash from a spell knocking her out cold was of no consequence. "No worries. I'm a bit tired, but nothing more. Oh, Katie! I think it really worked! I succeeded in performing a voodoo spell." She stretched toward the ceiling like a contented cat. "I feel like I've come back home, in a way, after turning my back on my childhood beliefs and practices. And I was able to honor the memory of my father, as well." Her arms dropped, and she gave me a dazzling smile. "I believe you will find the gris gris now. So, tell me: Where do you keep your broom?"

I stopped her as she turned toward the kitchen. "Cookie, you broke the box your father gave you," I said. "That was a huge sacrifice."

Tears gleamed for a split second before she blinked them away. "It was necessary, and I'm glad I did it. He would have been glad, as well. Now, even better than a regular broom would be a besom."

She seemed so happy that I let it go, but I tucked away the weight of what she had done to think about later. "In the gazebo," I said. "I keep my ceremonial broom out there."

Almost skipping, Cookie opened the French doors and went out back to retrieve the rough besom made of oat straw tied around a handle of polished oak.

"Well, Mungo. What do you think? Was that crazy business just now a success?"

Yip!

It was nearly one a.m. when Cookie left, with a spring in her step, to roust her husband out of bed and explain some things to him once and for all. We'd cleaned up all the broken glass that we could with the rough broom, then with the vacuum and microfiber cloths. Still, I knew I'd be finding sharp bits and pieces of red, blue, and green for weeks.

"You be careful," I admonished Mungo, worried about his tender paw pads. It was a miracle that none of us had suffered so much as a scratch from Cookie's breaking spell.

Had it broken another spell hiding the gris gris? Maybe. Cookie certainly seemed to think so. I considered trying to use Lucy's dowsing rod right away, but I didn't have a map of the city at home, and my injured shoulder was beginning to growl at me for not babying it enough.

So, I texted Declan that I was thinking of him, knowing that at that hour, he would either be on a call or asleep in his bunk. Then I took a pill, and Mungo and I went to bed.

At four-thirty, I was wide awake again, staring at the ceiling and wishing the tumble of thoughts in my brain would settle. Images pelted across my mental movie screen: desperate Dawn, comatose Dawn, her frightened mother, Poppa Jack in the witch's garden, dragonflies. Franklin Taite, fierce, balding, and determined to fight evil until he was no longer able. Oscar's bright smile, flashing brown eyes, and air of disapproval. Connell's brogue, fire licking at my feet, Declan's oceanic gaze enveloping me, calming me. His quiet snores, the half smile, and gentle hands. Mungo barking, Lucy's worried frown, Steve looking away as I tried to catch his attention. Then faster and faster: Mambo Jeni shouting at her son, Samantha smirking, Marie LaFevre pointing to the door, Cecelia riding away on her bike, snakeskin and poppets, Eulora stroking a stuffed hedgehog, Quinn holding up his hand to fend off the very idea of magic, Tanna's sharp gaze through the stairwell window at the hospital . . .

"That's enough!" I said, sitting up in bed. Mungo cracked an eyelid, unimpressed with my theatrics.

He changed his mind when he found himself bundled into the passenger side of the Bug and zooming toward the Honeybee. If I couldn't go for a run to clear my head, at least I could cook.

Chapter 22

"What on earth are you doing here? Katie!" Lucy stood with her hands on her hips, doing her best to glare at me. It was after six a.m., and the sky in the window behind her was beginning to brighten. Shreds of seashell-peach clouds hovered low on the horizon.

I held up my hands. "I couldn't stay home one second longer. I'm feeling pretty good, too. Please let me work, Aunt Lucy?" I put some extra whine in the last sentence for effect.

At least Iris laughed. "Glad to see you're much healthier than advertised."

"Oh, this little thing?" I said, pointing at where an edge of gauze showed beneath my T-shirt sleeve.

"Let me see your shoulder," Lucy demanded without so much as a smile. She hustled me into the restroom, where she carefully peeled back the layers of gauze covering the stitches. "Well!" she said after careful inspection. "I must say, you have remarkable powers of recovery."

I smiled at her.

A sudden grin split her face. "Why, Katie Lightfoot! Did you heal yourself?"

Craning my head to try to see the stitches, I said, "Not intentionally. It was probably the special tea you made me. Plus, you know how magic tends to energize me, and Cookie came over —"

"What?" she interrupted.

"Um, yeah." As she put a new, smaller bandage on my cut from the Honeybee first-aid kit, I told her about the hex breaking and the glass and my worries about Cookie and Oscar's marriage.

"Well!" she said as she finished. "That is something! Did you bring the dowsing rod? We can try to find the talisman with it again."

"Exactly what I was thinking," I said. "It's in my car."

She frowned, then shrugged. "As safe a place as any, I suppose."

Opening the restroom door, I said, "I thought maybe we could try after work again? Or even just you and me in the office — if we can get away."

We rounded the corner into the kitchen to

find Iris almost in tears.

"What's wrong?" I asked, wishing the bakery could be one place to escape drama.

She held up a small white disk and let it drop on the counter. It landed with a *thunk* and broke into several pieces. "The prep work is done for the day's baking, and the ovens are full, so I thought I'd try to surprise you."

Lucy and I peered at the pieces. "With . . . ?" I asked.

Iris sniffled.

"Meringue!" my aunt guessed.

Iris nodded. "Sort of. I'm trying to make *macarons*. I've been thinking about them ever since you made those coconut macaroon thumbprint cookies."

I felt my face clear. "Ah. Well, let's make them together, then." I looked at Lucy. "Today's special is oatmeal lace cookies, right? We can offer *macarons* as another, as long as they last. What flavor were you thinking, Iris?"

"Chocolate!"

"Okay, then. Chocolate, it is. Maybe with a bit of espresso and a hint of cinnamon?"

Our protégée's head bobbed enthusiastically. "Yum!"

"First you need to grind some almonds."

"You said something about almonds the

other day," Iris said, her tears forgotten. "I remember now."

"Many grocery stores sell preground almond meal, but we don't have any right now," I said. "So we'll grind up our own, and then toast it just long enough to dry it out and intensify the flavor. And we'll start with a French *macaron* meringue — it's easier and faster than the Italian version."

We set to grinding and roasting blanched almonds from the pantry, and whipping egg whites with lemon juice and a pinch of salt. Then I showed Iris how to fold in a combination of the cooled almond meal, confectioner's sugar, cinnamon, and powdered espresso while Lucy removed a batch of fig muffins — now a regular item on the Honeybee menu — from one of the ovens and put baking sheets in to preheat to 340 degrees.

"See, this batter forms a thick ribbon, much denser than the fluffy egg whites for traditional meringue. That's what gives the cookie outsides of the *macaron* their tender chewiness. And see the pretty speckles from the cinnamon and espresso?"

Iris nodded, as attentive as any pastry student I'd gone to school with. "Lucy said cinnamon draws love, happiness, and money."

Glancing at my aunt, who looked pleased as punch, I said, "That's right. And what about chocolate?"

"Oooh," Iris said, her eyes bright. "*Chocolate* has magical properties?"

Lucy laughed. "Good heavens, girl! What do you think?"

"It makes me happy, I can tell you that," she said.

"Chocolate creates serious feelings of euphoria, for sure," I said. "That's plain old science, I'm afraid. In culinary school we learned cocoa contains phenylethylamine, a chemical that reduces your appetite, makes you feel lovey-dovey — your brain makes the same stuff when you fall head over heels — and, like you said, makes you happy."

Lucy's expression held amused delight.

I shrugged. "Most people don't realize how much chemistry you learn in culinary school. Another food that has even more phenylethylamine than chocolate? Cheese."

"I'll have to tell Patsy," Iris said, referring to her stepmother, who owned the cheese shop down the block.

"I don't know about cheese," Lucy said, "But it certainly explains why chocolate is associated with romance and . . . you know," she finished, her cheeks turning pink.

"You mean sex?" Iris said, oblivious of my

aunt's discomfort.

I suppressed a laugh. "Back to the job at hand. Load some of the batter into this pastry bag, and I'll show you how to pipe out the cookies."

Ben showed up with several boxes from the bulk grocery then, and as he and Lucy opened the Honeybee and greeted customers, I directed Iris as she slowly and carefully formed uniform disks of succulent, gooey meringue on silicone baking sheets. When one was full, it went right on top of one of the preheated sheets in the oven, a simple method that prevented burning and encouraged even cooking.

As each pan came out of the oven, we let the cookies cool for a few minutes and then transferred them to a rack. In between batches, we mixed a simple chocolate ganache, adding more espresso powder and cinnamon.

"Now we fill," I said. "First, you have to make a little indentation in the bottom of each cookie with your thumb, so it will hold more of the filling." I gently pushed into the center of a meringue cookie to show her.

Iris did a little two-step before settling in to work. I began to realize that move of hers was a sign of joy.

"So these are kinda-sorta thumbprint

cookies, too!" she said, bending over and making a careful dent in one of the cookies.

"Ha! I guess you're right." I began piping ganache onto cookies and sandwiching them together, watching her out of the corner of my eye. "And you know what else? You're a natural at this. Whatever you decide to focus on at SCAD, I guarantee you that baking is one art form you'll excel at."

She answered with another two-step and a happy grin.

Making *macarons* with Iris — and sampling plenty of them as we worked — helped settle my thoughts. However, it didn't help me make sense of all the pieces of information I had. Part of the problem was that I didn't even know how many of the pieces even fit into the puzzle. And I felt sure there were still a few missing.

At least that night we'd have a better idea of where the talisman might be. And this time, I had a feeling Cookie wouldn't be kept from joining us.

Just to make sure, I called her first of the spellbook-club members. Her phone rang five times before going to voice mail. I looked at my watch, suddenly panicked that I'd called too early — it had certainly happened before. But the morning rush had come and gone, and it was well after nine-thirty.

On the other hand, Cookie had had a late night, and not everyone could get by on just a few hours' sleep, like me. I left a quick voice mail asking her to call me when she got a chance, and hung up.

Declan answered my next call, and we chatted for a while. He actually sounded worse off than I did, after being out all night checking for the source of carbon monoxide leaking into an entire apartment building. The residents had to be evacuated, and the fire crew not only had to track down the source of a poisonous gas, but also had to mollify a crowd of extremely cranky people who'd been rousted out of their beds in the middle of the night. Nonetheless, he still insisted on talking about my evening and how well I'd slept. When I told him about Cookie breaking the hex on the talisman, he grew quiet.

"Deck? This is good news. We have to be close to finding out who has the gris gris. That means we're close to finding Franklin's killer, and, hopefully, bringing Dawn out of her coma."

"I know," he said. "That's what I'm worried about. If you track it down — or if you track *someone* down — I want you to get ahold of me right away. And Peter Quinn. And Ben, of course."

All men. I smiled to myself. *Well, as they say down here: Bless his heart.*

Before returning to the front, I checked in with Candler Hospital. They wouldn't tell me more than that Eulora Scanlon and Dawn Taite were both still there, but that was enough.

Back out front, I found Bianca and Jaida sitting at one of the tables, leisurely flipping through sections of the *Savannah Morning News.* How long had it been since I'd simply sat down and read the paper? Things were fairly slow, so I grabbed a hazelnut biscotti and a cup of coffee and joined them.

"Hey, you two! Perfect timing." I sank into a chair.

"Katie! We wanted to see for ourselves how you're doing after that awful fire," Bianca said, setting aside the financial section.

Jaida examined my face, and then her attention flicked to my shoulder. "You had to get stitches in your arm?"

I nodded and grinned. "A baker's dozen."

Bianca rolled her eyes. "Naturally."

Jaida shook her head. "She's obviously fine, Bianca." She sat back. "Is our timing perfect because you can take a break? Or . . . ?"

"Ah. The break is good — don't get me wrong — but Lucy and I were going to call and see if you two could come here after hours."

"For, er, book-club business?" Jaida asked, surveying nearby tables to see if anyone was listening.

"Indeed. The same as the other night. Bianca, is this enough notice for you to get a babysitter for Colette?"

Her gaze slid away from mine.

"You know," I said, sitting back and regarding her through the steam drifting from my mug. "We haven't seen you as much as usual the past few days."

She looked up with a troubled expression and bit her lip.

Jaida's gaze sharpened. "Did you really have to stay home with Colette when we last gathered?"

"Yes!" Bianca said.

"You don't like that the spellbook club is involved in this voodoo business, though. Am I right?"

Bianca gave a slow shrug. "I'm sorry. It just makes me uncomfortable."

I set down my coffee. "You've never made a secret that you disapprove of Cookie's approach to magic, and we understand. But I've learned so much about voodoo that I never knew before. I think you might find some of it interesting."

Bianca's jaw set. Jaida shot me a look.

I lifted my palms. "Or not. It's entirely your choice. And if you don't want to come tonight, that's okay, too. I'm going to try Lucy's dowsing rod again." I directed my next words to Jaida. "Cookie is sure that last night she broke the hex that was hiding the gris gris." I didn't elaborate on the broken glass we'd had to clean up.

Interest sparked behind Jaida's eyes. "Well, count me in. Can I bring Anubis?"

"Of course!"

Bianca sighed. "I'll come, too."

I grinned and stood. "Thanks. Cookie should be calling me back soon, and I'm pretty sure Mimsey will be able to join us. So we should have the whole gang."

"Katie Lightfoot, as I live and breathe! What on earth are you doing at work today?" Mrs. Standish stood at the counter. Her hair was wrapped in a white turban that went nicely with her zebra-print caftan. Skipper Dean was nowhere to be seen.

I glanced down at Lucy's abbreviated bandage. It didn't show at all under the sleeve of my T-shirt. "Why, Mrs. Standish. I work almost every day except a few Sundays."

"Oh, but that *fire*. Darlin' girl, it's all over town how you survived that horrible blaze. How on earth can you be so *blasé* about it?"

"The woman who owned the house that burned down is in much worse shape than I am," I said quietly. "She's still in Candler Hospital."

"Oh, dear. That's right — the fire completely destroyed Eulora Scanlon's house, didn't it? I'm so very sorry. I don't know her well, but I'm aware that she is quite well respected in the community. She was hurt in the fire, then?"

I shook my head. "Not directly, but I'm sure the smoke did her no good." *Nor did fighting an antifire demon, or whatever the heck that was.* "She had a heart attack."

Her voice dropped to a faux whisper as she leaned closer. "Oh, no! Does the poor dear need help with her medical bills?"

I blinked. "I honestly don't know."

She straightened. "Well, you just leave that to me. I don't know if you're aware, but I am a fund-raising dervish."

I had to laugh. "Mrs. Standish, trust me — your reputation precedes you. Anything you can do to help will be much appreciated, by me and by her family, I'm sure."

Her eyes twinkled behind heavy eyeliner. "I might need more of those Brazilian cheesy biscuits your aunt Lucy made for the animal-shelter cocktail party. They were a huge success."

"You just let us know," I said. "We'll whip up as many as you want — of those or anything else you decide on."

"I can always count on the Honeybee! But for now, why don't you load up a half-dozen mixed pastries for me?"

"Of course. What would you like?"

She twiddled her fingers in the air. "Surprise me."

I selected two of the vanilla éclairs I knew she and Mr. Dean loved, a small brioche "pizza" drizzled with caramel and chocolate sauce, two savory scones — blue cheese and one of the cheddar sage scones Lucy had shown Iris how to make — and a peach pecan muffin, because I knew Mrs. Standish favored that flavor combination. Then I tossed in another small box with a half dozen of the oatmeal lace cookies for free.

She left, trailing the scent of expensive perfume in her wake, and I went back to the kitchen to arrange rows of pineapple macaroons next to the chocolate espresso *macarons.* As I refilled the glass jars of biscotti and bused the reading area, my thoughts kept returning to Cookie. After taking a fresh cup of tea to Martin, who was now typing so busily on his novel that he hardly noticed, I went back in the office and tried her cell again.

Again, there was no answer.

I didn't leave a message this time, and instead looked up the number of Cookie's employer. Listening for an influx of customers out in the bakery, I dialed. The phone was answered on the first ring.

"Quartermaine Realty. Amber speaking. How may I help you?" She sounded perky and friendly.

"May I please speak with Cookie Rios?" I asked.

"I'm sorry. Ms. Rios is not in at the moment. Would you like her voice mail?"

"No, thanks. Can you tell me when she's expected in the office?"

"Let's see here." I heard the clicking of a keyboard. "It looks like she's out showing a warehouse to a potential client."

Warehouse. Such a simple word, yet my internal alarm bells began to jingle jangle.

"Could you give me the address of the property?" I asked.

"Oh, are you interested, as well?"

"It depends," I flat-out lied. "On the location."

"Hang on a sec," she said. More typing. There were murmurs in the background. They grew louder, and I began to make out words.

"Did you see that snake? Keeps it in her *purse,* for God's sake." The voice was young and scandalized.

"Excuse me," I said in a trembling voice. "Amber?"

"Yes, I'm here."

"Did I hear someone say something about a snake?" I asked.

"Oh!" A hand covered the mouthpiece of the phone, muffling the urgent tone. Amber came back on the line. "Just a misunderstanding, ma'am. As for the warehouse property you were asking about, it's out on Old Louisville Road." She read off the street number. "Used to be a lumber warehouse, I understand. It's over seventeen hundred square feet. Does that sound like something you might be interested in?"

My heart was tripping over itself, unsure of whether to pound through my sternum or stop beating altogether. "I'll let you know," I said, my voice half-strangled. "Could you tell me the name of the client she's showing it to?" I scrambled for a good reason for her to tell me. "I have a partner, you see, and I was wondering if it might be, er, him."

A pause. "Maybe. Is his name Sam? Sam Hatfield?"

Goddess help me, I hung up on sweet, helpful Amber.

Samantha. New to town and recently met, as Connell had warned. With a perfect story for Steve about moving from Hilton Head, perfectly meeting him at his club, the perfect conversationalist, the perfect manicure, the perfect accent. Too perfect altogether.

The book she was reading in the Honeybee — *How to Get What You Want . . . Every Time.*

The big ole ring on her finger after only a few weeks. And, not least of all, the sardonic former crime reporter I'd grown to know and, yes, love in my own way, suddenly head over heels with someone who giggled and called him honeybuns.

The visit to a mambo who specialized in love potions.

Samantha. And a snake. In the warehouse where Franklin Taite died from a venomous bite. With *Cookie.*

"Lucy!" I shouted.

She came running. "Good Lord, Katie,

what's wrong with you? Shouting like that when there are customers . . ." She rounded the office doorframe and stopped cold when she saw my face.

"Something's happened," she said.

"I think Cookie may be in terrible danger." I rose quickly. Mungo had scrambled into my bag already, and I looped the handles over my shoulder. "Are Bianca and Jaida still here?"

She nodded. "And Mimsey's at her shop."

"We'll pick her up on the way," I said.

CHAPTER 23

In whispered tones, I hastily explained to Uncle Ben what was going on — at least as much as I knew. He wasn't happy about it, but agreed to stay at the Honeybee with Iris. When she started to ask questions, he shushed her.

"I'll tell you in a bit," he said to her, as he looked to me with a question on his face.

"Yes," I said. "If you're going to work at the Honeybee, Iris, you should probably know the kinds of things we get up to around here on occasion. Will you call Peter Quinn, too?" I asked Ben. "Let him know where we are and why. And mention the words *human sacrifice* if he balks."

Iris paled beneath her black, spiked hair.

"Sure thing, hon. How about Declan?" Ben asked.

I shook my head. "I don't want a bunch of sirens and fire trucks and the like, and, knowing him, he'll do whatever he can to save the day. At this point, we can't even be sure there's anything wrong."

Sure, Katie.

Jaida and Bianca joined Lucy and me out on the sidewalk. Lucy said, "Ben dropped me off before getting groceries this morning. So we only have his little pickup."

"No way we can all fit in that, unless we pile into the back," Jaida said, smoothing her summer dress.

"Bianca, you have your Jag?" I asked.

She nodded. "I can pick up Mimsey."

I hesitated. "Are you okay with whatever might happen at the warehouse? It might involve voodoo in a big way."

Her nod was decisive. "Don't worry. This is Cookie we're talking about. Get going. Mimsey and I will be there soon." She took off at a jog toward her sports car, and Jaida, Lucy, and I piled into the Bug with Mungo.

As I drove, I told them more details about Cookie breaking the hex on the gris gris the night before, and ended with, "She felt sure she was successful, but now I wonder if she didn't also open herself up to discovery by whoever has the talisman." I didn't mention Declan opening himself to Connell in an attempt to reach through the veil to Franklin, but it seemed that Cookie's spell breaking could easily have had the same effect.

I turned onto Old Louisville Road and pushed down on the accelerator.

"The warehouse is coming up on the right," Lucy said, peering at the GPS on her smartphone.

I slowed, searching for the address. It was pretty obvious, though, when the warehouse came into view around a curve in the road. It was a behemoth of a building, squat and long and set back from the road by a large parking area covered with pockmarked asphalt. Six oversized, garage-style doors marched down the front of the olive green building, waiting for months now for the big trucks to back up and take away loads of lumber from inside. Steering into the entrance to the lot, I guided the little car around the potholes, toward the people door set into the front corner.

As we tumbled out of the Bug, Jaida asked, "Where's Cookie's car?"

Her words gave me a sense of hope. Maybe I was wrong. Maybe this was just a property listed by Quartermaine Realty, Sam was looking at it for her dot-com father, and Cookie had shown it and was now back at her office . . .

Lucy tried the metal door. "It's locked."

Eulora's bracelet of protection warmed against my wrist.

Bianca zoomed into the parking lot, weaving the red Jaguar around the potholes much as I had — only four times faster. She braked to a halt in front of us, and a pale and shaking Mimsey exited from the passenger's side. Swaying slightly, she righted the purple bow on her pageboy, took a deep breath, and reached back into the car. Heckle emerged, gripping her arm hard and looking a bit wobbly himself. The fact that he didn't immediately deliver a rude greeting was enough to tell me he wasn't used to Bianca's driving, either.

"Heckle was with me at Vase Value, and wanted to come along," Mimsey said.

"No explanation necessary," I said as Mungo popped his head out of my bag

Bianca's Puck flowed out of her light jacket to drape around her neck, peering at us all from the black Zorro mask that covered his otherwise pure-white face.

"Are you sure Cookie is here?" Bianca's gaze flicked over the abandoned warehouse.

"Let's check the back," I said.

We trouped around the corner and along the side of the building. A few windows placed high in the long, metal-clad wall would allow a bit of light inside, but afforded us no view to the interior. We reached the corner, and I paused.

"There." I pointed. "Cookie's driving Oscar's car."

"There's another vehicle." Lucy had rounded the corner in front of me, standing exposed in the smaller parking lot behind the warehouse.

I stepped forward, an admonishment to be careful on my lips, when I saw where she pointed.

On the far end of the lot was Steve Dawes' Land Rover.

"Is that . . . ?" she asked as the others joined us.

I nodded. "I'd know that Rover anywhere." For a brief moment, hope flared. "Maybe he's here to help." Steve had certainly aided the spellbook club in the past, both with his druid clan and on his own.

For me. He's still keeping tabs on me, after all, and knows I might need . . . Then my mind's eye called up the blond hair flowing out of the window of the Rover, honeyed locks fastened with a long pink ribbon.

Samantha.

"Katie?" Mimsey asked.

I shook myself. "That's Steve's car, all right. But I don't think he's driving it."

The other witches exchanged a look.

"Cookie came out here to show the property to Samantha Hatfield. She's driven his car before."

"Steve's new girlfriend?" Mimsey asked.

"His new fiancée," I corrected.

Jaida's eyebrows shot up, as Bianca drew her breath in through her teeth. Lucy looked worried — and slightly embarrassed — but Mimsey's expression held quiet triumph. She'd never really cared for Sam.

"Come on, ladies," I said. "We have to find a way in. Oh, and be *careful.* That woman is not what she seems."

We fanned out, scanning the exterior of the building. Windows on this side were set much lower. Of the five panes, two were broken out.

No wonder Quinn figured animals could get inside. So could people.

Another metal door was set into the corner opposite the one in the front. We moved closer to the building, and I scurried down to the door. It probably wouldn't be unlocked, but it would be silly not to check. I was already trying to figure out how to break the rest of the glass in one of the windows without making a bunch of noise as I reached for the doorknob.

As I'd expected, it didn't turn. The door, however, glided silently open. Puzzled, I looked down and saw a small rock in the jam, preventing it from closing far enough for the latch to catch.

An accident? Or Cookie hoping we'd find her in time?

I motioned to the others, who hurried toward me, each woman stooping a bit in order to not be seen from the windows. Holding my finger to my lips, I pointed at the partially open door. Jaida saw the rock and shot me a look. I nodded, then shrugged.

Ever so slowly, I pushed open the door.

The faint scent of sulfur struck me as I peered into the dimly lit space. Though my eyes hadn't fully adjusted yet, I couldn't detect any light or movement. However, the light from the open door might be visible from anywhere in the warehouse. Quickly, I stepped in and to the side. The others followed, and Mimsey closed the door behind her.

We stood blinking for a few seconds, hidden in a short hallway leading from the back door to the cavernous, empty storage space in the middle of the building. Four offices opened off either side of the corridor in front of us, all but the closest with doors closed. The near one, I could see, was empty save for a cheap desk and dented file cabinet.

The sulfur smell grew stronger, burning

my eyes and reminding me of the fire at Mother Eulora's. A shuffling sound carried from closer to the front of the building, and I tiptoed down the hallway to lean around the corner. A light flickered about two hundred feet away, a live flame — no, several — at the base of a tall post.

A low moan came from the same direction.

I looked over to see Lucy visibly shaking beside me. Jaida and Mimsey had heard, as well, and shared equally grim expressions. Bianca was wide-eyed with fright. Then her jaw set, she caught my eye, and she gave me a firm nod.

Together we moved out of the hallway and toward the candles.

As we grew nearer, my mind struggled to identify what I was seeing. The post in the middle of the warehouse was part of the structure, and reached up to support the roof. There were others, but this one was surrounded by at least fifty votives. Something was scattered around and even under the candles. As I got closer I saw it was . . . food?

My, my, yes. The smell of the dishes tucked at the bottom of the post was enough to almost clear the sulfur from the air. There was a plate of fried chicken, a tureen of soup

— *crab?* — fresh tomatoes, and chunks of cheese. Over there, a jar of pickled okra leaned against a pile of fresh peaches, and a bowl of peppery coleslaw nestled in the middle of a platter of hush puppies. There was more, lots more, of whatever kind of offering this was.

Then I saw the bare feet standing on the concrete on the other side of the support beam.

"Oh, Cookie!" Lucy cried, rushing toward our friend.

"Back off!" The voice reverberated through the dank air, seeming to come from every direction at once.

I reached for my aunt, but she eluded my grasp and barreled toward Cookie. I ran behind her, the footsteps of our coven mates pounding behind me.

Lucy came up short, shrieking. Her arms flailed and her legs churned backward, almost knocking me over. I caught her, hearing the gasps of the others around me. When I saw why, my stomach did a slow flip beneath my unbeating heart.

Twenty feet away, Cookie stood with her back against the metal beam. She wore a black satin robe that fell to her knees. Her hands were tied to the post above her, and she blinked blearily at us, as if she couldn't see properly.

And at her feet swarmed the reason Lucy had shrieked like a little girl.

Snakes.

Lots and lots of them, slithering and flowing like a single entity.

My heart came online again, beating furiously as if to make up for lost time, but breathing was difficult. I couldn't tear my attention away from the roiling mass of red and yellow and black stripes.

The same color as the molted skin on Mother Eulora's altar. Coral snakes. One was poisonous enough, but this many? Terror arrowed through my solar plexus at the thought.

A lock of fuchsia-streaked hair flipped down over one of Cookie's eyes as her head lolled forward. The movement caught my attention, and I tore my gaze away from the horrid reptilian tangle and saw it at last.

The gris gris.

The amulet hung from a hook in the metal above our friend's head. It looked exactly like the talisman in the photo Mother Eulora had given me, except for one thing: The snowy white fringes tied into the lower corners were now inky black. As I stared, they seemed to rise, though there was no breeze to stir them. The silken strands moved toward us like alien antennae, sending a shiver down my back so violent that I shook all over.

Samantha Hatfield stepped out from the shadows to the right of Cookie. We must have walked right past her hiding place. Steve would have recognized his all-American fiancée despite her casual capris being stained with goddess knew what, and instead of pink she wore a simple blue, button-down shirt. But her gaze was calculating, and her thin-lipped smile the stuff of nightmares.

"I was hoping you'd come, Katie. I didn't expect you'd bring all these other people, though. What ever happened to lone-wolf heroes?"

I took a deep breath, reaching out to the tiny flames of each candle as I had the fire at Eulora's. I gathered the element of air all around us and mentally felt my way into and through the concrete at our feet, deep into the element of earth below. Silently, I called upon Gabriel and the element of water to join the rest.

Lucy took my hand, and I felt a jolt of hopeful energy. Mimsey took hers then, and Jaida and Bianca joined. It wasn't a circle, but a linking as effective as any I'd ever felt.

"We are stronger together," I said to Sam.

"You're alone and desperate."

She held up her hand as if to push us back, and her nostrils flared.

"We are stronger than you are, whatever drives you and whatever voodoo spells you plan to cast here," I continued. "I guarantee you that, Samantha. If that's even your real name."

"Oh, it's her real name," said another voice. My head whipped to the left as Mambo Jeni stepped out from the other side of the warehouse. "And she's not alone. Not at all."

My mouth gaped open as my mind scrambled to put it together. "But you said you didn't know Franklin Taite!"

"I also said I always tell the truth." She shrugged. "I lied about that, too."

How could I have been so stupid?

The other spellbook-club members looked confused.

"This is Mambo Jeni," I told them. "One of the voodoo queens Cookie and I went to see."

She went on. "Franklin Taite almost arrested my daughter and me down in Louisiana. But we got away and relocated here."

Daughter? So much for Steve's new love being a member of the dot-com nouveau riche in Hilton Head. I remembered the dark-haired girl in the picture on Jeni's fireplace mantel. Now that I could see them together and knew Sam's hair was dyed blond, the resemblance between mother and daughter was unmistakable. Samantha wasn't just a customer of Jeni's; she was her own flesh and blood. And yet the idea was hard to wrap my brain around.

"What about your son?"

Sam made a rude noise. Her mother shrugged. "He's uninterested in anything except his game console. He knows nothing of any of this." Jeni shook her head. "But then Detective Taite followed us here."

"Not terribly clever of you to choose Savannah, given that he used to live here," Jaida remarked.

Sam pointed at her. "How were we supposed to know that? We came here because the voodoo community is wide and deep. My mother could make a living without standing out, just as she had in New Orleans, while we fine-tuned our plans."

Plans.

Mambo Jeni grinned. "And the magic in Savannah is strong. We don't want to leave. When Taite showed up here, I decided that rather than running from him forever, he could help us."

"Help you what?" Lucy asked in a trembling voice.

Jeni said. "Well, you're a woman of a certain age."

I felt my aunt bristle at the words — and the tone.

"And I'm betting you've been wronged by a man."

Mimsey snorted.

The mambo glared at her. "A man who takes up with a younger woman and leaves you with two kids to raise and nothing else — no money, no house, no source of income."

Bianca rolled her eyes. "Sure. Happens to a lot of us. But we're women, for heaven's sake. We don't need men."

I suppressed a smile.

Jeni eyed her thoughtfully. "Exactly. And so I did what I'm good at. What I'm trained for."

"Voodoo?" I couldn't keep the disbelief out of my voice.

Between the two women, Cookie moaned again. One of the snakes began to coil around her ankle.

Samantha strode toward me. "Shut up. You don't know anything. My mother raised my brother and me by herself. When she asked for my help to finally set us all up for life, I couldn't refuse her."

"You mean Steve Dawes? No way would he marry you without a prenuptial in hand. His father wouldn't hear of it."

She smirked. "My mother's love potions are strong."

"You know he's a druid, right?"

Sam looked delighted. "All the better, when I take his power once and for all. It was more . . . difficult to convince him I was the love of his life than most men. That's why we decided to sacrifice your detective friend. For the extra power it gave to our spells."

I could feel Lucy's hand shaking in mine. And no wonder: What this woman was saying was terrifying. They could call it taking power, but we all knew they meant taking lives.

Cookie moaned again. The snake around her ankle began to slowly wind its way up her bare leg.

"Franklin's death provided enough power to the potion to convince Steve he should marry me," Sam went on. "But we needed more power to convince his father to give me access to the family fortune." Her smile was devoid of humor or kindness. "That's why we tried to sacrifice both you and the spiritualist by fire."

"You set it?" I asked.

"Oh, yes. But Mommy gave it the extra oomph to do you in." She laughed.

Mambo Jeni looked pleased. "That gris gris I took from Franklin before we killed him is a thing of wonder. Golly. If it had worked, we would have gained both your power *and* that of Eulora Scanlon."

"Didn't work, did it?" I didn't try to keep the smugness out of my voice.

"Nope. Came close, though."

The others had been listening in silence, and now Jaida's head tipped to the side. "Why are you telling us all this?" she asked.

"Oh! Because as long as you are all here, and we have the only member of your little group who knows anything about voodoo sedated, we're going to take all your power. Even Steve's family won't stop us from getting to the Dawes money then."

Chapter 24

Mambo Jeni began muttering words that sounded like utter gibberish. Still, they made Bianca's eyes grow wide, and her ferret, Puck, still curled around her neck, squeaked in the back of his throat. Mimsey closed her eyes and bowed her head, still gripping Lucy's and Jaida's hands. Heckle rose up on her shoulder and spread his wings wide, like a multicolored phoenix. My left hand was on Mungo, who stood up in my tote, quivering with canine outrage. Lucy grasped my other one so tightly, it was numb from lack of blood flow. Eulora's bracelet throbbed against my wrist.

"Oh, brother," Samantha said with a toss of her blond hair. "Save the theatrics, ladies."

The elemental power I'd called before had been waiting like a curled mongoose. Wordlessly, I asked it to augment my own now, and instantly felt my energetic signature grow. Mimsey nodded, her eyes still closed but a small smile on her face, acknowledging that she felt it too. I looked at the others. As one, they nodded, too.

Mambo Jeni's muttering grew louder. It sounded like she was speaking in tongues, and perhaps she was. Her eyes were locked on me, though, and I could see the frisson of alarm in them. Like Sam, she'd thought I'd come alone. I could see her doubt that she could overcome all of us.

"The snakes," Lucy whispered.

They were roiling harder now, a loose, slithering knot of evil. Above Cookie's head, the reversed talisman shone with a deep darkness, a vortex that felt like it would eat light like a black hole. At her feet, the snakes reared their heads, striking in our direction. One hit the back of another with its fangs, behind the head. The wounded snake fell away from the group, writhing alone on the floor.

Despite my revulsion, I found myself feeling almost sorry for it. These greed-driven women were using the spirits of animals that were not inherently evil for their own dark purposes. Snakes were disgusting and creepy and terrified the living daylights out of me, but it wasn't right for them to be used like that.

Then they turned their striking heads toward Cookie's bare legs. The one that had curled around her ankle was now halfway up her leg. As if in slow motion, I watched one of the striped beasts prepare to strike her slim ankle.

"No!" I screamed in a flash of white light. The word came out loud and long, echoing through the cavernous space and folding back upon the tableau in layers. The gathered energy of the four elements was in my Voice, as was the energy of my fellow witches and their familiars. As a result, the sound of the word grew louder rather than fading, increasing in volume and intent.

I was hardly aware as Mungo jumped to the ground and ran to the mass of coral snakes. But when I saw him barking and snarling, ducking their dripping fangs and drawing them away from Cookie, I couldn't breathe. Then Puck was there, too, fighting them, enticing them away, flowing away from their strikes like liquid fur.

Mambo Jeni was shouting now, and Samantha was running toward the snakes, stomping at them to move them back toward her captive.

Heckle launched himself from Mimsey's shoulder, blue-and-green wings beating the air as he rose and swooped toward Cookie.

No, *not* Cookie.

The gris gris.

The great parrot snagged the amulet's chain in mid-flight and circled back toward us.

"No!" Mambo Jeni screamed in rage, as Heckle dropped the talisman into my outreached palm. But as soon as I held the gris gris in my fist, her voice no longer had power.

Cookie raised her head, eyes completely clear.

And, boy, was she angry.

I didn't blame her a bit.

Silence settled on the room, strange after the booming echo of my Voice. Mungo and Puck returned to us. I let go of Lucy's hand to pick up my familiar and nuzzle his furry neck.

"That's not yours," Samantha said, advancing on me. Her eyes were wild, her pretty face ugly with hatred and greed.

"The gris gris? Oh, please. It's not yours, either. It truly belongs to the man you killed."

"Sammy, let it go. We can leave now and try again someplace else," Mambo Jeni said.

Sam turned toward her mother. "Are you out of your mind? I'm going to marry Steve Dawes, and I'm going to have the life I deserve — the life you've always told me I deserved!" She stomped her foot.

Behind her, one of the snakes turned.

"Um," I said.

"Shut up, Katie! Katie-girl, as Steve calls you. But he's not yours, he's mine."

"He's not either of ours, you sanctimonious, controlling —"

"All right, everyone stay right where you are!" Quinn rushed in from the back hallway, where the spellbook club had entered the warehouse. Ben was right behind him, and, bless his heart, so was Declan — in civilian garb. My uncle must have called him, anyway.

The snake struck fast, unexpected, burying its fangs deep into the flesh at the bottom of Samantha's calf. Her face went slack from surprise. All her calculation was replaced by simple fear. "Mommy!"

"Sammy? Oh, no! Sammy!" Mambo Jeni rushed to her daughter.

"Hold on there!" Quinn shouted.

I raised my palm and walked toward him, very, very careful where I stepped. But all the snakes seemed to have retreated to the outer edges of the warehouse. "Thanks for coming, Quinn. These are the women who killed Franklin. And I'm betting they put Dawn in a coma, as well."

"How did they do that?" he asked.

"With a curse," I said.

He rolled his eyes.

Jeni moaned. "My daughter needs to go to the hospital. She's been bitten."

"How many times?" Declan asked, running over.

"Once," I answered. "Coral snake."

His head came up and his gaze raked over me. "You okay?"

Power still thrummed through my veins. I looked down to where I grasped the gris gris in my left fist. Slowly, I opened my fingers.

The fringes were white again, shining against my palm as if illuminated from within.

I grinned. "I'm great."

Declan nodded and turned to a weeping Mambo Jeni. "She'll be okay, ma'am. Ben, call Five House. I want my guys on this." He bent to tend Sam's bite, efficient and tender even with someone he must have deduced was a truly bad person.

How I loved that guy.

Detective Quinn frowned. "You want to tell me what's going on, Lightfoot?"

I took a breath. "Mambo Jeni here is a voodoo queen. The real deal. Samantha Hatfield is her daughter. They killed Franklin to get power to seduce Steve Dawes."

He blinked. "You're kidding."

"Nope. Did you check on coma victims?"

"Um, yeah. As it turns out, there was a John Doe in a state rehab facility over in Pooler for about three months. Then one day he disappeared. They reported it to the police, but the general assumption was he came to and got up and left of his own volition. From the description, I'm sure it was Frank."

I looked at the ashen-face Samantha, prone on the floor, while my boyfriend elevated her foot. "You sweet-talked your way in to the facility and took him out, didn't you?"

Licking her lips, she nodded.

"I want to know more about these comas," Quinn insisted.

Jeni rocked back on her heels and raised her face. "I placed a voodoo curse," she said.

He snorted.

"You used poppets?" I asked.

"It helps if you believe in such curses, and both of the Taites did," she said. "I gave them both empty dolls so they'd know, but the dolls held only intention."

Only intention. Ha!

"It was the power of the talisman that accomplished my ends," she said.

Quinn shook his head. "I still don't get it."

"Katie! Would you mind untying me, please?" Cookie sounded impatient.

I hurried over, laughing. "Sheez, I can't believe we left you —" I stopped cold. All the other snakes had slithered away except one.

The one still coiled around her leg.

"Any day now," Cookie said.

"Hold very, very still," I said.

She lifted her leg so she could better see the snake. "Can't you tell the difference between a coral snake and a king snake? Just untie me."

"Uh, no," I said, feeling confused but reaching for the length of clothesline wrapped around her wrists.

" 'Red touch yellow, kills a fellow,' " she said." 'Red touch black, venom lack. Yellow touch red, soon you'll be dead. Red touch black, friend of Jack.' " Freed, she put her arms around my shoulders. "Thank you for saving me."

It was all I could do not to cringe away from the monster on her leg. "Um, sure. What were you just nattering about?"

"The stripes," Ben said, his arm now around Lucy's still-shaking shoulders. "Coral snakes and king snakes are often confused." He pointed to Cookie, who was now holding the two-foot length of reptile in her hands. "That's a king snake. They're the good ones."

She held it out to me. I shuddered. "Katie, meet Rafe. My new familiar. He found me early this morning, after Oscar and I came to an understanding. He was in my purse when Samantha and her mother overpowered me, but was protecting me this whole time."

After everything that had happened over the past few days, that was when I came the closest to passing out.

"Have another macaroon," I urged Dawn Taite.

She sat across from me in the Honeybee reading area. The doctors were just as baffled by her sudden emergence from unconsciousness — at the same time the gris gris had reverted to its intended state — as they had been by the cause of the coma in the first place. Her peanut-butter-colored hair was drawn into two adorable ponytails on either side of her head, and her eyes were clear and a bright robin's-egg shade of blue. Even her skin seemed more alive than the other times I'd seen her. She was still thin as a rail, however.

She laughed. "I think three is enough. Maybe you can talk my mother into a couple when she comes to pick me up. She's checking out of her hotel, but I told her I wanted to talk to you alone for a few minutes. Then we're driving back home to Saratoga Springs."

I leaned forward. We'd already covered the basics of what she'd been doing for Franklin.

Now she continued. "Uncle Frank told me to come to you if anything happened on the, er, occult front if I couldn't reach him. When I came back to Savannah, I learned from one of the guys at his rooming house that he'd up and disappeared. I tried to find him for weeks, but the trail was cold by then. And then the empty poppet showed up at the cheap motel where I was staying. I knew what it meant. That was when I came to find you."

I nodded. "You knew you were cursed. But how did you know the gris gris was missing?"

"Because I could actually feel the curse. I didn't know who unleashed it, but I'd learned enough from Franklin to know a regular voodoo curse doesn't carry weight unless you believe in it."

"And you don't?"

"Well . . . not enough. At least I don't think so. Uncle Franklin had shown me the gris gris, though, had told me that if anything happened to him, I should take it. But it wasn't where he said it was, so I knew someone else had it."

I took a bite of sweet macaroon, swooning at the combination of sticky pineapple and coconut. "Where was it supposed to be?" I asked after swallowing.

"He always found a hiding place wherever we were. Outside. At Cozie Temmons' house, it was behind one of the loose bricks in the foundation on the side."

The dowsing rod hadn't lied, then — only been a bit behind the times.

"But you weren't in Savannah with him? We found something about a cult."

Dawn nodded. "I infiltrated a group headed by a prophet of sorts. Guy calls himself Astroy."

I'd been reaching for my cup of coffee, but paused. "What?" I rose. "Hang on." I went to the bookshelf, where one of our enterprising number had placed a copy of the spellbook I'd chosen for the last meeting. I showed Dawn the picture of Astroy.

"Oh! Now, what a strange coincidence that you'd have this. That's the guy, all right. And that's her."

"Her? Rowanna Bronhilde?"

She laughed. "Her name is really Hazel Smith. She's the one I went in to get."

I stared at her.

"What?"

I shook my head. "Nothing."

"Oh, there's Mom." She stood and waved at the woman in the doorway. Mrs. Taite included me in her return wave, looking far better than the last time I'd seen her, as well.

"Wait a sec," I said, and reached into my pocket. The gris gris felt heavy in my hand. I held it out to Dawn. "I believe this is yours."

She looked at it for a long moment, then shook her head. "I don't think so." She raised her eyes to mine. "It's yours, Katie."

I sat across from Mother Eulora in the rehabilitation center. She'd had a pacemaker put in, and she practically bounced in her seat with excess energy. Tanna sat in another chair a few paces away, eyeing Eulora with a combination of possessiveness and embarrassment. From what the spiritualist had told me, her apprentice was still upset about not saving her mistress from the fire herself.

Tanna wasn't the only one embarrassed. Steve hadn't returned my calls. Fearing

Mambo Jeni's love potion might not have worn off, I'd told his father about it. Whatever had happened next had sparked a terse text message from Steve:

Utterly mortified about Samantha. Thanks for looking out for me. Glad you're okay. Taking some time away to think about things.

"I'm getting out of this place tomorrow," Mother Eulora said. "Aaron pulled a few strings to get them to keep me a bit longer so the family could find someplace for me to live."

"Are you going to live with your son's family?" I asked.

She shook her head. "Oh, no. They'd never let me be. At least Tanna and I understand each other. There was a wonderful woman who held some kind of fundraiser and got me the down payment on a little house over in Midtown. Mrs. Standish. Do you know her?"

I laughed. "Doesn't Mrs. Standish know everyone? She asked us to provide the pastries for that party, by the way. I'm glad to hear it was such a success."

Eulora looked pleased. "It was so nice to know so many people wanted to help. Evelyn Coopersmith got her whole church group to contribute. It was really something else."

I made a mental note to thank Margie again. "Of course they did. You're an important part of the Savannah community."

She surprised me with a giggle. In a low voice, she said, "I think I'll be around for a long time, now that I have this contraption in my chest."

I grinned. "Good to hear."

Sitting back, she surveyed me. "And how are you doing after all the excitement with Mambo Jeni? Is she in jail?"

"Oh, yes. She and her daughter both. The police linked physical evidence in the warehouse to items they found at Jeni's house. Plus, she confessed to murder in front of six people, so there's that." I shook my head. "But Jeni isn't fighting it. When she thought her daughter was going to die, it changed everything. After all, Samantha's happiness was the reason she was willing to kill Franklin."

Eulora looked away, and I saw tears threaten. "I'm glad you found his killers, Katie. I know it wasn't easy."

I patted her hand. "I'm sure you miss him."

"I do."

"Dawn gave me the gris gris," I said.

Interest sparked in her eyes. "Did she, now?"

"What am I supposed to do with it?" I asked.

She settled her deep purple gaze on me. "That, Katie Lightfoot, is your choice."

RECIPES

KATIE'S THUMBPRINT MACAROONS

Naturally gluten-free, coconut macaroons pack a sweet punch made even sweeter here with the addition of a gooey filling. Easy to make, they can be topped with any kind of jam you might want, like a typical thumbprint cookie, or try a bit of homemade pomegranate jelly or pineapple jam for a different twist.

Yield: about 30 macaroons

3 large egg whites
1/2 cup sugar
1/2 teaspoon vanilla extract
Dash of salt
1 package (14 ounces) shredded, sweetened coconut
1/2 cup jam or jelly of choice

Preheat the oven to 325 degrees and line a baking sheet with parchment paper.

Whisk together the egg whites, sugar, vanilla extract, and salt. Fold in the coconut until combined. Portion heaping tablespoonfuls of the mixture onto the baking sheet about one inch apart, and, using wet fingers, tidy the coconut shreds around the edges so they don't burn. Bake for 15 minutes. Remove from the oven and make an indentation in the middle of each macaroon with the back of a spoon, being careful not to puncture the bottom of the cookie. Fill each with jam or jelly (see below), and bake 10 more minutes or until golden brown around the edges. Allow to cool on the baking sheet for 10 minutes, and then transfer to a rack to cool completely.

Pineapple Jam
Combine 1 can (20 ounces) crushed pineapple, 1/2 cup sugar, and the juice of half a lime in a saucepan. Bring to a simmer over low heat and, stirring frequently, cook until reduced to a sticky jam — about 40 minutes. Makes about a cup. Leftovers are great over ice cream or as a topping for baked Brie.

Pomegranate Jelly
Combine 1 cup of bottled pomegranate juice from the grocer's refrigerator case (so

it has not previously been heated in a canning or bottling process) with 1 tablespoon of water and 2 cups of sugar (be exact) in a saucepan. Heat to a full boil, stirring constantly. Stir in 1/4 cup of liquid pectin (there might be some left over if purchased in premeasured packets) and boil for exactly 1 minute, continuing to stir. Ladle into clean jars and fasten lids. Let them stand on the counter until cool, and then put the jars into the refrigerator. It may take a full day for the jelly to set. Makes about 2 1/2 cups. Leftovers will keep in the refrigerator for up to two months, or jars can be sealed in a boiling water bath for 5 minutes.

LUCY'S BRAZILIAN CHEESE BREAD (PÃO DE QUEIJO)

Crispy on the outside, soft and airy on the inside, this addictive cheese bread goes perfectly with any soup or stew. They keep for several days in an airtight container — they will soften (and make fantastic sandwich rolls) but can be re-crisped in the oven before serving. As an added bonus, these puffs are naturally gluten-free. Tapioca flour is made from the root of the cassava plant, so you may find "cassava flour" in international groceries. Most regular grocery stores and natural food stores carry tapioca flour. Bob's Red Mill is a popular brand.

Makes 2 dozen puffs — or 1 dozen if you make them twice as large for sandwiches.

1 cup whole milk
1/2 cup vegetable oil
1 teaspoon salt
2 cups tapioca flour, sifted

2 large eggs
3/4 cup Parmesan cheese, grated
3/4 cup sharp Cheddar cheese, grated

Preheat the oven to 450 degrees. Note: you will reduce the heat once the bread goes in the oven, so arrange the racks to accommodate two baking sheets at once. Line the baking sheets with parchment paper.

Combine milk and oil in a 2-quart saucepan, and bring to a boil over medium heat while stirring. As soon as it begins to boil, remove from heat and add the salt and all of the tapioca flour at once. Stir until combined. The dough will be slightly grainy in appearance.

Put the dough into the bowl of a standing mixer. (You can do the next bit by hand if you're looking for a workout.) Beat the dough for 2–3 minutes at medium speed, until it is smooth and has cooled enough to easily touch for several seconds. Crack an egg into a ramekin and scramble slightly. Add it to the dough and mix on medium until incorporated. Repeat with the second egg. The dough will be smooth and slightly golden. Add the Parmesan and Cheddar and beat the mixture on medium until the cheeses are thoroughly incorporated.

The dough will be sticky with a consistency between a dough and a batter. With an ice-cream scoop or using two soup spoons, portion the dough into mounds a bit more than an inch apart on the lined baking sheets. Smaller puffs take about two tablespoons of dough, but you can double that size to make larger rolls (add extra space between them), or use less dough for bite-sized appetizers.

Place the baking sheets into the oven and immediately reduce the temperature to 350 degrees. Bake for 25 to 30 minutes until the dough has puffed, the exterior is dry, and the outside begins to color.

Serve immediately, or store for up to a week in an airtight container.

ABOUT THE AUTHOR

Bailey Cates believes magic is all around us if we only look for it. She's held a variety of positions, ranging from driver's-license examiner to soap maker, which fulfills her mother's warning that she'd never have a "regular" job if she insisted on studying philosophy, English, and history in college. She traveled the world as a localization program manager but now sticks closer to home, where she writes two mystery series, tends a dozen garden beds, bakes up a storm, and plays the occasional round of golf. Bailey resides in Colorado with her guy and an orange cat that looks an awful lot like the one in her Magical Bakery Mysteries.

The employees of Thorndike Press hope you have enjoyed this Large Print book. All our Thorndike, Wheeler, and Kennebec Large Print titles are designed for easy reading, and all our books are made to last. Other Thorndike Press Large Print books are available at your library, through selected bookstores, or directly from us.

For information about titles, please call:
(800) 223-1244

or visit our Web site at:
http://gale.cengage.com/thorndike

To share your comments, please write:
Publisher
Thorndike Press
10 Water St., Suite 310
Waterville, ME 04901